impressive because Mary Handley is based on a real person. An added delight is the number of well-known historical figures who are intertwined with the story."

—Rhys Bowen, *New York Times* bestselling author of the Molly Murphy and A Royal Spyness historical mysteries

"Lawrence H. Levy brings Mary Handley to life with deft hands, giving readers who love strong and capable female sleuths a character bound to be their new favorite. *Second Street Station* is the perfect combination of wit blended with an engaging and clever plot."

—Tasha Alexander, *New York Times* bestselling author of *And Only to Deceive* and *The Counterfeit Heiress*

"What do you do with a young Victorian woman so intelligent, yet so insubordinate that she is sacked from her last position? If you are the Brooklyn Police Department and she happens to be Lawrence H. Levy's delightful heroine, Mary Handley, the only sensible thing is to make her the city's first policewoman. A fun setting, a resourceful heroine, and a plot that combines danger, humor, and proper sleuthing. . . . What more could anyone want?"

—Will Thomas, author of *Some Danger Involved* and *Fatal Enquiry*

"An ingenious story with unforgettable fictional characters, crossing paths with well-known historical ones. I learned a lot from this book, the main thing being that I could never write one."

—Larry David

"*Second Street Station* is a great read. Following Mary Handley through this Victorian adventure makes you feel like you've found some lost Sherlock Holmes story. It's impressive that the characters, many based on actual historical figures, are always funny, but the greatest delight is the mystery itself."

—Matthew Weiner, creator of *Mad Men*

BROOKLYN
ON FIRE

BROOKLYN ON FIRE

A Mary Handley Mystery

Lawrence H. Levy

B \ D \ W \ Y
Broadway Books
New York

Copyright © 2016 by Lawrence H. Levy

Reader's Guide copyright © 2016 by Penguin Random House LLC

All rights reserved.
Published in the United States by Broadway Books, an imprint of the Crown Publishing Group, a division of Penguin Random House LLC, New York.
www.crownpublishing.com

Broadway Books and its logo, B \ D \ W \ Y, are trademarks of Penguin Random House LLC.

Library of Congress Cataloging-in-Publication Data
Levy, Lawrence H.
Brooklyn on fire : a Mary Handley mystery / Lawrence H. Levy. —
First edition.
pages ; cm
1. Women detectives—New York (State)—New York—Fiction.
2. Murder—Investigation—Fiction. 3. Brooklyn (New York, N.Y.)—
Fiction. I. Title.
PS3612.E9372B76 2016
813'.6—dc23

ISBN 978-0-553-41894-1
eBook ISBN 978-0-553-41895-8

PRINTED IN THE UNITED STATES OF AMERICA

Book design by Anna Thompson
Cover design by Tal Goretsky
Cover illustration by Mark Summers

10 9 8 7 6 5 4 3 2 1

First Edition

To my mother, Betty, who was an avid reader;
to my father, Bernie, who wanted me to choose a
safer profession but still supported my efforts;
and to my brother, Michael, who has always had my back.

PROLOGUE

IT TOOK QUITE some time for the old lady to undo the mess her friends had wrought. Vicky and Albert had done the unthinkable by having a domestic spat in front of her, a physical one, too, and right in the middle of her living room. Anyone else would have been banished from her home, but Vicky and Albert were such close friends they had become family. And family was always given a certain leeway. Besides, the old lady was alone now, a widow for some time. She was well into her seventh decade, sixty-four years old to be exact, and even though it was 1890 and improvements in medicine seemed to occur daily, she was painfully aware she had outlived most of her contemporaries. Vicky and Albert were all she had left.

Their spat had strewn newspapers every which way, but the old lady had corrected that. She carefully perused her work; ten years of her beloved *Brooklyn Daily Eagle,* in four-month stacks, approximately one hundred and twenty in each, spaced evenly on her living room floor in chronological order. The old lady took great pride in the fact that, at any moment, she could relive the major events of any specific day over the past decade—not that she had done so as of yet, but it was available to her and that was the important thing. She smiled and tossed some of her long, gray hair off her cheek to its proper resting place on her back. It was almost down to her waist by now. Years ago, she had given up frivolous things like haircuts and makeup. Her skin was wrinkled, her teeth yellow, and her dresses ancient, but who did she need to impress? Certainly not Vicky and Albert. They were family, and occasionally family needed to be corrected.

"You two are incorrigible. When I saw what you had done, I was beside myself."

"You're always beside yourself," snapped back Vicky in her high yet haughty voice.

"There must be a hundred of you by now," Albert added. His voice was deeper, with a deliberate cadence, almost a monotone.

"Probably closer to a thousand," the old lady admitted. Vicky and Albert could always defuse a tense situation, and the old lady could never stay mad at them.

She glanced at her coffin clock and saw it was inching toward five P.M. She had promised Vicky and Albert she would prepare a special dinner for the three of them, and at the stroke of five, she would start the process. The old lady was on a strict schedule.

"Without a schedule, all that is left is chaos," she had often said.

"And chaos is the enemy of civilized people," Albert would always reply.

"Have I ever told you how very intelligent you are, Albert?" the old lady would say, complimenting him, and Vicky would inevitably react.

"Of course he's intelligent. Do you think I would marry an idiot?"

And the old lady would laugh every time. Vicky and Albert were younger than her, but the old lady didn't know their exact age. They were clearly well into midlife, but their behavior was much more youthful, and that energy seeped into her old bones by osmosis, a word her husband had taught her that was invented by some Frenchman. She truly missed her husband and her son, both of whom had been felled by a cholera epidemic in 1871. They had survived the Civil War only to be erased by a bacterium, an infernal bug, and she lived with that heartbreaking irony every day, never letting it go.

The coffin clock struck five.

"Ah, it's time!" the old lady exclaimed. She patted the clock as if thanking it for the reminder, and some of the dust that covered it flew into the air.

Although it was daytime, it was dark inside. The shades were drawn, and the only light came from two small kerosene lamps. The old lady's house was large, but her voluminous collections made it seem cramped. As they carefully navigated their way around the newspapers, past the boxes of porcelain dolls and tea canisters, and into the dining room, where years of mail smothered the table, the old lady mused about coffin clocks.

"Can you believe the imbeciles out there are calling them grandfather clocks? They're tall, rectangular, and made of wood, like a coffin. What that has to do with a grandfather is beyond me, unless you're burying the old fool."

They all agreed. The world had definitely gone mad. Danger and disrespect ruled. The pages of the *Brooklyn Daily Eagle* were filled with evidence of a dying culture: robberies, murders, young people being allowed to marry whomever they wanted. Everyone knew that "young" was synonymous with "dim-witted" and if left to their own devices, the nation's youth would most certainly lead them down the path to hell. That was why the old lady decided to withdraw from society, if you could call it that these days. It didn't matter that she lived in Clinton Hill, one of the best neighborhoods in Brooklyn. According to her, no place was safe. She had her grocer deliver staples and her butcher deliver meat. Each time they did, she gave them a list of what she wanted next. Her only concession to the modern world was a telephone she had installed in case of an emergency.

As the three of them entered the kitchen, the old lady reached for one of the many pots that filled the sink and counters. That's when she heard it.

"What was that?" she asked as she turned toward Vicky and Albert, who were looking in the direction of the noise. "You heard it too, didn't you?"

Then it happened again. It was a loud clank followed by what sounded like a scrape.

"It's not the grocer," the old lady remarked, full of concern. "He delivered yesterday."

There was a third clank and scrape, then, seconds later, a pounding on the front door. The three of them flinched at the loud sound, fear of the unknown racing through their brains. They all stood still for another moment, not sure what to do.

Another pounding, even louder.

This time the old lady marched out of the kitchen, through the dining room, and into the living room as if she were about to take decisive action. Vicky and Albert paused, then followed.

Yet another pounding, the loudest yet. The three of them halted immediately.

The old lady had had enough. "There is a horrific beast out there that is planning our demise, and I won't have it." She walked to the telephone and picked up the receiver. "Hello, operator, get me the police, and do hurry."

There was an eerie silence as she waited on the telephone. No more pounding.

"Of course I'll hold on, but understand, this is a grave situation."

Suddenly, coming from outside the front door, a man's screams shot through the room. "Oh, oh, oh, no-o-o-o!" It was shortly followed by the sound of scraping and clanging metal, a crash, and then a thud. Seconds later, the man began moaning in a low, sorrowful voice. The old lady clung to the receiver and stared at it as if willing someone at the police station to speak up.

"O-o-o-oh, o-o-o-oh!" the man continued. In spite of her resolve, she couldn't help being curious. The old lady set down the receiver, went to the right of the door by an entry window, and slowly bent back a tiny portion of the shade, hoping to sneak a peek without being noticed. What she saw astonished her.

Limestone covered her front courtyard and lying on it was a small man, about five foot six or so, with a metal brace covering his entire left leg. Next to him was the object over which he had probably tripped—a three-foot stone statue of an angel whose head was now separated from its body. The man was still moaning, the volume of which ranged from hushed, almost melodious tones to loud outbursts. The old lady felt relieved and foolish all at once.

"It's a poor cripple. I can't believe we've been fretting over a cripple," she said.

"O-o-oh, o-o-o-oh." The man's voice seeped into the house like a cold, wet draft.

The old lady turned to Vicky and Albert. "Stop giving me those sorrowful looks. There will be somebody along soon enough," she reasoned.

"Consider the consequences," Vicky said. "He fell on your property and he could sue you. Which is worse—helping him now or paying him later?"

The old lady had to admit that Vicky made sense, but the task ahead of her was daunting. The last time she had ventured outside was three years before, when she was stricken with a bout of pneumonia. Two strong men carried her out on a stretcher and drove her to the hospital in a carriage. *This is different,* she thought.

The old lady took a deep breath, then slowly opened the front door, the hinges creaking from years of neglect. She stuck out her left foot, carefully pointing it downward like a dancer and setting the tip of her shoe on the limestone, then quickly removing it, as if testing the temperature of the water at a bathhouse. Feeling bolder, she ventured outside one small step as Vicky and Albert watched intently.

"Sir," she softly called to him. There was no answer. He just continued to moan in a low, almost whiny tone. "Sir, do you need medical assistance? Shall I call a doctor?"

But there was still no answer, and the moaning increased.

She decided to take a different, more aggressive tack. She stepped toward him. "Now, look here. You can't lie in my entryway all day whimpering. What will the neighbors think? Besides, you broke my statue and—"

Before she could finish, he sat up with amazing swiftness and grabbed her around the waist. "Gotcha," he said.

It was then that she first noticed the massive muscles bulging from his arms, the thickness of his chest, and the wild look in his eyes. She was in shock for a brief moment, but it was long enough. In no time, he was on his feet, one arm around her waist, the other covering her mouth as he lifted her in the air. She struggled, but he was much too strong. Her legs flailed helplessly as he carried her inside her house, the clanging of his metal leg brace ever present.

The old lady was not one to surrender. She kicked walls and slapped wildly at him. Several items—a vase, the telephone, a small table—were knocked over as he dragged her further into the house, but even she knew this was one fight she would not win, not without help.

Vicky and Albert saw their friend in trouble. Albert immediately jumped on the man's back, but he too was no match for him. With a violent shake of his powerful body, the man easily dislodged Albert, then kicked him very hard with his one good leg, sending Albert reeling across the room. The man turned back to the old lady. He leaned her over a stack of the *Brooklyn Daily Eagle* and started choking her.

Suddenly, the voice of a man with an Irish accent emanated from the telephone receiver on the floor. Bored, he was in midyawn. "Hello, this is the police. What can I do for ya? Hello?"

Vicky ran to the receiver, but with the old lady silenced,

she couldn't manage much. She stared at it quizzically as she stretched her long feline body. Albert joined her, then licked his right front paw, which had been injured when he was knocked across the room. The old lady had assigned them names in honor of her two favorite monarchs, Queen Victoria and Prince Albert, but without her speaking for them, words would never come out of their mouths.

"Anyone there?" asked the male voice. There was a click, and the telephone went silent.

Vicky and Albert looked at each other, then at their friend, who by now was completely helpless. They knew there was nothing they could do as her body fell limp and lifeless.

Vicky turned to the open door. She saw a mouse charge inside, scampering toward the back of the house. She took off after it with Albert right behind her. After all, it was dinnertime, and they were on a schedule.

1

THERE WAS NO mention of Alice B. Sanger in the Saturday morning edition of the *Brooklyn Daily Eagle*. It was the middle of April 1890, over three months since her appointment to President Benjamin Harrison's staff, and still not a word, no acknowledgment whatsoever. One would think the first woman in United States history to be added to the staff of the president would be of some import, but not in the eyes of the *Eagle*. Instead, the newspaper was filled with details of the Brooklyn Bridegrooms, a professional baseball club that had moved from the American Association to the National League, and the new reserve clause in all baseball players' contracts, a mere paragraph that bound them to their teams. Baseball was apparently more newsworthy than a historic moment, especially when that moment involved a woman.

Mary Handley shook her head. She realized Miss Sanger was only a stenographer, but up until this point no woman had been trusted by a president to perform even the most menial of duties on his staff. Her appointment had significance.

Still, Mary wasn't going to dwell on it. Changing the inequities of the world was a slow process. Most people, both men and women, welcomed change as they would a bill collector seeking payment on an overdue note.

What was more important to Mary at that instant was that the *Brooklyn Daily Eagle* was resting on her very own pedestal desk in her very own office. The smile that crossed her face was hard to contain. The desk was a new addition, a gift from her friend Sarah, who was cleaning out her house in preparation to move to a larger one now that she was pregnant with her fourth child. Also on the desk was another gift from the wonderfully supportive Sarah: twenty business cards neatly tucked into a small wooden tray. In the center of the cards, it read "Mary Handley—Consulting Detective" and on the bottom left corner was her business address. The title of consulting detective was a private joke between Sarah and Mary. Sarah knew of Mary's admiration for the new series of novels about a detective called Sherlock Holmes. Holmes had labeled himself a consulting detective, so Sarah had been referring to Mary as one. The business address was the address of Lazlo's Books, the bookstore in which Mary worked about five blocks from her tenement apartment on Elizabeth Street in Brooklyn. Her office was situated in the back, in what had previously been a storage room. Mr. Lazlo, the Lazlo of Lazlo's Books, had provided her unlimited use of the space along with a small filing cabinet, two chairs, and a kerosene lamp. The desk was the finishing touch and she now had everything she needed, except for cases.

After Mary had so spectacularly solved the Goodrich murder as an outside hire for the Brooklyn Police Department, her expectations for continuing the detective work she loved were high. That had been a good year and a half earlier. Unfortunately, police departments were still not officially hiring women, and except for one case that had sent her briefly to Chicago, gender apparently outweighed competence when it came to hiring private investigators. Since eating was an essential bodily need, a few months after the Goodrich case she had procured a job as a salesclerk at Lazlo's Books, where Mr. Lazlo believed her notoriety as a woman who had solved a sensational murder case would draw curiosity seekers to buy his books.

"Do you really believe the type of person who might come to gape at me actually reads?" Mary had asked in her usual blatant manner when Lazlo had interviewed her for the job.

"Possibly not, but wouldn't it be grand if it were so, and we played a part in elevating someone's intellectual pursuits?" Lazlo crinkled his forehead, a habit he had when musing on a subject he deemed worthwhile. In his midfifties, he still had a full crop of gray hair and was thin, his face accented with a bushy gray mustache. His creased brow gave him a professorial look. He liked that, and it was probably why the expression had become such a habit.

"I believe your goals are a bit too high, sir."

"One must always aim high, Mary, or you're left without an excuse for failure. . . . And do call me Lazlo. I abhor formal titles like 'sir.'"

Lazlo was very informal, especially with those whom he liked, and he had liked Mary from their very first meeting. With her thick blond hair, blue eyes, and pretty visage, he realized it would have been easy for her to sail through life relying on looks alone. But that was not Mary. He saw she had a certain intelligence and awareness that was rare in people of any gender or age. Their relationship from their first meeting had consisted of an intellectual sparring that eventually grew into mutual respect, their most oft-discussed topic being Lazlo's hero, Benjamin Franklin.

"I don't understand his appeal or why the man deserves such praise," she had once told him.

"He was a modern-day Renaissance man. What more need be said than that?"

"That term has mistakenly become equated with brilliance. A more accurate description would be 'jack of all trades, master of none,' a phrase which I believe is in Mr. Franklin's *Poor Richard's Almanac.* Quite apropos, don't you think?"

"Apropos for the uninformed. That term is not and has never been in Mr. Franklin's book."

Mary smiled, amused that Lazlo had caught her. She hadn't believed what she said, but she couldn't resist needling Lazlo about his idol. While working on the Goodrich murder case, she had learned from her interactions with Thomas Edison that idols could be very disappointing, and possibly even deadly if adoration obscured reason. Her conclusion was that they were good for inspiring people but unhealthy to meet. Of course, since Benjamin Franklin had been dead for a century, there was no danger of Lazlo ever meeting him, so their conversations were pure fun.

It had been five months since Mary had returned from her Chicago adventure. Lazlo had graciously given her the time off from work, voicing the hope that her solving a new case would attract even more customers. In reality, her success would have brought him an extra satisfaction that could not be counted in coin.

As far as adventures go, Chicago was a minor one. Mary had been hired by a woman to find her husband, who had disappeared in a torrential rainstorm. Her contention was that he had met with serious harm or foul play or both. She maintained he would have never disappeared on his own, not because of his love for her but rather for that of his dog, whom he had left behind and whom she loathed. When Mary found the husband and returned him to his wife, she discovered the dog was an elaborate ruse. He had no love for the animal; rather, his disappearing was his way of having her experience a taste of the misery she had fostered on him during their marriage. Mary left them trying to push the dog on each other in a twisted game of seeing who could make the other's existence more wretched.

On the train ride back to New York, Mary had contemplated the nature of relationships. The Chicago couple did not have an arranged marriage, so at some point they had chosen one another. How did that love disappear and turn into such vehement antagonism? Had sexual attraction blinded them to their differences or could life somehow change people so drastically?

Either one or both, she had thought, *possibly along with a lack of human perception.*

Now, as she stared at her pedestal desk, Mary's eyes wandered to the business cards, and her sense of pride faded into disappointment. Sarah had given them to her on her twenty-fifth birthday. *That was nine months ago,* she thought, *and except for one card, they're all still there.* She had given that one card to the couple in Chicago, though she really had no desire to hear from them again.

Two cases over two years were not a career but an avocation. She still had her reward money for solving the Goodrich murder. She had once considered using it to finance her way through medical school. As she was considering that once again, she was interrupted.

"This lady needs your assistance, Mary," said Lazlo, standing in the doorway and indicating the woman next to him. She was about Mary's age and had dark brown hair. She was also tall, big boned, and ungainly in a slightly stooped-over sort of way.

"I'm sorry. I didn't realize the store was open. How may I help you?"

"The store isn't open yet," Lazlo replied with a twinkle in his eye, and then left Mary alone with the woman. The woman stepped further into the office and offered Mary her hand.

"I'm ever so pleased to meet you, Miss Handley," she said in a thick Southern drawl. "My name is Emily Worsham."

As they shook and Emily's huge hand engulfed Mary's, Mary couldn't escape feeling a bit odd. She realized it was a stereotype, but that accent had always conjured up thoughts of dainty, delicate women. Emily Worsham was far from that.

"I'm pleased to meet you, too. How may I be of service to you, Miss Worsham?"

"I believe my uncle John Worsham was murdered, and I need you to prove it."

Murder was never pleasant news, but Mary almost smiled as she handed Emily Worsham her card and they both sat, getting down to business.

2

COLLIS HUNTINGTON HATED Saturdays. He used to love them. Saturdays had meant burying the competition and wooing politicians, all in his pursuit of accumulating more money than one human being could possibly spend in several lifetimes. Saturdays now meant currying favor with people he despised and from whom he knew he would never see a cent. He was sixty-eight, bald, and sported a full white beard, a constant reminder that he was too old for this type of nonsense. Huntington couldn't have cared less about art and yet there he was at a board meeting of the Metropolitan Museum of Art. He was also part of the committee to bring the 1892 International Exposition to New York and involved in countless other activities that he deemed boring and fruitless. The reason for his participation was simple. He was hell-bent on becoming a pillar of New York society, but not because he had any desire to rub noses with the insufferable hypocrites who populated it. It was because of Arabella.

Huntington was a master at business and had come a long

way from his farm-boy roots in Connecticut, where his family lived on the edge of a swamp. Drawn by the California Gold Rush of 1849, he had the good sense to avoid the boom-or-bust mentality that went with panning for gold and established a successful hardware business in Sacramento. Using business ingenuity, political influence, and ruthless tactics, he eventually became the driving force behind the "Big Four": Mark Hopkins, Leland Stanford, Charles Crocker, and Huntington. Due to his finagling, they had used mostly government grants and subsidies to build the Central Pacific Railroad, which was the western portion of the First Transcontinental Railroad. Needless to say, each of the Big Four had amassed millions. In business, Huntington was a force of nature. Grown men who had never feared anyone cowered before him. His fiercest competitors, forces in their own right, shuddered when they had to go up against him, but he was helpless when it came to Arabella.

Arabella was Huntington's second wife and almost thirty years his junior. The new Mrs. Huntington was particular and demanding, yet he was completely smitten. He would move mountains to get her what she wanted, and she knew that.

Arabella had come from humble beginnings, a likely root of her desire for acceptance into the ranks of New York Society. Truth be told, she yearned to be the grand dame of New York society, but first, she and Huntington had to overcome the fact that neither of them had been born into it. It also didn't help that rumors still persisted about their relationship having started before Huntington's wife passed away. Add to that the fact that Huntington was perceived as being gruff and unmannerly, and they had a much higher hurdle to jump than most nouveau riche business tycoons who desired entry into "proper" social circles.

It's the rare person who enjoys bootlicking, though, out of necessity, some are quite good at it. Huntington was terrible at it, and he had no desire to perfect that ability. On the occasions when he wanted something, he'd simply threaten reprisals or write a check. But entrance into New York society didn't work that way. Writing a check to what was deemed a noble cause was a prerequisite, though donating time and moral support was considered more valuable. If Huntington's name became associated with a cause célèbre of the elite that was triumphant, certain requirements for acceptance would be overlooked, and he'd get the admission ticket he was seeking.

Image was everything. Huntington saw it for what it was—insincere, superficial hogwash—but he had to comply if he was going to get his beloved Arabella what she wanted. For that, and for no other reason, as the board meeting adjourned, he put on his best forced smile and approached Andrew Haswell Green.

"Any news on consolidation, Andrew?"

"We're running into the usual resistance. The Brooklyn Ring is spreading lies about us. It's to be expected with these things, but combating it is costly." The Brooklyn Ring was the name given to the political machine that ran Brooklyn. Brooklyn was a large city in its own right and not part of New York City. Green sincerely believed that consolidating New York and Brooklyn would be mutually beneficial for all concerned. For many reasons, however, not the least being their fear of losing their political clout, the Brooklyn Ring was against it.

"Don't worry about the costs, Andrew. I'll take care of that."

"Your generosity is greatly appreciated, Collis, but you've already contributed so much of your time and money. I can't help feeling we're taking advantage of you."

The next words were difficult for Huntington to utter, but he managed to get them out. "None of that's important. What's important is what's good for New York and its people." *And especially for Arabella.* "Anything I can do—it would be my pleasure."

Green heartily shook Huntington's hand, thanked him, and left. His wealth didn't approach that of the New York elite, yet Green was a New York darling. He was the protégé of the late Samuel Tilden, who had been governor of New York and in a controversial election had barely lost to Rutherford B. Hayes for the presidency of the United States. Tilden had won the popular vote, but Hayes had won in the Electoral College. Together, Green and Tilden had staged a campaign to rid New York City of political corruption and successfully rooted Boss Tweed out of Tammany Hall and into jail. Green had also been the driving force on many projects to beautify New York and improve the lifestyle of its residents, including the creation of Central Park, the Metropolitan Museum of Art, the Museum of Natural History, and many other projects that were in the works. Being associated with Green and his projects could get Arabella the status she craved whether others wanted them on their precious lists or not. Most important and frustrating to Huntington, Green was considered squeaky clean and untouchable. So Huntington had to be humble and ingratiate himself, two actions that made his skin crawl.

As Huntington turned to leave, he noticed three men conversing in a corner: Andrew Carnegie, John D. Rockefeller, and Cornelius Vanderbilt II. Carnegie, with his graying beard and receding hairline, was the eldest of the three at fifty-four. Rockefeller was fifty and had a dark mustache with closely cropped hair that was beginning to gray. That, coupled with his sharp features and conservative dress, often gave him a dour look. At forty-six, Vanderbilt still had his jet-black hair and was the most stylish of the three. He whispered something to the other two, then they glanced at Huntington, laughed, and returned to their conversation.

Huntington would not let this go unchallenged. Currying favor with Green was one thing, but these men played his kind of game, a game at which he considered himself a master. He approached them.

"Andy, John, Junior, glad to see you're in good cheer." Huntington was fully aware that Cornelius Vanderbilt II had been named after his grandfather and not his father, yet he insisted on calling him Junior because the name implied inheritance and lack of accomplishment. It also annoyed the hell out of Vanderbilt.

"Give my regards to the lovely Arabella," said Carnegie. "She's a fine woman, Collis. I'm sure even Elizabeth would have approved."

Elizabeth was Huntington's first wife. She had died of cancer a short nine months before Huntington married Arabella six years ago, and Carnegie was alluding to the rampant rumors of an affair, which continued to haunt Huntington and Arabella.

"And be sure to give my regards to Louise, Andy," Huntington shot back at Carnegie. "I'm absolutely certain Margaret wouldn't have approved." Louise was Carnegie's wife. Margaret was his mother, and it was well-known she didn't want him to marry her. He didn't get engaged until he was forty-five, and, the dutiful son that he was, he made Louise wait seven years until after his mother died for them to get married. *Two down, one to go,* thought Huntington. *You're next, John. Come on, let's have it.* He didn't have to wait long.

"I can't recall you ever being such an art connoisseur, Collis," Rockefeller interjected. "It must be Arabella's marvelous influence. I'm pleased to see she's widening your horizons."

Huntington knew what Rockefeller was implying, and it was spot-on. He wouldn't have been there, doing everything against his nature, if it weren't to please Arabella. Still, no matter how true, it was an assault on his manhood, and he couldn't let Rockefeller get away with it. Besides, this was the only fun he had had all day.

"Believe it or not, John, sometimes an old dog can learn new tricks. Speaking of which, have you had any luck in finding a good maid for that lovely house of yours?"

Huntington was hitting Rockefeller on two levels, both having to do with his renowned frugality. It was widely known among the wealthy set that Rockefeller's wife, Laura, was her own housekeeper, and that the Rockefellers maintained significantly fewer servants in the house than others with much less money. The Rockefellers claimed it was due to their spartan religious beliefs, but most believed Rockefeller was just cheap. Huntington had also previously owned Rockefeller's mansion and had sold it to him. Rockefeller later discovered he had paid over market for the house. As a man who prided himself on knowing value and getting bargains, it irked him to no end that someone had gotten the best of him.

Confident that he had wiped the snide smirks off the three men's faces, Huntington took his leave, now sporting a genuine smile. It had turned into a good day after all.

~⚬~

"From what little I can recollect and from all accounts of my relatives, my uncle John—actually, he was my great-uncle—was no saint," Emily Worsham told Mary. "Of course, there were reasons."

"There always are for poor behavior," Mary interjected. "Funny how people never cite reasons for behaving properly."

"I couldn't agree with you more," Emily Worsham responded, "though extenuating circumstances did exist. Richmond was destroyed during the war—"

"I take it you mean Richmond, Virginia?"

A tinge of hauteur crept into Emily Worsham's voice. "Is there any other Richmond?"

"Yes—in Texas, Michigan, and California," Mary replied in a matter-of-fact manner.

"My, you are a geographic wonder," said Emily Worsham, genuinely impressed.

Mary laughed. "I read a lot. So, in the spirit of our discussion, can I also assume the war you mentioned is the Civil War?"

"You mean *the* war. It's the only war where I come from."

"I wanted to make sure. That was twenty-five years ago."

"We're still fighting it. Southern gentlemen call it the War of Northern Aggression, but most describe it in other terms a lady doesn't repeat."

"It was an awful war with tragedies on both sides."

"We were cruel and moronic, and we deserved what we got. But you Northerners tend to overlook that there are Southerners who abhor slavery."

"I never doubted that. Human beings are human beings, and in spite of Northern propaganda, logic alone dictates that there had to be a decent amount of people who opposed it."

Mary could see that if she let this conversation continue the way it had so far, they'd soon be discussing the moon. That would be okay if that was where Uncle John was killed, but she highly doubted it.

"Though I am a history buff of the first order, we should return to your uncle John."

"Yes, of course. I don't know what's wrong with me, getting sidetracked so." Emily Worsham was suddenly filled with sadness. She pulled a handkerchief from her purse, wiped a tear that had emerged from the corner of her right eye, then continued getting sidetracked.

"I was only six years old when I last saw Uncle John, but I'll never forget him. He was always so gentle with me, so kind. I had a very stressful childhood, Miss Handley. It's not easy growing up in the South looking like I do."

"Children can be very cruel, and you're being much too hard on yourself."

"Please, I came to terms with who I am many years ago."

Mary sympathized with this woman, but she wanted to avoid any further digressions in order to get to the facts of the case. "So you haven't seen your uncle in about twenty years?"

"Twenty-one to be exact."

"How do you know for certain that he was murdered?"

"My uncle was a good faro player, and he opened a faro parlor in Richmond after the Civil War. A fairly successful one, too. Nearby, an Isabella Yarrington ran a boardinghouse of questionable repute. Even though Uncle John was well into his forties, he became infatuated with Isabella's nineteen-year-old daughter. In no time, they were married, and she got pregnant. Uncle John moved the whole family, including Isabella and her other children, to New York City, where he bought a home large enough to house them all. It was there that his son, Archer, was born. Within a year, Uncle John was dead, and the Yarringtons had all his money and the house."

"That's a very compelling story, but, again, how do you know it was murder?"

"Everyone in Richmond knew the Yarringtons were social climbers, but it wasn't until I was older that I heard about my uncle's wife carrying on an affair with a much wealthier man. Divorce would have tainted her, and there was absolutely no chance my uncle would have given up his son. There was only one way out." Emily Worsham sighed. "So there you have it. I can pay you two weeks in advance if you're amenable to it."

"That's perfectly fine. And you've told me everything?"

"Everything I know." And Emily Worsham was finally quiet.

In one respect, Mary wanted to celebrate the silence, but the detective in her knew the information she had been provided was thin at best.

"To be honest, your story is full of unproven accusations, but considering what few facts we do have and your strong feeling, it's worth investigating. When exactly did your uncle die?"

"In the fall of 1870. I'm sure you'll find it was murder for profit."

"A twenty-year-old murder will make it more difficult, but the wait is understandable. You were a child when it happened. Is your uncle's widow still alive?"

"Indeed she is. After living with this torturous information for many years, I finally decided to save up for this trip north, if for nothing else than to soothe my conscience. I got as far as her front door, then realized I wouldn't know what to say when she answered. It's a wonder how people like that seem to live forever and thrive where truly good, upstanding human beings—"

Mary's look was enough to make Emily Worsham realize she was rambling off topic again. She stopped and got to the point.

"She's remarried and is living quite well now, on Park Avenue."

"It would help if I knew her name."

"Of course. I don't know what's wrong with me. How are you supposed to find her if—"

"Her name, Miss Worsham."

"Arabella. Arabella Huntington."

3

SHORTY WAS IN a terrible mood. It had been two weeks since he had completed his last job, and he still hadn't received his final payment. Granted, the old witch hadn't given him much trouble, though setting foot into that pigsty was enough of a challenge. *I'll never understand how rich people—hell, anyone—can live like that,* he thought. *And somebody should've told me about the cats. Dogs are fine, but cats are sneaky little shits.* His problem with most clients was that they would swear they had told him everything, and they had always overlooked something. But that had nothing to do with getting his money. The work was done. An agreement was an agreement.

Shorty tried to calm himself. He hated freelancing, but full-time employment wasn't an option in his line of work. Most of his clients had jobs that paid them regularly, yet they still didn't think twice about making him wait to be paid. *I wonder how they would feel if their weekly checks were delayed,* Shorty thought. *Then maybe those bastards would understand what they do to me.*

Calming himself wasn't working. He needed to let off some steam. He was in his favorite place for it, too: a barroom in Brooklyn. Shorty had honed his skills in barrooms all over Brooklyn.

In 1858, as a five-year-old child, little Kieran Timothy Kilpatrick, Shorty's birth name, by which almost no one ever called him, had contracted infantile paralysis. It made his right leg flaccid and useless. The doctor shook his head, not really knowing what to do. He suggested making a brace for his right leg, then expressed his relief that at least his particular case was an anomaly and not part of an epidemic.

Shorty asked what those words meant. His father, the class act that he was, replied, "It means you've been fucked."

Shorty had no idea what that meant either, but being a street kid in Brooklyn, he only had to go outside and ask. It obviously wasn't good, but he still needed to know about the doctor's words. He couldn't read yet, so he went to the nice lady next door, the one his father would visit for hours a day, and she looked them up in her dictionary. She told him that "anomaly" as the doctor used it meant an exception, most probably an unusual case that happened to only one person, whereas an epidemic was something that had spread to a lot of people.

Shorty stunned the nice lady when he screamed, "The old man's right. I've been fucked!"

He was angry. Why should he be the only one with this disease? If he had it, everyone else should have it, too.

As his nickname indicated, Shorty was little for his age, but that didn't stop him from getting into his share of scrapes—in fact, much more than his share. Kids would mercilessly taunt the little boy with a leg brace, and without exception, Shorty would see red and attack. Eventually, he became so overly sensitive that a mere look, sometimes even an innocent one, would set him off. He didn't win many fights, but he acquired a reputation as a kid who never gave up no matter how badly he was losing.

When he turned twelve, Shorty realized he was never going to grow to be very big and decided to do something about it. He was tired of losing, and he needed to get stronger. Giving up fighting was never a consideration. The release he felt from it was by far his greatest joy in life. And as he grew into adulthood, it became apparent to him that fighting provided him with even more pleasure than sex ever would.

Shorty's family was poor, bordering on indigent. His father had abandoned them soon after Shorty was diagnosed, and his mother was a drunk. He lived with her in a shanty on Myrtle Avenue in Brooklyn, an area that was aptly named Young Dublin for the vast number of poor Irish immigrants living there. Shorty knew purchasing barbells would cut too deeply into his mother's whiskey money. He had to get creative about his bodybuilding.

He found a metal bar at a construction site, then got two old milk pitchers, filled them partially with dirt, and attached them to either end of the bar. He worked out religiously with his makeshift barbells for hours a day. Pretty soon he was filling the pitchers with more dirt to make them heavier and eventually had to get larger pitchers. When those pitchers became too light, he swiped a bag of cement from another construction site, dumped the dirt out of the pitchers, mixed the cement, poured it in, and let it harden. By the time Shorty was fifteen, his arms and chest were huge for his size, or really any size. None of the kids dared to tangle with him. Shorty seemed to be missing that tiny switch in a person's brain that turned off the rage, telling him to stop when a person was beaten and helpless. He'd sent more than a few opponents to the hospital.

On his sixteenth birthday, Shorty received what he described as his "best birthday present ever." He saw the doctor who had diagnosed him with infantile paralysis walking toward him on the street. With a quick, "Hi, doc," Shorty decked him with one powerful punch. As the doctor lay there, moaning, Shorty planted his braced leg firmly on his chest.

"Don't worry, doc. What just happened is an anomaly and not part of an epidemic. I'm real happy about it. How about you?" Then Shorty removed his braced leg from the doctor's chest, stepped over him, and went on his way, a snide, satisfied grin on his face.

The incident with the doctor was Shorty's epiphany, and any epiphany involving Shorty also involved fighting. It was time for him to start fighting grown men. So Shorty began frequenting barrooms in Brooklyn, the rougher the better. He'd approach the biggest man there and pick a fight. For a while, it didn't go very well. He was often beaten senseless. But Shorty never gave up, and he learned. He started winning some, and then he won them all, even rematches with men who had previously pummeled him. After six months, Shorty would walk into a barroom and grown men would hastily leave in order to avoid tangling with him.

Now, over twenty years later, Shorty looked around the barroom. There were slim pickings, just a few neighborhood drunks. He was disappointed, but he soothed himself with the fact that it was late morning and it wouldn't be too long until the lunch crowd arrived. Just as he was getting antsy, itching for some fisticuffs, a ten-year-old boy dressed in rags stepped through the doors.

As the bartender was telling the boy to get lost, Shorty raised his hand, shushing him midsentence. The bartender immediately obeyed. No one wanted to risk upsetting Shorty, whose mind at that moment was churning away. His last job had been different from most. He had never met the client in person. Instead, he had been handed a sealed envelope by a local prostitute containing the details and a generous offer. All he had to do was nod to accept. The next day a carriage drove by him, and he was tossed an envelope with a sizable advance. And so now, maybe, just maybe, this kid was his payoff. The boy approached him, dug under his pants, and pulled out a thick envelope.

"Here you go, mister," said the boy, then he started to leave. Shorty opened the envelope, saw the wad of bills, then called to the boy.

"Hey, kid, how did you know this was for me?"

The boy looked at Shorty, then down at his bad leg and up again. "Think hard. I'm pretty sure you can figure it out."

Shorty winced, his eyes narrowed, and he gritted his teeth. The air in the barroom got very tense. It was abundantly clear to everyone that Shorty was going to pound the little boy, and they were all helpless to stop him. The boy also realized he had made a mistake. His mother had always warned him that his smart mouth was going to get him in big trouble one day, and this looked like it was going to be that day.

Shorty took two steps toward the boy, gave him a chilling stare, and then burst out laughing. "You've got balls, kid, a giant set for such a little tyke."

The whole barroom broke into laughter, mostly out of relief. The boy instinctively knew he had tempted fate and had gotten away with it. He wasn't going to do it again. He smiled at Shorty and got out of there as fast as he could.

Shorty had just gotten paid a nice sum for a job that was relatively easy, and he was feeling really good. He shouted, "The next round's on me!"

His declaration was met with cheers, and as he stepped back to the bar, he motioned the bartender over to him. With lightninglike speed, Shorty flattened him with a roundhouse right. Suddenly, the room got very quiet.

"Change of plans," Shorty announced. "Drinks on the house!"

The cheers returned as Shorty stepped behind the bar and over the bartender to serve drinks.

∽

AFTER EMILY WORSHAM left, Mary searched for Lazlo. He wasn't in the bookstore. She went outside, peered down one side of the street and then the other, but didn't see him. It wasn't until she heard a sound from above that she looked up. The bookstore occupied the ground floor of a two-story building. Lazlo lived on the second floor, but the sound hadn't come from there. Mary took several steps away from the building, until she was in the middle of the street. It was only then that she saw Lazlo on the roof with a metal pole in his hands.

"Lazlo," she called. "You've certainly chosen an odd spot to play Don Quixote."

"Don Quixote?" he replied. "I'm up here alone, unless you happen to see Sancho Panza by my side or an errant windmill. And if you did, I'd be concerned."

"I do spy a pretend lance, and Don Quixote was all about imagination."

"Ah, I see where you were led astray." He raised the metal pole in the air. "This is a lightning rod. I'm finally getting around to installing it."

"Mr. Franklin and his inventions; I should have known."

"Wait there. I want to speak with you."

"Isn't that what you're doing?"

Lazlo didn't answer. He put down the lightning rod, and in a few moments, he was down on the street with Mary.

"What was so important that you couldn't shout it from the rooftop?"

"I wanted to know how your meeting went," uttered Lazlo in a low voice with a very secretive, conspiratorial tone. He was almost childlike in his excitement.

"She believes her uncle was murdered, and she wants me to investigate."

"So you've been hired. Good going."

"She paid me two weeks in advance, which begs the question—"

"Of course. By all means, take the time off. I am your biggest fan."

"You may be my only fan."

"Don't forget the lady who's paying you."

"And don't you forget to ground that lightning rod, or you might burn down the house and God knows what else instead of saving it."

He removed a manual from his suit jacket pocket and held it up. "Don't worry. I am following Benjamin Franklin's explicit instructions."

"Make sure you follow the section on the lightning rod

and not on flying a kite, or we'll all be gone in a puff of smoke."

Lazlo smiled. "Not you. You'll be off on a case."

Mary smiled back. It did feel good. She then turned and took off down the street.

Lazlo watched, possibly even giddier than Mary over the fact that she had been given another opportunity to follow her dream. He would have felt differently if he knew what danger it would soon put him in.

4

ALFRED CHAPIN WAS feeling a great deal of stress, which was not a familiar sensation for him. If anyone could be said to have lived a charmed life, he certainly qualified. His family was well-to-do with a lineage in the United States that dated back two hundred and fifty years. Chapins had witnessed the colonial period, the revolution, the Civil War, and everything in between. Alfred had attended private schools, Williams College, and Harvard Law School. He had married Grace Stebbins, whose family had been similarly blessed, and had started a successful law practice. When he decided to enter politics, he won every election he ever entered and at forty-two was presently mayor of Brooklyn. Chapin exuded class and breeding. There was talk of his running for governor of New York or possibly senator, and for that he needed Hugh McLaughlin.

Hugh McLaughlin's life experience was almost the polar opposite. The son of Irish immigrants, he had come to the United States as a boy, and he had grown up in a Brooklyn slum where school took a backseat to survival. Using his fists, he worked his way to the leadership of a Brooklyn street gang, and the respect he earned on the streets translated to the flow of Irish immigrants when he got a job at the Brooklyn Navy Yard. Once he had the trust and respect of the people, it was a natural step to politics, and though he wasn't very good at winning elections for himself, he found he was excellent at getting others elected. Now the head of the Brooklyn Ring, he had become the local kingmaker. McLaughlin ruled Brooklyn like Boss Tweed had once ruled New York City with his Tammany Hall machine. He doled out city contracts and supported candidates, receiving very handsome remuneration in return. The difference between McLaughlin and Tweed was that Tweed had been caught and prosecuted. McLaughlin had so far eluded the "do-gooders."

McLaughlin had backed Alfred Chapin for mayor. It didn't matter that he was sixty-three and weathered; McLaughlin was at the height of his power. Unlike Chapin, he had lived with stress his whole life. It was a constant for him, and he thrived on it.

Both men were in Chapin's office, along with Liam Riley, a seemingly innocuous yes-man in his midthirties who obsequiously followed McLaughlin around and whose main purpose was to support and verify every point McLaughlin made. For this reason, he had earned the nickname of "the Echo," but no one dared call him that when McLaughlin was in earshot.

"It shouldn't surprise ya, Yer Honor, that New York was gonna call out the big boys," said McLaughlin. "That's what those Tammany fellas do when they see they're in for a fight. Eh, Liam?"

"Every time, Mr. McLaughlin. Never fails," Liam answered, performing his job with the amount of enthusiasm that McLaughlin required.

"It's not Tammany, Hugh. It's Andrew Green. Millionaires flock to him like—like—"

"Like flies to shit. I can say it, but ya never will. Yer too elegant. And that's why the public likes ya so much." This time McLaughlin solicited his sidekick's response with a glance instead of words.

"They love you, Your Honor. Always have," Liam chimed in.

McLaughlin pointed to Liam. "That comes from a man who doesn't lie. It's bred in his family. He has a framed letter from Abraham Lincoln on his wall, the president who never lied."

Chapin knew that the legend of never lying was about George Washington and not Lincoln, but he saw no advantage in correcting McLaughlin. It would only anger him, and it was easier to endure the smoke he was blowing his way.

"The point is, they have big money and big names on their side, all pushing for a consolidation between Brooklyn and New York. Who and what do we have?"

"We have right on our side."

"Hugh—"

"You've paved more streets, opened more schoolhouses, and set up more parks than any other mayor in Brooklyn's history. Ya did all that and balanced the budget, too. The people of Brooklyn are not gonna let those damn New Yorkers in here to ruin the wholesome family lifestyle ya established for 'em with ya hard work."

"I'm not debating my credentials. I'm questioning our

power. They're lining up with Gatling guns and all we've got are peashooters."

"Now ya insulted me." McLaughlin puffed up his chest. The nice talk was over. "Do ya think I would ever let any of my people go into battle unprotected? I've bested more blowhards, tumbled more bullies, and beaten more wealthy shites than ya can imagine! Let those downtown assholes try to come in here! They'll crawl back bloodied if they can crawl at all!"

In the moment of silence that followed McLaughlin's tirade, Liam knew not to say a word. He just nodded his approval.

"I'm sorry, Hugh. I didn't mean to doubt you. I'm just concerned. Collis Huntington is getting very vocal, which means he's writing a lot of checks."

"No worries," McLaughlin said, calming down as quickly as he had risen to anger. He stood to go, and of course, Liam followed suit. "Don't fret about those New York fellas. I'll handle 'em. You just do yer job like ya have always done, helping the good people of Brooklyn." McLaughlin stuck out his hand and Chapin shook it.

"By the way," Chapin said, "that other thing is almost done. There was a delay for a while, but it seems to have been rectified. It looks like clear sailing from here on."

McLaughlin chuckled. "Clear sailing. I like the way you talk, as if we're all on a yacht, sippin' cocktails."

"Seriously, Hugh, are you sure this is the right move?"

"Well, ya gotta ask yerself another question, really, in order to answer that one: is this good for Brooklyn?" Before Chapin could speak, McLaughlin continued: "And the answer is: yes, of course, in the long run, in the short run, in any run. Are ya hearin' me, Yer Honor?" His stern stare served a double purpose. It assured Chapin that he meant business and that there would be repercussions if he failed to follow through.

Chapin felt foolish. He'd mistakenly hoped that somehow a miracle had occurred and McLaughlin had changed his mind.

"Loud and clear, Hugh, as always."

"Good." McLaughlin smiled his approval and left with Liam.

When they were alone in McLaughlin's carriage outside, McLaughlin turned to Liam.

"Did ya do what we discussed?"

"Yes, sir. It's already in place."

"Excellent. We have to come in punchin', fast and hard. I'm not sure how much longer I can prop up our pissant of a mayor before he starts blubberin' like a little girl."

McLaughlin rapped the wall of the carriage twice with his fist, signaling the driver, and they drove off.

∽

MARY HAD BEEN to City Hall Park and checked the death certificate for John Worsham. It stated that he had died of heart failure. No doctor's name was on the certificate, but that was not unusual. Most death certificates were filed just to verify a death for inheritance purposes. She had expected little from her trip to City Hall Park, and that's exactly what she had gotten.

How to proceed? She was on her own now, unlike in the Goodrich murder case, during which she had acted on behalf of the Brooklyn Police Department. Though even then her access to the privileged was limited. And Arabella Huntington certainly qualified as privileged. Mary knew she had to tread lightly. She couldn't just knock on Arabella Huntington's door and start asking questions about her first husband and how he came to be deceased. Instead, Mary had opted to watch the house on Park Avenue for a while in the hope that Arabella would eventually emerge, at which point Mary might be able to find a way to strike up an inconspicuous conversation in a public setting. She was aware that her plan was far from being foolproof or even clever, but it was all she had. Luckily, she had finished her business at City Hall Park early enough to arrive at the Huntington mansion late morning, avoiding having to make two separate trips from her home in Brooklyn to accomplish these tasks.

She spent an hour or so trying to be as unnoticeable as a woman of her lower social class could be amid the homes of the elite. She had brought a notebook and a pencil and pretended to be sketching the roofs of the mansions in the area as if she were an architectural student. This allowed her to hold the pad high up as often as she could to conceal her face. Her knowledge of architecture was practically nil and her artistic ability severely wanting, but she hoped no one would ever see her drawings.

Finally, a carriage stopped in front of the Huntington mansion and a woman emerged from her house with a young man at her side. As the driver opened the carriage door for them, he greeted her as Mrs. Huntington. From the way Emily Worsham had described Arabella Huntington, Mary had expected a svelte, sexual vixen. But, at forty, she was considerably overweight and dressed very conservatively, more like a wealthy schoolmarm than a seductress. Mary reasoned that the young man with her was probably her son, the one she'd had with John Worsham. He seemed the right age—about twenty—had dark hair and a mustache, and wore wire-rimmed glasses.

After they entered the carriage, Mary stuffed the notebook in her pocketbook and hurried over just in time to hear Arabella Huntington's command to the driver, "The Metropolitan Museum of Art and make it smooth for a change. I'm tired of being knocked about like a ball in a game of table tennis."

Mary shook her head. Arabella Huntington had presented the driver with an impossible task. Most streets in Manhattan were still cobblestone, and their journey would inevitably be "rocky." Mary detested how the working poor would often lose their jobs over their inability to cater to the unrealistic demands of the pampered rich. In any case, she had to get to the Metropolitan Museum of Art and couldn't afford to hire a carriage. She rushed one block over to Lexington Avenue and took the trolley to Eighty-First Street. Then she walked the three long blocks to Fifth Avenue, where the museum was located. She knew the Huntingtons would arrive before her, but she hoped she could scour the museum and find them, which she eventually did. As she pretended to be fascinated by an Édouard Manet painting, she was actually trying to decide how she could "innocently" strike up a conversation with them.

"I find it awful, positively tragic, that a man can spend his whole life creating such magnificent pieces of art and not be recognized as the genius that he is until after his death."

Mary turned to see that the man addressing her was fashionably thin and in his late twenties with pleasant, delicate features. He was dressed in expensive, bespoke clothing. The slight twirls at the ends of his mustache, almost imperceptible, were the only hint that, beneath his very conservative appearance, he might possess a bit of a rakish quality. Yet, in spite of her quick observation, she had been taken by surprise and couldn't manage much of an immediate reply.

"Excuse me," she said.

"*A Matador,* the piece of art you're admiring, was painted by Édouard Manet. His work is only just now becoming recognized, years after his death."

"Yes, poor man," Mary said, her wits returning, "he spent the last of his inheritance exhibiting his work to no avail, shared the same mistress with his father, and died of syphilis. None of those accomplishments are fitting to write on anyone's epitaph."

It was now his turn to be taken by surprise. "And I thought you had no interest in Manet."

"Why would you think that?"

"You appear to be much more interested in Arabella Huntington. Or is it her son, Archer?"

Mary had thought she was being discreet, but she obviously wasn't and needed to cover. "Arabella who? What in the world ever gave you that idea?"

"The lady doth protest too much, methinks."

"I'm impressed. That line from *Hamlet* is often misquoted. Most people make the mistake of placing 'methinks' at the beginning of the sentence. Bravo, Mr. . . . ." Mary strategically paused, hoping this man would identify himself. He bowed as all gentlemen did when greeting a lady.

"Vanderbilt. George Vanderbilt. Pleased to meet you, Miss Handley."

"A Vanderbilt recognizes me and yet I am oblivious to his identity. Has the world gone completely insane or have I?"

"Please go easy on yourself. Unlike the rest of my family, when in New York, I keep a low profile, and I've been a big fan of yours since the Goodrich case."

"Really? I had thought my dubious notoriety had been forgotten by now."

"Hardly. I followed your exploits in the newspaper with great interest and was almost disappointed when you caught the killer. I couldn't get enough of you." He stopped very briefly. "That may have sounded improper. Please excuse me—"

"You're excused. I doubt whether that was your intention. You appear to be quite balanced."

"I appreciate that, though my family might disagree with you."

"Then the rich and the poor do have some things in common. My family is similarly inclined toward me."

"Now that we've found common ground, maybe you can divulge why you're following Arabella Huntington. Please tell me it involves a case you're currently working on. I so want it to be."

His enthusiasm was childlike but at the same time it took on a self-mocking tone. Mary found it oddly charming, but she wasn't about to divulge everything to a man she had just met.

"You're right in one respect. I do want to have a conversation with her."

"Well then, let's have it." And he started walking toward the Huntingtons.

"Wait. I can't just walk up to them and start chatting."

"*You* can't, but I can," he said as he stepped back toward

her. "Arabella Huntington has been pursuing a friendship with my family for years. Being the snobs that we are—not me, my kindred—every effort has been rebuffed. Believe me, she'd be more than happy to chat with me and meet my friend." He smiled, and the glint in his eye betrayed the slight devil-may-care quality she had seen in the twirls of his mustache. *What an odd pastiche of contrasts,* Mary thought as she walked with him over to Arabella and Archer Huntington.

"Mrs. Huntington, Archer," George exclaimed as he bowed, "what a nice surprise to run into you here."

"Please, George, no need to be formal with me. Call me Arabella," she cooed, her tone infinitely warmer and friendlier than the one she had taken with her driver. "And where else would we be? Archer is back from Spain, and, like you, the two of us can't make it through the day without our requisite amount of great art."

"You know me well, Arabella, and it appears you'll get to know me better. I understand you're building a home just a stone's throw from my brother."

"Yes, we've bought a small piece of land and—"

"Small? From what I'm told there's not much of Fifth Avenue left. They're thinking of changing its name to Arabella Way."

She emitted a short bellow of a laugh. "Oh, George, you do have such a wonderful sense of humor."

"Thank you. You're being generous as usual. Arabella and Archer, I'd like you to meet a friend of mine, Mary Handley."

"Well," said Arabella, "I am more than pleased to meet any friend of George's. How do you do, Miss Handley?"

After the requisite bows and pleasantries were exchanged between Mary and the Huntingtons, George turned to Archer. "Archer, I know how fascinated you are with Hispanic culture. Have you seen the Goya the museum just acquired?"

"Really, a Goya? Where is it?"

"Come, I'll show you. Please excuse us, ladies. We'll be right back."

And they left, but not before George nodded his good-bye, casting an almost imperceptible sly glance at Mary. There was definitely an element of the rogue in him, and Mary liked that. She was also impressed by how smoothly he had orchestrated her being alone with Arabella Huntington—without even a hint of suspicion.

"Well, it looks like we have an opportunity to have a little get-to-know-you chat," Arabella remarked with a smile.

"Yes, I'd like that very much, Mrs. Huntington."

"Good," responded Arabella as the coldness she'd exhibited with her driver crept into her voice. "But first you must explain why you, a neophyte detective, were pretending to sketch houses outside my home."

5

ABIGAIL CORDAY WAS an actress of little repute, her accomplishments unable to fill the smallest footnote in the annals of New York theater or any theater at all. Much to her chagrin, besides having a few small roles in some less than noteworthy melodramas, her biggest break had come a few months earlier when she was cast in a production of Sophocles's *Electra*, where she was merely one of many in the chorus of the Women of Mycenae. Since a Greek chorus required a uniformity of look and movement, individual actors rarely stood out. But Abigail had managed to circumvent that.

She had long admired the Italian actress Eleonora Duse, who was known for her naturalistic acting style and for portraying real, raw emotions. She felt only disdain for most actors of the day. Their set facial expressions and hand gestures indicating what emotion they were supposed to be feeling were superficial, phony, and almost comical to her. Abigail had worked hard on her part in the Greek chorus of *Electra*, making sure every word, every gesture, and every movement was completely genuine and truly felt. She had even created a detailed background for her character. It had nothing to do with the action of the play, but it had helped her to understand who she was and why she was there.

Abigail realized early on that the director had no concept of reality, urging the actors to make one untruthful move after another. So she approached him after one of the rehearsals. She pointed out that the chorus was looking up when they should have been looking left and they were moving to the right when they obviously should have been moving forward.

"Why would I look up? What's my motivation?" she had asked.

He had simply replied, "Your job, my dear."

On opening night, after three weeks of rehearsal following the director's lead and feeling like a complete fraud, she had come to the conclusion that she was going to show the American audiences what real acting was. True, she was part of a chorus, but all the Women of Mycenae were real people who had very real lives. If the director had been more receptive to her ideas, he would have understood. How could anyone contest that they were all human beings?

When the curtain rose and the play had begun, she was a living, breathing person, and the others in the chorus were the lifeless automatons of the director's creation. She had rationalized that the fact that she was not performing the same movements and gestures as the others was minute compared to the clear difference between being truthful and being artificial. So when the chorus looked down, she looked up. When they stepped to the right, she stepped to the left. At one point, Abigail collided with another actor.

In a very short time and after howls of laughter, the curtain came down, only to be raised a few minutes later with one less Woman of Mycenae in the cast. Abigail wasn't nearly as upset at being fired as she was at the audience's reaction. She thought, *How could people be so shallow? How could they fail to see what was so clearly presented in front of them?* She had decided from that moment on that no one's opinion would matter except for her own. She would not only dig deeply into each role she played and become the truthful incarnation of the playwright's intent, but she also had no need for her art to be confined to a theater. She would no longer be Abigail Corday in everyday life but rather the characters she portrayed or wanted to portray. That way she would not only attain more insight into her roles but also give people who never went to the theater, like her local grocer in Brooklyn, the benefit of experiencing true art anywhere, anytime. One day she would be Ophelia in Shakespeare's *Hamlet,* another she'd be Agnès in Molière's *The School for Wives,* and yet another Clytemnestra in Aeschylus's *Agamemnon.* When she got bored with portraying someone else's creation, she would invent her own characters or portray people she knew or had casually met, making up histories for them to fill in what she didn't know. Shakespeare had written, "All the world's a stage," and she would take it literally.

Abigail dismissed the many who snickered at her. And much to her delight, there were some who appreciated her efforts. An occasional pedestrian would toss her a coin. Her butcher gave her a free piece of meat, and she got hired to play the part of someone's mother at a birthday party. It filled her with hope and encouraged her to continue.

Abigail Corday was no more. Only greatness remained.

～∞～

MARY, GEORGE VANDERBILT, and the Huntingtons were
having cocktails and lunch at a crowded saloon on Third Avenue and Fifty-fifth Street. Mostly frequented by Irish labor-
ers, it was a rowdy place, hardly known for catering to the
upper crust of New York.

"My goodness, Arabella," exclaimed George, surprised
and enjoying the atmosphere, "I learn more about you every
time I see you. I never would have imagined you patronized
places like this."

"I must confess I've never been here before. But I thought
Miss Handley might feel more comfortable dining here."

"Mother!" Archer interjected. "I'm certain it wasn't your
intention, but I do believe you've insulted Miss Handley."

"As usual, you're absolutely correct, Archer," Arabella said
with a sigh. "I apologize for my behavior. I do tend to get testy
when people aren't being forthright with me. I'm sure Miss
Handley can understand that. Can't you, Miss Handley?"

As she turned to Mary with a pointed stare, the waiter delivered their food to the table. He was an unshaven, grubby-
looking man whose clothes were as unkempt as his person.
The chill running through Arabella's body was almost visible,
but Mary decided that no matter how amusing the woman's
discomfort might be, she had to stay focused.

"Please excuse my little charade near your home earlier."

"A charade?" George interrupted. "That sounds like fun."

"Not now, George," Mary replied.

"But I insist. I want to know. I *need* to know."

"I will tell you at another time. I promise."

"Good. It's a date then." George slyly smiled. Intrigued
and interested, Mary smiled back.

"Mrs. Huntington, it might be more prudent if we have this discussion in private."

"Please, there is nothing you can tell me that I can't share with Archer, George, and even these reprobates." She nodded toward the boisterous crowd that offended her senses.

Normally, Mary would have pushed the point further, being more concerned with not embarrassing the person she was questioning. But Arabella Huntington's proclamation insulted her twice over. She was implying that nothing Mary could say would have any chance of being important enough to require a private discussion, and the "reprobates" to whom she referred were honest Irish workingmen, the very stock from which Mary came.

"As you wish, Mrs. Huntington. I have been hired to look into the death of your first husband." And Mary handed Arabella Huntington her card.

Arabella Huntington flinched ever so slightly, but it was enough to show she was concerned. As she put Mary's card in her pocketbook, she asked, "Who hired you?"

"I'm not at liberty to tell you."

"Then I'm not at liberty to discuss it with you."

"It's been suggested that he might have met with foul play."

"That's absurd!"

Shocked, Archer quickly turned to face Mary. "You think someone killed Father? Who . . . who would do such a thing?"

Arabella was quick to respond. "No one killed your father, Archer. Miss Handley here is just trying to drum up tawdry gossip."

"I assure you I am not, and there is a simple way to put this to rest. I'd like permission to exhume the body."

"What on earth will that accomplish? The man's been dead for twenty years. There's probably nothing but dust in his coffin."

"Did you have him embalmed?"

"Of course. I'm not a barbarian."

"Then there is probably still a good amount of him preserved and a reasonable chance that a cause of death can be determined." Mary knew forensic science had advanced by leaps and bounds in the last two decades, but she really had no idea if this was possible. She would cross that path when she got to it. For right now, she was more interested in Arabella Huntington's reaction.

"I am in no way inclined to entertain your ridiculous notion. John Worsham died of a heart attack, and not prematurely, I might add. John was forty-nine, and I believe the average life of an American male is several years less. *N'est-ce pas,* Miss Handley?"

"Mother, there's no need to get upset. She's just doing her job."

"Archer, you are a sweet, trusting boy and unaware that there are people in this world who derive pleasure from causing others harm. Exhume your father's body and gossipmongers will appear on every street corner."

"But those same gossipmongers will immediately disappear," Mary quickly pointed out, "if his cause of death is finally confirmed."

"And what if nothing can be determined of what's left of him? What then? We will live with a cloud of doubt over our heads for the rest of our lives." She stood up. "Come, Archer, let's go home and have lunch. I have no intention of eating this gruel."

Archer rose, then bowed appropriately. "Good day, George, Miss Handley."

"Always wonderful to see you, George," Arabella said, making a considerable effort to plaster a smile on her face. "Next time I hope you bring more pleasant company." And she left with Archer, purposely ignoring Mary.

George turned to Mary. "Are you always this controversial?"

"You think this is controversial? You should attend one of my family dinners."

George laughed. "Ours are similarly trying." A moment passed as Mary became lost in thought. "Do you mind telling me what the wheels in your brain are churning up?"

"Arabella made a good point."

"She did," George agreed, "but there seemed to be more to it. . . . The lady doth protest too much, methinks."

"My sentiments exactly," said Mary.

Arabella Huntington was hiding something, but Mary had to tread carefully. The Huntingtons were powerful people.

6

FRIDAY-NIGHT DINNER AT the Handleys' was a tradition that Mary would've liked to abolish. Family had a facility of staying with you beyond its welcome, like a bad piece of cheese in your stomach. She had always gotten along well with her father, Jeffrey, and though her relationship with her brother, Sean, a Brooklyn policeman, was still somewhat acrimonious, it had improved over the years. Mary's major difficulties had always been with her mother.

Elizabeth Handley's view of the world was governed by her belief that there was a finite amount of happiness and sadness on this earth, and that they balanced out. If someone was happy, it meant that someone else was equally sad. So whenever something good happened to one of them, she expected something bad to happen to one of the others. This philosophy had made it impossible for her to enjoy any family member's good fortune. And overall, she felt the Handleys hadn't gotten their fair share of happiness and was intent on changing that through her stern leadership.

"Let someone else suffer," Elizabeth would say. "We Handleys have already had more than enough."

Elizabeth's definition of happiness almost always conflicted with the rest of her family's, but that never deterred her from judgment. Nothing Mary did seemed to please Elizabeth. Her goals and desires simply didn't match the ones her mother had imagined for her. Elizabeth's opinions were mostly influenced by societal norms, many of which Mary found irrationally restrictive. But she couldn't argue with her mother's roast.

"Delicious as usual, Mother," Mary said, savoring the meat as she chewed.

"I'm glad you like it," responded Elizabeth. "How's work at the bookshop? You *are* still employed there?"

Elizabeth was referring to the time, approximately two years earlier, when Mary had rebelled against her oppressive boss at the sweatshop where she used to work, and consequently was fired. It had given Elizabeth the leverage to refer to Mary as "an unemployed sweatshop worker," which she had hoped would push her in the direction Elizabeth had always wanted her to go: forgetting about any silly notions of a career, finding a good man to marry, and having children. But that leverage didn't last, because soon after Mary left the sweatshop, she had been brought on by the Brooklyn Police Department to sleuth the Goodrich murder.

"Elizabeth, dear," Jeffrey addressed his wife with as much sweetness and love as he could muster. "You know perfectly well Mary is still working at the bookshop. Why do you keep—"

"The girl has surprised us in the past, Jeffrey, or have you forgotten?"

"I'm sorry if it surprised you, Mother," Mary interjected. "But I did tell you the moment it happened, and that moment was two years ago."

"That didn't lessen the surprise and shock that my *brilliant* daughter couldn't keep her job at a place where eight-year-olds managed to stay employed?"

"The point is, Mother," said Sean, coming to his sister's defense, "Mary has a good job now, and that's all that matters."

Mary smiled at Sean, thankful for his support. Their relationship over the years had never been easy. Sean had yet to get over the fact that he had a younger sister who was much brighter and more competent at many things at which males, especially big brothers, were supposed to shine. One of their many sticking points was chess. Mary had always beaten Sean at chess, and to this day, Sean maintained that Mary only won because she cheated. Mary found it especially annoying, which prompted Sean to repeat it as often as he could. But now Mary preferred to view the positive. It hadn't been that long since, upon hearing his mother's verbal attack, Sean's first instinct would have been to sink Mary even further. So she had to admit their relationship had progressed. In fact, though it was purely by accident, Mary was responsible for Sean's meeting his girlfriend Patti, whom he had been dating for over a year.

Patricia Cassidy worked at Lazlo's Books with Mary, and they had become close friends in the time Mary had been employed there. She was twenty-two and had thick, curly red hair; a face full of freckles; and a smile that was contagious. Though not as smart as Mary (few were), she was self-educated like her, bright, and an avid reader. The two of them would discuss great literature, philosophy, and other intellectual pursuits. In that respect, Patti reminded her of her childhood friend Tina Chung, who now lived in San Francisco. Patti was also a complete and hopeless nature lover, and the small room she rented was full of a variety of plants, to which she constantly tended. Mary completely understood why she and Patti were friends, but she had never dreamed that Patti and Sean would ever be a good match.

Sean wasn't the least bit interested in an education or in reading books, and he couldn't think of anything more boring than a day in the country surrounded by nature. He was very much a "city boy." And yet, the laws of attraction are strange and sometimes incomprehensible.

One day, Mary and Patti were on their way to a lecture on the poet Walt Whitman. Whitman had resided in Brooklyn a good deal of his life. The first edition of *Leaves of Grass* was published by a Brooklyn printer and Brooklynites considered him "a local product." They had been waiting for the streetcar when Sean happened by. Mary introduced him to Patti, and whatever instant attraction two people can have when they first meet, those two had it tenfold. Sean and Patti had started chatting immediately, as if Mary weren't there. Finally, Patti beckoned to Sean.

"We're going to a Walt Whitman lecture. Would you like to join us?"

Mary would've bet the fifteen-hundred-dollar reward she had earned for catching the Goodrich killer that that would drive Sean away, but she would have lost.

"I'd love to," Sean had exclaimed. "That man is spectacular!"

Again, Mary would have bet everything that Sean didn't

know who Walt Whitman was. She had originally thought the word "lecture" would have been enough to deter him, but she had no desire to comment and be a spoiler. So Mary decided to let them discover whatever differences they might have. And that they did . . . eventually.

Months later, their fights became epic shouting matches, witnessed by neighbors at both their residences. They had even broken off their relationship several times, but it had never lasted more than a few days.

Mary tried to be the voice of reason in the middle of this madness. It was apparent how much Sean loved Patti, and being Patti's friend and confidante, she knew the feeling was mutual. She didn't want to see either of them in a constant state of forlorn.

"Be smart and give in on some of the small matters, Sean," Mary had advised Sean one day. "You'll see. Pretty soon she'll return the favor, and in no time the two of you won't even be able to remember what you used to argue about."

Sean had decided to reject Mary's counsel the moment he had heard "Be smart," those words striking at the heart of his insecurity with his sister. And so, Sean and Patti's tumultuous relationship continued as it was.

At the dinner table now, Mary had to focus on her mother's negativity and not Sean's drama with Patti or competitiveness with her. She was heartened that at least she had some good news to report.

"Just so everyone here will be the first to know," Mary said, really only meaning her mother, "I've been hired on a new case."

"That's wonderful, Mary!" exclaimed Sean with genuine joy.

"I'm proud of you, sweetheart," said Jeffrey.

"What kind of case is this one?" Elizabeth asked with the usual skepticism she harbored pertaining to anything involving Mary's career aspirations.

"It's a private client, and I'm not allowed to divulge that information."

"And Lazlo knows about this?"

"Yes. Lazlo believes in me and is incredibly supportive," said Mary with a tone that implied what she thought but did not utter: *Like you, Mother, should be.*

"Well," said Sean, "as long as we're sharing good news, I've just been promoted and put on my first murder case."

This time Mary was the first one to chime in. "Fabulous news, Sean. I'm sure you'll crack it in no time!"

"I'm very proud of both my children," announced Jeffrey, beaming.

"As if I'm not?" Elizabeth said, challenging him with a scowl.

"I didn't say that, Elizabeth. I—"

"Congratulations, Sean, and"—she paused, the rest difficult for her to say, but she finally spit it out—"you too, Mary."

Mary knew her mother's compliment was backhanded at best, but she decided to leave it alone and concentrate on Sean's good fortune.

"So, Sean, I know I can't talk about mine, but can you tell us anything about your case?"

"There's not much to tell yet. You know Gabrielle Evans, that rich old woman who was found strangled in her home?"

"Mary, would you pass the salt, please?" Elizabeth asked.

Concentrating on Sean and without looking at her mother, Mary passed the salt. "The one in Clinton Hill?"

"Yes, that's the one. The obvious motive is robbery, but her house is filled with so much garbage, it will take us weeks to go through it all, and even then it'll be hard to know what might have been taken."

"The pepper, please, Mary."

"Are there any clues to the intruder?"

"Not yet. It's hard to decipher between her mess and what the killer might have left."

"Mary, the pepper."

"You'll find the killer in due time. I have every bit of faith in you."

"Thanks, sis. Who knows? Maybe someday I'll even beat you at chess," he remarked with a smile.

Mary shook her head, thinking, *A step forward and then a step back again. Sean will be Sean.*

"Mary," Elizabeth blurted out, trying to control her anger. "How many times have I told you? When you pass the salt, you always pass the pepper, too."

"Oh, sorry, Mother," Mary said as she quickly passed the pepper to her mother. But Elizabeth couldn't control her frustration.

"How are you ever going to find a husband or even a date if you don't know common table manners and all you talk about is murder?"

"I don't know, Mother. Maybe I'll wait until the right murderer gets out of jail and marry him. We'll have a lot to discuss, don't you think?"

"That's not at all funny, especially since your last serious beau was a dope fiend."

Jeffrey and Sean knew Elizabeth had gone too far and immediately protested.

"Elizabeth!"

"Mother!"

Elizabeth's outburst hurt Mary, and she knew it was probably meant to do just that. It was one of her tactics, "a hard lesson to wake her up." Elizabeth was referring to Charles Pemberton, the son of John Pemberton, who had invented a soft drink known as Coca-Cola. Charles was a witty, charming, and handsome young man who hid his addiction to morphine very well. Shortly after it came to light, they broke up. Charles knew his resistance was weak and didn't want to bring Mary down with him. Still, they were very much in love, and it had been devastating to both of them.

Mary gathered herself. "Well, Mother, you're right about Charles, but you're absolutely wrong about my dating. In fact, I have a date tomorrow night."

"Really, and who are you trying to save this time?"

"You may have heard of him. His name is George Vanderbilt."

Elizabeth's mouth dropped wide open. "George Vanderbilt, as in . . . Stop fooling with me, Mary. I don't appreciate sick jokes."

"It's no joke, Mother. I met him while I was working on my case at the Metropolitan Museum of Art, a place that, along with my profession, you think is a waste of time. Now, if you'll excuse me, I have to go. I just realized I have a prior engagement."

Elizabeth's mind was swimming with excitement and anxiety. As Mary rose to go, she tried to stop her. "Tomorrow night, George Vanderbilt, there's not much time to prepare . . ."

With a nod and smile to Sean and her father, Mary was

gone, leaving Elizabeth all at once excited, frustrated, and in the dark.

Jeffrey and Sean were not used to seeing Elizabeth so nonplussed. They looked at each other and were about to laugh when Elizabeth noticed.

"Oh, shut up, you two!" she screamed.

But they couldn't help themselves. Their laughter was uncontrollable.

⁓

LAZLO WAS ALONE and laughing out loud. Sitting in a cushy club chair in his living room, he had in his hands *The Wrong Box,* a novel written by Robert Louis Stevenson and his stepson Lloyd Osbourne. He was reading it for the third time, and its dark humor still tickled him immensely. It was somewhat out of character for him—not that Lazlo was above having fun. He enjoyed a good repartee with Mary or anything that involved intellectual jousting as long as the other person was at least close to his level. If not, he labeled it "cerebral massacre" and found no pleasure in it. Outright laughter was entirely a different matter.

He reached over to the side table that was next to him. Besides a kerosene lamp, resting on it was a box, out of which he removed a Japanese *washi* and wiped his nose, which had been running from his laughing so hard. Lazlo liked his creature comforts, and he admired the Japanese for inventing simple items that made everyday life so much easier. A *washi* was an extremely soft, almost silky paper with which one could wipe one's nose and then just toss it away. He also preferred to lounge around his apartment at night in a kimono. He had a dark blue one with some gold stripes that was loose fitting and extremely comfortable. He had reasoned that no one would see him, since he was alone most of the time. Years earlier he had been married for a short while, but they were both so headstrong and so feverishly erudite that eventually each had found the other insufferable and they had divorced, glad to be free of one another.

His apartment above the store was roomy enough for just him. There, he could indulge in whatever scholarly pursuits he desired with little interruption from the outside world. It had two bedrooms, one of which he had turned into an office to do the bookkeeping for his business. There was a large living room with a fireplace and a decent-sized kitchen with, of course, a Franklin stove. Matching his personality, all the furniture was comfortable, though a few pieces were worn. He had a hard time getting rid of something he liked just because it was showing its age. As far as conveniences were concerned, it had been cheaper for Lazlo to build a toilet with plumbing downstairs in the back of the store. It was somewhat off-putting, but it was still significantly better than venturing outside in the cold to an outhouse. And he was very much impressed by a fairly recent invention of the Scott brothers: putting toilet paper on a roll. Their product hadn't caught on because most people thought that any discussion of what went on in the nether regions was in poor taste, and that made advertising difficult to attain.

It was about this time that nature gently tapped him on the shoulder, and having remembered that he had run out on his last visit, Lazlo rose to get a new roll of his precious toilet paper, which he stored in a kitchen cupboard. As he ventured downstairs, thinking about *The Wrong Box* and the bizarre adventures of the Finsbury family, he paid little attention to his surroundings. But as he reached the bottom level, a man's shadow crossed his path. He turned toward the bookstore window and saw a man pacing outside his shop, stopping periodically to peer in the window. He was wearing a hat and had his collar turned up, so his face was indiscernible. What was discernible was an urgency, almost a desperation in his behavior. Then there was a knocking at the door, which quickly escalated into more of a pounding.

Lazlo had been safely ensconced in his self-made cocoon over the past two decades and rarely experienced anything out of the norm or the slightest bit alarming. This was radically different and cause for concern. In a closet in the back of the shop he kept a rifle that was reputed to have been used by Benjamin Franklin when he was a military commander in the French and Indian War. It was a Brown Bess, a flintlock smoothbore musket that was over one hundred thirty years old, and besides not being absolutely sure that it was Franklin's, more importantly at this moment, Lazlo had no idea whether it could still function. Still, he knew it would have to do. It could possibly scare someone off . . . he hoped. As the pounding increased, he got Brown Bess and was headed for the door when it occurred to him how unthreatening he looked in his kimono, holding an ancient musket in one hand and a roll of toilet paper in the other. The only thing he could do to rectify the situation was to drop the toilet paper.

Lazlo's rendezvous with the intruder was imminent. He reached for the doorknob and felt something he hadn't felt since he was a schoolboy: fear.

7

COLLIS HUNTINGTON, ANDREW Haswell Green, Alfred Chapin, and Hugh McLaughlin were sharing a booth in a saloon in lower Manhattan that was practically under the Brooklyn Bridge. It was meant to be a clandestine meeting, and as evidence that it was, McLaughlin hadn't brought Liam Riley with him. None of them were familiar with the saloon, nor would they have chosen it as a place to dine and drink. The meeting place was a compromise, so that the two men from Manhattan and the two men from Brooklyn would be on neutral ground.

"Well, well," McLaughlin exclaimed. "I never thought I'd see the day when a poor son of Irish immigrants like me would be sittin' face-to-face with New York's golden boy Andrew Haswell Green and the great Collis Huntington. God, America's a wondrous country, isn't it?"

"It certainly is," responded Huntington, "and I bet you've found others naïve enough to fall for that humble immigrant crap."

Both Green and Chapin were appalled at Huntington's

crude remark, but Huntington knew no other way to do business. He was fully aware that Chapin was just a puppet and that McLaughlin was the real decision maker. He needed McLaughlin to know right off that if he planned to shovel any shit, he'd better not throw it in Huntington's yard. McLaughlin wasn't unnerved, or at least if he was, he didn't show it.

"As a matter fact, I have," said McLaughlin calmly, "and they're all in Brooklyn." He paused for effect, then continued. "I heard yer family's been here so long they greeted the pilgrims at Plymouth Rock. Ya may have forgotten how sturdy we immigrants are. By the way, is it true? Are ya part Indian?"

Thinking the insults had gone too far, Green quickly interrupted. "Gentlemen, we have come here to put aside our differences, not to create more."

"Don't worry, Andrew," said Huntington. "This is just a mating dance we Indians do before the romance begins. Right, Hugh?"

"I'm already in love," said McLaughlin, staring straight at Huntington, who returned his gaze. There was no way either of these two gigantic egos was going to give the other the satisfaction of blinking first.

After an uncomfortable pause, Chapin finally spoke. "Gentlemen, we have weighed the pros and cons of the situation, and I think it behooves us to explain why Brooklyn sees no advantage in becoming part of your city."

"Brooklyn or you?" Huntington interrupted.

"We *are* Brooklyn," McLaughlin quickly answered.

Concerned that, like two cocks trapped in the same barnyard, Huntington and McLaughlin would get lost in another standoff, Chapin jumped back in. "The fact of the matter is, our people like things the way they are. They have good schools, wholesome neighborhoods, and have no desire to take on big-city problems."

"Brooklyn on its own is the fourth-largest city in the United States," Green calmly answered. "True, we're number one, but don't fool yourself. You're already a big city with big-city problems. There is strength in consolidation. A unified harbor alone will please your banking and merchant community, and the civic improvements we can make will increase real estate values. With our pooled resources, we can solve any problem that arises."

"Our people like being part of a smaller community."

"That doesn't make sense, Alfred. A good portion of them are already commuting to Manhattan for work. Don't you think they'd rather work and live in the same city?"

Chapin paused, stuck for an answer, but McLaughlin wasn't. "Look, His Honor is a nice fella. He doesn't like sayin' things that may sound unpleasant, so let me put it in plain English so there can be no misunderstandin'. We don't want yer immigrant mongrels with their poverty, disease, and crime comin' here and soilin' our fair city."

"I'm confused, Hugh. Are immigrants mongrels or are they sturdy, and where do you fit in?" asked Huntington.

"Yer family's been here so long ya think all immigrants are the same. That's yer mistake, and it's a real jim-dandy. The ones comin' in today, the Eastern Europeans and the Jews, are from a different stock, and we don't want 'em. Is that clear enough for ya?"

"We all have our prejudices," responded Green. "I do have one question though. You have over eight hundred thousand people in Brooklyn. What are you going to do for water?"

"There's no water problem," McLaughlin answered with a touch of disdain in his voice.

"That's not what I hear. You have four hundred thousand more residents than you did twelve years ago, and the water supply has stayed the same. Your aqueduct has already broken several times and left the whole city without water. We have plenty of water, and we can help."

"Mr. Mayor, will ya please tell these gentlemen from Manhattan that they're barkin' up the wrong tree?"

"Yes," said Huntington, "please do that, *Your Honor.*" And Huntington's steely stare fell right on Chapin. In fact, Chapin felt it going through him. He seemed shaken.

"To be perfectly honest, Andrew and Mr. Huntington, it was a concern, but we've recently addressed it and we'll be fine. Thank you."

McLaughlin indicated Chapin. "See? I told ya he's a nice fella. He's tellin' ya to take a walk, and it sounds like he's gonna invite ya to dinner."

Huntington looked right at McLaughlin. "It may be foreign to your ears, but it's called having class, Hugh."

"Then try something that's foreign to your ears: *no.*" McLaughlin looked at Chapin, then they both rose and left.

Green finished his drink before turning to Huntington. "So, Collis, which is it? Are they just angling for power or do they really think they can survive without us?"

"Most probably a bit of both, but one thing is for sure. The mayor is bothered by something, and to use his words, it may *behoove us* to find out exactly what that is."

Green had noticed it too, but he was the epitome of an upstanding gentleman and had given them the benefit of the doubt. He wasn't a fool. He knew people lied, but he thought the contingent from Brooklyn was being clandestine in order to get a better deal. Huntington knew something sleazy was going on. He could smell it.

                                             ◈

As THE MAYOR's carriage crossed the Brooklyn Bridge on its way home, Chapin tried to rationalize his behavior at the meeting.

"I think I handled the water issue fine, Hugh. I don't think they noticed anything."

"If I noticed it, you don't think Collis Huntington caught it? The man's not just a snake. He's a cobra. And you know how a cobra thrives. . . . It feeds on its own."

"Look, I—"

"Relax. Do you see me worried? I'm not, and do ya know why? Brooklyn's gonna be fine and we're gonna be fine because yer holding our ace up yer sleeve, and it's about to win us the hand. Ya *do* have the ace, don't ya, Mr. Mayor?"

"Like I told you earlier, it's almost done. But it's unnerving going up against Huntington. I get the feeling he's completely aware of what we're doing."

"Let me worry about that fella. I bet Collis Huntington never tangled with an ol' street fighter like me before. He doesn't know it yet, but he's about to get hit right where it hurts the most."

                                             ◈

MARY HAD TOLD her mother she had a prior engagement, but it was a lie. She needed to get her mother out of her head and decided the best way to accomplish that was to focus her energy on her case. At least that was something on which she might make progress.

At this point, her only chance of determining John Worsham's cause of death would be to exhume and examine the body. She knew that even if that were possible, it would be a long shot to get any concrete answers, but it was all she had. Arabella Huntington was going to be of no help, and so it was up to Mary to find some legal precedent to allow her to dig Worsham up. That required knowledge of the law she didn't possess. Lazlo had a section on law in his bookstore, and now that she had an office there he had given her a key to use at her will. Mary wasn't tired, and thanks to her mother's hurtful mention of Charles Pemberton, she wouldn't be for a while. So, in an effort to turn a negative into a positive, she headed for Lazlo's Books.

She was half a block from the bookstore when she noticed light was emanating from the shop. Usually at night, Lazlo was safely ensconced in his apartment upstairs, rarely going below except for the occasional trip to the toilet, and then there was no reason to turn on lights in the store. She cautiously approached and found the door ajar. Mary became instantly alert. She was glad she had kept up on her jujitsu, a discipline she had been practicing since she was a child. It had come in handy on the Goodrich case, and now it gave her the confidence to venture farther into the store.

She heard scuffling coming from the back bookcases, followed by the loud sound of books crashing to the floor. Mary knew Lazlo was too old and much too slow to handle any youthful intruder, and at no age would he have been able to deal with a criminal. She quickly but cautiously moved toward the back bookshelves.

When she arrived there, she found Lazlo on the floor

moaning, surrounded by fallen books. There was another man on the floor facedown, unmoving.

"Lazlo, are you all right?"

"Yes, of course," he said as he slowly sat up. "I was just demonstrating *juego de maní* to our friend here, and I'm afraid I'm not as good at it as I thought I was."

"Our friend?"

The man slowly turned, brushing off the books, and Mary immediately recognized him.

"Archer!" And it was indeed Archer Huntington.

"I had told Lazlo of my interest in Hispanic studies, and when he discovered I wasn't familiar with *juego de maní,* which is a combination of dance and martial arts, he decided I had to see it. Apparently, the dance part needs considerably more practice."

Archer smiled and so did Lazlo as they slowly rose. Mary didn't share their amusement. She was confused.

"What are you doing here, Archer?"

Lazlo said, "Oh, that's right, you don't know. You see—"

"Please, Lazlo, I want to hear it from Archer, and later you can tell me why you're wearing that hideous outfit."

"It's called a kimono."

"I know that much."

"No one would've seen it if Archer here—"

"Please, Lazlo, from Archer."

Archer Huntington straightened himself and his clothes, then looked directly at Mary.

"I need to know what happened to my father. I want you to exhume his body, Miss Handley."

∽

COLLIS HUNTINGTON HAD adopted Archer shortly after he married Arabella. Archer was fourteen at the time, and Huntington was the only father he had ever known. John Worsham had died when he was a baby.

"If my father had abandoned me, I might not care who he was or what happened to him," Archer explained as he and Mary sat in her office after Làzlo had gone back upstairs. "But that's not the case. He just . . . died."

"You realize your mother won't be happy about this."

"That's quite an understatement, but thank you for the warning. Ever since our lunch today, the question of my father's death has been haunting me. I'm afraid I might have spooked Lazlo with my exuberance, but I doubt whether I'll get any rest until it's settled."

Mary almost smiled at the inability of certain rich people to deal with discomfort. She knew of others with far worse problems who had to live with the horror of their circumstances every day, because they didn't have the financial wherewithal to free themselves. But Archer seemed like a decent enough fellow, so Mary decided not to hold his privilege against him.

"How did you know where to find me?"

"I saw my mother put your card in a drawer, and when she left the room, I fished it out."

"I'm sorry. It must be uncomfortable having to sneak around."

"Frankly, Miss Handley, I can't imagine having a better mother. She was always there to support me and give me anything I needed. But I'm fairly certain that Mother is trying to shield me from any possible scandal that may arise from this. What she doesn't realize is that if such a situation does arise, I feel perfectly equipped to handle it."

Archer's words reminded Mary of her trouble with her own mother and how she had always yearned for Elizabeth to be supportive. "You're a lucky young man to have a mother who cares about you so much. Are you sure you want to do this?"

"Most certainly, and I am prepared to pay for any expenses involved. I want it done properly."

"I understand, and it will be." Mary was particularly pleased with this offer. In her eagerness to acquire a new client, she had failed to discuss possible expenses with Emily Worsham in addition to the two weeks' pay she had received. It was her oversight, and in this instance, Archer had saved her from appearing unprofessional by having to return to her client with an "oh, by the way" speech.

Mary liked Archer Huntington, but she had purposely held back one important detail. If anything untoward had happened to his father, it was most likely his mother who had done it.

8

SHORTY DIDN'T JUST like fire. He loved it. He hadn't been born yet when fire destroyed most of Wall Street in 1835, and the Great Chicago Fire of 1871 was much too far away for him to witness. He yearned to see blazes of that magnitude. And about the only thing Shorty enjoyed more than watching fires was starting them. So as a personal bonus to himself, he'd finish each assignment by setting everything aflame. It added to his enjoyment of the job, and it also had the extra benefit of getting rid of any evidence that he might have accidentally left behind. But in this last job, he had been told to kill her and get out. The note that he was given with his instructions specifically read, "There will be no fire." It was disappointing, but he was being paid infinitely more than his usual fee and he saw no benefit in questioning the client.

This left him with a dilemma: the unknown. Did he leave something at the scene that could be traced back to him? Shorty didn't think he had, but he didn't know for sure. As a result, he continually found excuses to walk past the old lady's house, and even though it had been more than two weeks since he'd completed his assignment, he observed that police were still busily running in and out.

On this particular Saturday he had been watching from behind a tree across the street when he saw two policemen, one considerably older than the other, emerge from the house and engage in what looked like a serious, animated conversation. He needed to get closer. He crossed the street and hid behind a carriage on the other side.

The older officer talked with a thick Irish accent. "I know this is your first murder case, Sean, and ya want to make a big splash, but take my word for it, lad," he said as he gestured toward the house, "ya won't be findin' a thing in that pile of garbage."

"You're wrong, Billy," Sean replied as he held up a coat button. "This button is something."

"She has so many collections of whatnots, how can ya say that's from the killer?"

"She had no collections of buttons."

"But the ol' nutcase had every piece of clothing of her poor deceased husband and son."

"I checked all their clothing, and there's not one match."

"For all we know, one of her filthy cats brought it in from the street."

"If you want to visit the lady who is taking care of the cats and use your cat talk to interrogate them, go ahead. I'm going to see what I can do with this."

Billy rubbed his bald head and smiled. Billy O'Brian had known Sean and his family since Sean was a little boy. In fact, he had recommended Sean to Second Street Station when he first told Billy he wanted to be a policeman.

"Yer almost as stubborn as yer sister, Sean Handley." Billy laughed and went back inside as Sean took off down the street.

Shorty waited until it was safe, then crossed back to the other side. *I better keep an eye on this Handley kid,* he thought. *He's not stupid like most cops.* As he started to put distance between himself and the house, he felt his coat. He had wondered where he had lost that button. Now he knew.

∽

ABIGAIL CORDAY WAS simply effervescent. Nothing could contain her joy. She was preparing for the role of a lifetime, the role she was destined to play, Nora in Henrik Ibsen's *A Doll's House.* She had read that her idol Eleonora Duse was going to play the same part in Europe, and the thought made her giddy. Together they would show the world what the art of acting really was.

One minor detail remained. She needed to be cast in the play. According to Abigail, it was indeed minor, a fait accompli. Once the director saw her he'd realize she was the walking embodiment of Nora. No one could have been more perfect, not even Duse. For days, Abigail had been living as Nora, only answering to that name. She spoke as Nora would, ate as she would, and dressed like her, too. And today her journey would begin. Today was her audition.

There was a knock at her door. "Who is it?" she asked.

"It's Robert."

She opened the door and standing there was thirty-four-year-old Robert Davies, a fellow struggling actor who was Abigail's friend and had spent many hours with her rehearsing different parts and sharing their theories on acting.

"Come in here, Torvald, and see what I have bought," Abigail said, reciting a line from the first scene of *A Doll's House.*

Playing along, Robert entered the room and looked

around. "Bought, did you say? All these things? Has my little spendthrift been wasting my money?"

Closing the door, Abigail didn't miss a beat. "Yes but, Torvald, this year we really can let ourselves go a little. This is the first Christmas that we have not needed to economize."

Robert dropped the pretense. "Very convincing, Abby. I'm sure you'll get the part."

But Abigail would not break character. "What part, Torvald? We are who we are."

Robert decided not to push it further. He didn't want to chance an argument, thus upsetting both of them right before they auditioned for the lead roles in a play. He was a dedicated actor and loved everything about the craft of acting. What he didn't like, what he couldn't tolerate, was the lack of paying work. He looked around the room again. Abigail lived in a tiny, one-room hovel where insects and occasional rodents scampered about freely. He couldn't imagine "suffering for his art" like she did. That was exactly why he had another job that allowed him to live decently, and that was also why he was jealous of Abigail. She was living the life he didn't dare try to live. And her talent was growing while his felt stagnant.

He returned to the text of the play. "Still, you know we can't spend money recklessly."

"Yes, Torvald, we may be a bit more reckless now, mayn't we? Just a tiny wee bit!"

Abigail beamed, thrilled to be back in her fantasy world, a world Robert feared would come crashing down on her one day. He hoped that wouldn't happen until he got what he needed from her.

∽✲∾

MARY, ARCHER, AND Police Superintendent Patrick Campbell stood by John Worsham's grave in Trinity Churchyard near Wall Street and Broadway as the cemetery workers dug away. Archer fidgeted nervously. In his twenty years, he had never before experienced this amount of anxiety. Mary was sympathetic, but considering the entitled life into which Archer had been born, she couldn't help thinking that before this there had likely never been anything for him to be anxious about.

Superintendent Campbell had been Chief Detective Campbell when he brought Mary on for the Goodrich case. He was her mentor, and he and his wife were now also her friends. The police commissioners at the time were afraid his sterling reputation would usurp theirs and he would take their jobs. In a preemptive move, they had decided to fire him with no real cause. A year later, he had been made police superintendent, their boss, which enabled him to return the favor. Besides the perk of being able to dismiss the police commissioners, Superintendent Campbell had found little joy in his job. He loved being out in the field solving cases, and police superintendents didn't do that. The pay was much better but his job mostly entailed mounds of paperwork and politics. He couldn't decide which of the two he loathed more.

Mary decided it would be prudent to have someone of authority at her side when they dug up John Worsham, and Superintendent Campbell more than filled that bill. Though it was perfectly legal to request the exhumation of a body with just the permission of the son, the Huntingtons were powerful people, and she didn't know what they might do to stop her if they found out in time or what sort of retribution they might seek afterward. She had reasoned that if either case should arise, Superintendent Campbell's presence could only serve to alleviate the situation.

When she had arrived at his office earlier that day, his secretary, a Miss Quincy, informed Mary that he was in a meeting. Mary knew Superintendent Campbell well, and she especially knew that "I'm in a meeting" often was code for "I need some time to be alone and not be disturbed by any more idiots." Mary went right to his door and listened. When she didn't hear any voices, she marched right in, ignoring Miss Quincy's pleas.

She found Superintendent Campbell sitting at his desk with a stack of playing cards in his left hand. With his right hand, he was in the midst of tossing one across the room toward a wastebasket, around which several cards lay on the floor. When he saw Mary, he smiled.

"Mary, what brings you here?"

"I was hoping you'd join me in a card-tossing contest, but I can see you need more practice."

At that moment, Miss Quincy rushed in. "I'm sorry, Superintendent. I had told Miss Handley you were in a meeting—" She stopped midexcuse, having seen the cards in his hand and the ones on the floor. She would never have said it, but she was obviously thinking, *I wish I had your job.* Instead, she said, "I'll close the door and let you two be alone."

"It's nice to see you inspire such admiration and respect in your employees."

"I don't blame them. How do you admire someone whose main function is to be a figurehead?" Superintendent Campbell had always been heavyset but solid. Mary couldn't help observing that in the six months or so since he had been promoted to superintendent, he had put on a decent amount of weight and looked puffy. The sedentary life didn't agree with him, and the banquet circuit made it worse.

"I need your help, Chief."

"In case you hadn't noticed, Mary, I'm no longer chief."

"You'll always be Chief to me."

Mary meant what she said, but she also knew those were the exact words he wanted to hear. Superintendent Campbell immediately perked up.

"Well, let's get going then." And he started ushering her toward the door.

"Don't you at least want to know what it's about?"

"You can tell me in the carriage. If I spend another second in this office, I may do something undeniably sane, like quit."

⌀

ABIGAIL'S AND ROBERT'S auditions were at the Thalia Theatre in lower Manhattan. At one point it had been called the Bowery Theatre, but the name was changed in 1879 when new ownership took over. They were German and had produced mostly German plays. A change in strategy had prompted them to hire a new artistic director who wanted to return the Thalia to its heyday when it was established in 1826 by the Astor family. The artistic director—a distant relative of Andrew Carnegie's wife, Louise—thought he could revive the theater with one successful play and boost his career in the process. For that reason, he had chosen *A Doll's House*. It was a critical favorite, and a great production would attract New York's elite, helping the theater regain its popularity among "those who mattered."

Abigail and Robert requested to be audition partners, and

the casting director saw no problem with that. They were both unknown and likely to stay that way after the audition. When they were called onstage, the artistic director, who was also directing the play, took notice. The actress looked exactly the way he had envisioned Nora. She dressed like her and even walked like her. *Now, if she could only act,* he thought.

When their scene started, the director became entranced. *This girl is good,* he thought, *very good.* He got up from his seat in the audience and moved a few rows closer to the stage. He needed to be sure. When the scene was over, he asked them to do another scene, and then another. It didn't change his opinion one iota. In fact, she got better with each scene. He finally returned to his original seat and, holding up a piece of paper, asked the actress to step forward.

"What's your name, dear? It's not on your résumé."

"My name is Nora Helmer," Abigail responded as if it were obvious.

The director chuckled. He had heard of this new brand of actor who "lived the character." He had been to Rome, where he had witnessed the great Italian actor Tommaso Salvini mesmerize audiences with his brilliant and very real performance in *Othello*.

This is what this theater needs to make a real splash, he thought, *a fresh approach.* Little did he know that Abigail was more than fresh. She was at best deluded and quite possibly insane.

❧

"FIRST THOMAS EDISON and J. P. Morgan," Superintendent Campbell had said in his carriage, referring to suspects in the Goodrich case. "And now Collis Huntington. Mary, can't you go after someone less powerful, like possibly the president of the United States?"

"I'm not going after Collis Huntington. I'm just digging up the body of his wife's first husband. He likely has nothing to fear."

"Collis Huntington never fears anything or anyone. But you're leaving something out. Is it Arabella?"

"We'll cross that bridge when we come to it."

"Longfellow! You're using a Longfellow quote to avoid my question?"

"Truthfully, that's not an exact quote . . . but it is close."

His subsequent look had told her it was time for her to stop dancing around the subject.

"If John Worsham met an untimely death, the most obvious suspect would be—"

"Arabella."

"Yes."

"And you don't think Collis Huntington will do everything within his power to protect her, which might involve destroying you?"

"Chief, by now you must know that I refuse to be bullied, no matter how much money or bite an individual has. And Collis Huntington is no exception."

"Did you ever consider what he might do to me?"

"I've never seen you back down from a fight, but there's always a first time."

"Nice attempt, Mary, but do you really think that kind of psychological claptrap will work on me?"

"No, but I know you too well to think you're actually concerned. Besides, we don't yet know if there's a problem with Worsham's death. Odds are, there won't be, or at least not anything we can prove."

"Maybe not, but I want to be there if there is. You may need protection, and besides, the fireworks will be spectacular."

Mary had seen the little glint in his eye before, and she now knew for sure he was enjoying this break from the monotony of his job.

It was time. The cemetery workers were now hauling the casket out of its hole. Mary and Superintendent Campbell could both see Archer tensing.

"No point in fretting, son," Superintendent Campbell said, trying to calm him. "As the Spanish saying goes, *Que será será*—what will be, will be."

"Actually, Chief," Mary chimed in, "that phrase was made up by the English."

"And," added Archer, "the Spanish version is grammatically incorrect."

Superintendent Campbell grimaced. "Then fret away. Are you two satisfied now?"

His comment cut the tension in the air. Mary and Archer laughed, and even Superintendent Campbell, who rarely allowed himself that type of release, smiled. But the humor was short-lived, cut by the arrival of a very distressed Arabella Huntington.

"What is the meaning of this, Archer?"

"Mother, what are you doing here?"

"I received a phone call from the coroner's office, apparently for you, saying they'd be a little late to the cemetery to collect the body."

"Please understand. I just want to know what happened to Father. Is that so awful?"

"I've told you a million times what happened to him. He had a heart attack. And this won't bring him back!" She then turned to Mary. "This is your doing, Miss Handley. Archer's a very impressionable young man, and you took advantage. Shame on you!"

Archer started to defend Mary and take responsibility, but his mother quickly put up her hand to shush him and turned to Superintendent Campbell. "I must say I'm surprised to see you here, Patrick. I shall mention your lack of discretion to Mayor Chapin the next time we have dinner." Both Superintendent Campbell and Arabella knew her threat was a hollow one. Mayor Chapin was McLaughlin's man, and she had absolutely no sway there. Arabella then turned her attention to the cemetery workers.

"I demand that you put that casket back in the ground this moment. Do as I say, and do it now!" She stepped closer to them, hoping her proximity would intimidate them enough to make them do her bidding.

But the men were Italian immigrants who only spoke a few words of English and didn't know this woman. They did know what their boss had told them to do, and so they followed his orders: they opened the coffin. Mary rushed over to have a look. If Arabella Huntington succeeded in returning John Worsham and his coffin to the ground without his being examined, she wanted to at least see the condition of the body. But that would not be.

"It's empty!" Mary exclaimed.

"What?!" screamed Archer as he ran over to look. "There's nothing but rocks in here. Someone stole my father's body!"

It was fortunate that Superintendent Campbell also came to look. It enabled him to catch Arabella Huntington as she fainted into his arms.

9

DESPITE THE BIZARRE turn of events in the cemetery, Mary had been looking forward to her dinner that night with George Vanderbilt. He was attractive and charming and even seemed to share the same sensibilities as her. She wanted to get to know him better. So, after they had revived Arabella Huntington and once Archer had calmed down, Mary had a brief discussion with Superintendent Campbell, then went home to change in order to meet George at the prestigious Hoffman House in Madison Square. As they sat down at a well-positioned table next to a picture window, the conversation immediately veered from the beautiful eleventh-floor view.

"So, I understand you had an interesting day," George intimated with a sly smile.

"Have you been spying on me, George?" Mary responded with a decidedly light touch.

"I didn't know you'd tolerate that, but I'd love to."

"I'm not sure if I'd tolerate it . . . yet," Mary coyly responded. "But what *do* you know about my day?"

"Let's just say a certain individual, a very cold, very deceased one, has mysteriously disappeared."

"How did you find out?" asked Mary, surprised that he already knew.

"You must understand that we are a small, yet very influential, community."

"By 'we,' do you mean the absurdly rich?"

"You left out pampered, a very important ingredient."

Mary laughed. She was glad to see George had a sense of humor about himself.

"And because we are who we are," George continued, "people like to pass on information on the off chance that at some point in the future they might reap benefits."

"And when one of you finds out—"

"Exactly. It spreads like wildfire."

"So Arabella Huntington wasn't exaggerating when she claimed that if we exhumed the body, gossipmongers would appear on every corner?"

"Not on every corner, just on any corner she would ever consider populating."

"And it's my fault." Mary paused, letting the result of her actions sink in. If John Worsham had been murdered, Arabella Huntington would certainly be a prime suspect, but there was no proof yet, and she might have been suffering needlessly.

"What else could you have done? It was your job, Mary."

"That's true, but I don't like what it has wrought. I need to find that body and finish the job I started. That's the only way this mess can be cleaned up."

"Of course, you realize that may not 'clean up' anything? Let's say you discover Worsham was murdered. It's been many years, and it might be hard to prove who did it."

"And Arabella Huntington will live with the taint of tasteless gossip for the rest of her life."

"Precisely."

"Then we must get at the complete truth in order to dispense with all the idle chatter."

"I was hoping you'd say something like that. Can I be your assistant?"

"I can't afford an assistant, George. I can barely afford fare for the streetcar."

"Problem solved. I don't require a salary, and we can use my carriage."

As Mary mulled over George's outrageous yet somehow tempting proposal, they were interrupted by a visitor to their table: Andrew Carnegie.

"Hello, George, good to see you," Carnegie said in a very friendly tone.

George immediately rose and shook his hand. "Good to see you, too, Mr. Carnegie. I'd like to present to you—"

"No need at all, George. I'd recognize Miss Handley anywhere."

Mary immediately responded. "It's a pleasure to meet you, sir."

"The pleasure is all mine. I was a big fan of yours during the Goodrich case. So pleased when you nabbed the culprit."

"And I had thought my notoriety had vanished."

"Nonsense," Carnegie declared. "And after today's events, well, it will only grow."

There was no mistaking Carnegie's delight in the Huntingtons' unfortunate circumstances. Mary didn't care if he was Andrew Carnegie; he was exhibiting poor form, and she was about to let him know it as only Mary could. George sensed her disapproval and was quick to make a preemptive move.

"Thanks so much for stopping by to say hello, Mr. Carnegie."

"Please, George. Louise and I were dining with John and Laura," Carnegie said, indicating a table where his wife was sitting with John D. Rockefeller and his wife. "What would your family think if I didn't at least come over and say hello? And besides, you *are* with the celebrity of the day." He motioned toward Mary. "Nice to have met you, Miss Handley."

"The pleasure was all mine," Mary replied with a tinge of sarcasm. Carnegie either didn't catch it or chose not to, returning to his table with a grin.

"You didn't have to shield me, George. I can hold my own."

George sat down. "I assure you, Mary, you weren't the one I was shielding."

Mary laughed at the implication that Carnegie needed to be protected from *her,* a former sweatshop worker. She looked over at the Carnegies and Rockefellers, who were immersed in animated conversation with each other, taking an occasional glance in their direction. Mary turned to George in amazement. "Is everyone in the upper classes an incurable busybody?"

"I'm afraid they've spent so much time and effort acquiring their fortunes that they never had time for hobbies. Now that they're flush and have an overabundance of leisure time, there's not much for them to do besides give away their money and talk about each other."

"If I weren't aware of the ruthless methods they used to obtain their wealth, I might feel some sympathy for them."

"That is exactly why I want no part of them or their businesses."

"What is it you want to do, George, besides being my assistant, of course?"

And between ordering dinner, leisurely consuming it, and drinking fine wine, George told Mary about his life's plan. His two passions were art and nature. He had already bought land in Asheville, North Carolina, where he was building a house. He had chosen Asheville for its wonderful climate, it being the perfect place for his mother to recoup from her bouts with chronic malaria. In the long term, he was going to gradually buy fine art to adorn the place, and then also, hopefully, purchase more land. His main purpose was to start a farm where he would employ the latest agricultural methods and the best breeding techniques, and, most importantly, adhere to the principles of the new science of ecology. He cared greatly about creating a place that was safe and healthy for both animals and the land. He loved trees, and he wanted to preserve forests.

"For every tree I've used in building my farm, I've planted two more and placed them in a protected area that will never be touched."

"So," Mary said, summing up George's ambition, "you not only want to live in nature but also to improve it while being surrounded by art."

"Well, not the sort of living in nature that implies tents and sleeping outdoors. That isn't me. I'll have all the comforts of a mansion on Fifth Avenue and more, including the extra perk of being without all the gossipmongers."

"George Vanderbilt—country gentleman." Mary smiled.

"You're making fun," he said, suddenly insecure. "Does it sound foolish?"

"Please excuse me, George. I have a tendency to joke sometimes instead of expressing real emotions. That's my problem, not yours. And no, your plan doesn't sound foolish. Quite to the contrary, it sounds . . . perfect."

Mary reached over and touched his hand affectionately, and he looked back at her, relieved and grateful that she understood. That's when she knew that, not then but someday, she and this very gentle man were going to fall in love.

10

ARABELLA HUNTINGTON SAT in her Park Avenue garden staring off into the distance with a faraway look on her face. After what had happened three weeks earlier in the cemetery, her upset had transitioned to sad resign, which she couldn't seem to shake. Her eating was now intermittent at best, and she had lost a good amount of weight. Arabella had always loved going out and socializing, but lately her "going out" had been limited to these solitary visits to her garden.

Collis Huntington watched his wife from his office. He was a man of action. He had always met problems straight on and solved them. That's how he had made his fortune, and people marveled at his ability to remove seemingly insurmountable obstacles in order to get his way. But this was different. He was at a loss as to how to help Arabella. His hands were tied, because he was hopelessly in love and had to make sure that whatever he did wouldn't ruffle a hair on her head.

Huntington rose from his desk and opened the French doors that led directly outside. The garden was enclosed by the mansion on three sides, and several rooms had doors facing it. His office was on the northeast end, and Arabella was so lost in her reverie she wasn't aware of his approach.

"Lovely day, isn't it, dear?"

Arabella looked up, acknowledging him. "I guess it is. I hadn't really noticed."

Then, once again, she turned to gaze blankly out into what was a magnificent backyard, filled with exotic flowers, lush bushes and trees, and even a small vegetable patch. But she wasn't looking at anything. Hers was the stare of someone either emotionally drained or trying hard to avoid feeling anything at all. Huntington was upset, too. The recent gossip and social snubs they had begun to suffer meant little to him, but they mattered greatly to his family, and that disturbed him. However, he had learned that men like him could not show weakness. Besides, he had to be an absolute rock for Arabella's sake, especially now.

"You need to eat, darling. Let me have the cook prepare something for you."

She turned to him, this time her eyes filled with desperation. "They're going to find out, Collis. They're going to uncover what we did."

He knelt down next to her and took her hand. "Don't worry, dear. No one's going to uncover anything."

"They will," she said as her panic built. "And then we'll be destroyed and all will be lost!"

"Arabella—"

"I can somehow cope with whatever may happen to us, but what will all this do to Archer? He's an innocent. What will become of him?"

She laid her head on his shoulder and started crying. In no time, she was sobbing. He put his right arm around her and with his left hand he gently patted the back of her head.

In a way he was relieved she was finally letting out all of that emotion. It might allow them to return to some semblance of normalcy.

"It's all going to be okay, Arabella. It'll be just fine. I'll take care of everything, darling."

Somewhere in the unspoken code that couples share, Huntington knew Arabella had just given him permission to act. And he could do what he did best: go after what he wanted and destroy anyone who got in his way. That included Hugh McLaughlin, Mayor Chapin, and now Mary Handley.

⁓

CHIEF MCKELLAR, WHO had replaced Superintendent Campbell at Second Street Station, didn't think Sean's "button theory" had any merit. In fact, he scoffed at it.

"In all that junk, you really think that silly little button means something? We should send you to Governors Island and have you pore over the garbage. Maybe you can piece together the killer's whole coat."

Chief McKellar laughed, but that didn't lessen Sean's resolve. It just made his job more difficult. He'd have to investigate the button on his own time. So he spent his one day off a week on Fulton Street and other shopping streets, going into clothing stores and questioning salesclerks and store owners. After a while he caught a break. One of the owners recognized the button and remembered seeing it on the coats of a particular clothing manufacturer. He rambled on about how he hated the owner of that line and how he overcharged for cheaply made clothes. Sean patiently listened and got an address from him.

He wrote to the manufacturer, who had a factory in Lowell, Massachusetts, and enclosed in the letter a drawing of the button. The owner wrote back, confirming that he had indeed used that button on one of the jackets he manufactured, and was kind enough to enclose a sketch of the jacket. The jacket was similar to the peacoat the navy used for its seamen except for a few adjustments, the most dramatic being that it came only in a brown color, whereas the navy's peacoat was dark blue. Most importantly, the owner enclosed a list of half a dozen stores that carried his jacket in the New York area. Sean decided to visit the ones in Brooklyn first.

This was the third week in a row Sean had spent his one day off working, and he invited Patti to join him. He missed seeing her, and he saw no harm in her accompanying him to clothing stores. At each store he'd ask the salesclerks about the men who had bought that particular jacket. Since there were no exact records, he'd have to rely on their memories, some good, some bordering on awful. Still, after visiting the third store, Sean had a list of about twelve men. He was eager to continue on to the stores in Manhattan.

By this time, Patti was bored and began to complain. Sean, growing weary of the constant jabber, especially since he had also started getting it at work from Chief McKellar, decided on something highly unusual: he followed his sister's advice. Instead of challenging Patti and letting their little tiff blossom into a full-blown argument, he conceded that he might have been a bit selfish. After all, this was also her only day off. So Sean put off the rest of his search until the next week. He suggested they visit some women's clothing stores and then, knowing Patti's love of nature, have a late afternoon picnic in the park.

At first puzzled by his quick acquiescence, Patti was thrilled that this new Sean existed and hoped it signaled a turn in their relationship. And Sean was surprised how one small concession could make Patti so pleasant and amenable. As the happy couple left the store, they were too wrapped up in each other to notice a man with a leg brace quickly scurrying into a nearby storefront doorway.

SHORTY HAD BEEN keeping an eye on Sean Handley, and now he had found the store where Shorty had bought his jacket. He was sure the salesman would remember him. How many men with leg braces could have bought clothes from him? *I have to do something soon,* he thought, *but what?* He needed to speak with his employer about what type of action to take, but he didn't know who his employer was. If he couldn't contact him, he'd have to find a solution. And whatever that solution was, it had to stop Sean Handley.

∽

HUGH MCLAUGHLIN IMPLORED his driver to go faster. He had gotten a frantic call from Alfred Chapin demanding to see him immediately. Chapin had seemed completely panicked. McLaughlin leaned back in his seat and vented to Liam.

"Our mayor should be wearin' short pants, Liam. He doesn't have the balls to be dressin' in full-length trousers."

"Maybe it really is something serious."

"Yer right, lad. It is possible. It's also possible that he shit his pants!" McLaughlin burst out with a hearty laugh and Liam joined in. Then McLaughlin added, "Again!" The laughter got even louder as McLaughlin's carriage thundered through the streets.

When they arrived at Chapin's office, they were immediately shown in, and sitting there with a wry smile on his face was Collis Huntington. As for Chapin, he did have the deeply uncomfortable look of a man whose sphincter muscles had just given way.

Huntington pointed to Liam and said, "Who's he?"

"He's my associate," McLaughlin answered.

"Let him *associate* with Mayor Chapin's secretary in the outer office."

"Liam's my right-hand man. He's no slouch, and he's got a letter from Abraham Lincoln to prove it."

"And Mary Todd pleasured me before they fit her for a straitjacket. Now get him the fuck out of here!"

McLaughlin glared at Huntington, who glared right back at him. Once again, the two cocks in the barnyard were at it, neither one willing to give an inch to the other. However, McLaughlin sensed that this was different from the last time they'd met. He needed to know what was on Huntington's mind and was willing to cede a small concession to find that out.

"Go, Liam. I'll fill ya in later." When Liam was gone, McLaughlin calmly turned to Huntington. "Yer obviously in a tizzy over something. Let's hear it."

"You two have made the fatal mistake of fucking with my family. Did you think I was going to just take that lying down? You have incurred my wrath, and you're about to find out exactly what that means. I will—"

Chapin cut in shakily. "I don't know what you're talking about, Collis. We—"

"Shut the hell up . . . *Your Honor.*" And Chapin did just that as Huntington continued. "I know you're not calling all the shots around here, if any at all, so that leaves Hugh." Huntington turned to face McLaughlin. "I'm going to give you one chance. Call off that Handley woman."

"Handley woman?" McLaughlin asked with a crinkled brow. "I have no idea what yer talking about."

"See, Collis?" Chapin interjected. "I told you we—"

But Huntington rode right over Chapin's words and continued addressing McLaughlin. "Claiming ignorance, eh? You had absolutely nothing to do with hiring Mary Handley to soil my family's reputation?"

"Absolutely nothing."

"Okay, Hugh, if that's the way you want it. I'll put an end to the Handley woman's snooping myself, and it won't be pretty. And one other thing. It was abundantly clear from our little meeting the other night by the bridge that you two have something, how shall I say . . . clandestine going on."

"No, we don't!" a rattled Chapin protested. "Honestly, Collis, I don't know where—"

"Shut up!" Huntington and McLaughlin simultaneously shouted, and Chapin immediately followed orders. Then Huntington looked at McLaughlin.

"How do you like that, Hugh? We finally found common ground, and soon we'll be getting a lot closer. I'm going to investigate every aspect of both your lives. If I don't uncover what naughty little thing His Honor was so concerned about the other night, I'm sure I'll dig up something. Your Brooklyn Ring isn't composed of choirboys. And don't make the mistake of doubting me. That would be tragic."

As Huntington headed for the door, McLaughlin stopped him.

"What is tragic, Collis, is yer comin' to Brooklyn and thinkin' ya can order us around. So, get in yer fine carriage, get yer ass across the bridge, and don't come back. Next time I won't be so nice."

"Excellent. Now that we've both put our proverbial cards on the table, you have no excuse. You can't say you didn't see it coming when the train hits you." With that, Huntington was gone. Chapin looked at McLaughlin with a panicked look.

"Not a word, Alfred." McLaughlin took out a handkerchief and tossed it on Chapin's desk. "Use that to clean yerself up. I'm sure you've soiled yer pants a couple of times over."

McLaughlin left and was met instantly in the outer office by Liam, who was eager to know what had transpired. McLaughlin leaned toward him and whispered, "The cobra's snappin', hissin', and makin' a fuss, but our mongoose has its teeth in deep and won't let go."

They both smiled and left.

NORMALLY, TUESDAY NIGHT would have no significance for the artistic director of the Thalia Theatre, but this one was different. It was opening night for *A Doll's House* and he was beyond thrilled. He had called in every family chip he had and found a second cousin who indeed knew Louise Carnegie and was willing to approach her about the play. All he needed were bodies to fill the seats, the "right" bodies that could spread the word to the "right" people about his brilliant production. And there was no doubt in his mind that the production was brilliant. His instinct about the unknown actress he had cast as Nora was 100 percent correct. Her performance was transformative. Soon the whole world would know about Abigail Corday, and more importantly, his production of *A Doll's House*.

He had found out Abigail's name purely by accident. A week before opening he had asked her for a name to put in the program. She kept on insisting that she was Nora Helmer, so, not wanting to upset his lead actress, he had dropped the subject. A short time later, an actor he had cast in the bit part of the porter, Robert Davies, who had overheard their discussion, was forthright in giving him Abigail's name. Of course, he had also taken that opportunity to inform the artistic director that he was aware they had no money for understudies but that he was current on the part of Torvald and was ready to go on if sickness or anything else befell the actor playing the role. *Actors,* the artistic director thought, *everything they do is about their careers.*

A few days later, when the programs came out, the lead actress was furious to see her name in them. She went to the artistic director insisting that she was Nora Helmer and that he correct the mistake. He apologized to her and explained that they didn't have the budget to make the change, then blamed it all on Robert Davies.

A short while later, he overheard a quarrel between his lead actress and the bit player.

"There's life beyond this play, Abby," Robert Davies argued.

"What play? Stop talking rubbish. I am Nora, you are just a porter, and a porter doesn't give me advice or tell me what to do."

"Abby, I know you're inside there. I'm trying to get through to you, Abby, *you!*"

"You're obviously unbalanced. Carry my Christmas tree

like you're supposed to or I'll have to get another porter." Carrying Nora's Christmas tree was the porter's one short appearance in the play.

And Abigail Corday walked off, sweeping away in grand-dame-of-the-stage fashion.

"You've gone too far with this, Abby. Please! Come to your senses!"

But she did not return. The artistic director shook his head and shrugged. *Actors*, he thought. *You'd think there was enough drama for them onstage, but they always create more in their lives.* Still, he had to admit that Abigail Corday was, to be kind, a bit unbalanced. *I just need her to give me a month. After that, she can go foaming-at-the-mouth, straitjacket crazy for all I care.*

BESIDES REVIEWERS FROM the top newspapers in New York, sitting in the audience were Andrew and Louise Carnegie; Cornelius Vanderbilt II and his wife, Alice; and much of New York's elite. Collis Huntington was also there with Arabella and Archer. It was three and a half weeks after the coffin incident and just a couple of days since Huntington had his confrontation with McLaughlin and Chapin. The Huntingtons were determined to show everyone that they had absolutely nothing to hide. Of course, their plans for acceptance had suffered a serious setback earlier that day when Andrew Green had asked to meet with Huntington.

"I'm sorry, Collis," Green had said. "But I have to ask you to step back from our consolidation project."

"What's going on, Andrew?"

"Frankly, the rumors surrounding Arabella's first husband—"

"Somebody stole the man's body. That's all there is to it."

"I know that, and you know that, but . . ." He stopped and took a breath. "This consolidation is a delicate matter. A tinge of scandal, even if it eventually is proven untrue, could set us back just enough to lose."

Huntington was no dummy. He knew Green's mind was made up long before they had met, and changing it was not an option. So, for the sake of Arabella, he did something he wasn't used to doing. He bowed out gracefully. He saw no need to apprise Green that he was plotting revenge on those who had launched an attack on his family. However, little did he know that in that theater at that time—and just across the aisle—was one of his greatest adversaries: Mary Handley.

MARY AND GEORGE Vanderbilt were sitting next to George's brother Cornelius and his wife, Alice. She and George had been seeing a lot of each other over the past few weeks, as Mary had taken George up on his offer of being her uncompensated assistant. She knew the appeal for him was due partly to a dilettante interest in detective work but mostly to a desire to spend more time with her. She was more than happy with that, and their relationship had been blossoming. This was the first time she had met any of George's family, and the meeting was incidental; they had simply decided to attend the same play. Mary felt it was too early for anything more formal. The upper-crust gossip mill also knew of their relationship, but it hadn't reached the newspapers yet.

George had been a gentleman in every sense of the word. He was courteous and considerate, and had even brought her flowers on several occasions. They had started kissing, usually in his carriage and frequently for a prolonged period of time, but he had never once tried to carry it further. It made that part of their relationship easier because it spared her the responsibility of telling him that it was still too early. Yet, she did wonder why he didn't at least try. It could just have been the fact that he was a complete gentleman, or it could have been something more troubling: that he wasn't attracted to her.

As far as the case was concerned, she had reached an impasse. There were just so many places one could look for a body without starting to spin one's wheels. She had interviewed almost everybody who had worked at the cemetery in the last twenty years—those who were still alive, that is—and had received no important information from anyone. Mary had even gone to medical schools and hospitals, both of which had the occasional habit of buying corpses for teaching purposes, turning a blind eye to the fact they were usually purchasing them from body snatchers. Nevertheless, John Worsham's body was nowhere to be found.

Though it pained her to do so, she had written to Emily Worsham, who had returned to Richmond shortly after their meeting. Mary hated admitting defeat, so she didn't. She vaguely informed her of the success of unburying her uncle's coffin and the temporary setback of not being able to find the body inside it. It was four weeks since Emily Worsham had given Mary a two-week advance salary, but she didn't mention it in the letter. Mary had already decided she was going to continue no matter what. She prided herself in solving puzzles, and this one was gnawing at her. She had to find out what had happened to the missing body of John Worsham whether she was paid to or not.

But it was time to put aside all thoughts of work. She was

at the theater and the play was about to begin. Rumor had it that this was supposed to be the "definitive" production of *A Doll's House* and that the actress playing Nora, a newcomer named Abigail Corday, was magnificent. Mary enjoyed Ibsen's plays, and the lights on the stage were going up.

Nora entered and stumbled, emitting a grunt that garnered some uncomfortable laughter. She recovered and straightened, but as she began to speak her first line, blood gushed from her mouth and Nora collapsed to the stage floor. Everyone was shocked, especially Mary, who had recognized the actress the moment she'd entered.

It was her client, Emily Worsham.

11

EMILY WORSHAM WAS dead. Whether that was indeed her name, or whether it was Abigail Corday, or something else, that fact was undeniable. Examining the body, Mary was fairly certain about the cause of death: two stab wounds, probably to the right lung and stomach. After Emily's fall, Mary had made her way quickly to the stage. Actors were surrounding her body, and she had to push her way through. One man, whom she later found out was an actor named Robert Davies, was kneeling over the body weeping. Mary gently moved him aside in order to examine her.

Just seconds after she made her determination, someone cried out, "Fire!" And indeed, smoke was seeping into the theater from backstage. In a complete panic, everyone in the crowd—audience members, actors, stagehands, and theater staff—charged for the exits. There was pushing and screaming and people being thrown to the ground. Before she knew it, Mary was alone onstage with the body and the wailing Robert Davies. Mary turned to Robert.

"Help me carry her out of here."

He nodded and bent down to help her but drew back after touching his friend's corpse. Mary could see that he was not going to be of much help and was trying to figure out how she could drag Emily out by herself when she heard, "Let me help you with that."

It was George. The consummate gentleman, he had ignored his brother's pleas to leave and had stayed, first helping some people to their feet who had been knocked down in the scramble and then braving death by fire in order to help his lady. Mary smiled, chiding herself for any doubts she may have had about him. She informed George that the unfortunate actress was the woman who had hired her, and the two of them, with a minor assist from the bawling actor, carried the body of Emily Worsham/Abigail Corday outside to safety, albeit an odd way to note the state of a deceased person.

Out on the streets they found pandemonium. A few people who had been trampled in the panicked exit were being cared for by doctors who happened to be in the audience and were waiting to be transported to the hospital. Others had been jostled, some slammed against walls, nursing their bruises but not seriously hurt. The vast majority of the rest were at a total loss as to what to do next. Some were genuinely upset over the death of the lead actress. A few actors were bemoaning that the loss of the theater probably meant the loss of their jobs, and some of the affluent audience members were more put out by the fact they had no transportation planned for the early exit. They had told their drivers to pick them up after the play, which was supposed to be two hours from then, and were forced to search for hansom cabs.

Cornelius Vanderbilt approached Mary and George. As

the fire started to engulf the theater and people were either fleeing or standing around, oddly mesmerized by the disaster, Cornelius was more concerned with the proper thing to do.

"As luck would have it, my driver decided to stay here and eat his dinner in the carriage, so he didn't have a chance to wander off," Cornelius informed them. "Why don't you two come with us? Alice and I would be happy to drop you off wherever you like."

Mary looked at George. "Go with them, George. I need to stay here."

"Are you joking?" he replied. "I can't desert my employer."

Mary smiled and George turned to his brother. "Go ahead, Cornelius. I'm going to stay with Mary." He gestured toward the deceased actress. "This poor lady was her client."

A voice came from behind them. "So that was your client." Mary turned and saw an older, bald man with a white beard step forward.

"Hello, Collis," George said. "This is an unusual moment for an introduction, but Collis Huntington, may I present to you Mary Handley."

"Ah, the infamous Miss Handley," Huntington responded. "It's a pity about your client. They're so hard to come by nowadays."

"Yes, almost as difficult as first husbands," Mary said, looking him directly in the eye, never one to back down from what she perceived as a challenge.

"And speaking of the deceased, as tragic as this poor woman's fate may be, it serves as a cautionary tale to those who mingle unwanted in others' affairs. We all hold our families dear. Don't we, Miss Handley?" Huntington paused and stared at Mary with an adversarial look that leaned heavily toward threatening. "Well, I wish you luck in your endeavors." He started to leave, but there was little chance he was going to get the last word with Mary.

"Thank you, but I find that luck is rarely part of the equation. It's the facts that count," she said, then pointedly added, "and I assure you I will get them all."

If Huntington had played any part in this murder, his behavior didn't show it, but then Mary hadn't expected a man like him would ever be easily rattled.

George leaned over to his brother and whispered, "See? I told you she was magnificent." Cornelius nodded and also left.

At that point, the firemen finally arrived with their steam pumps and began fighting the fire. The flames were shooting out of the rooftop and smoke smothered the night sky. To the layman, it looked like the theater would be totally lost, but the general consensus of the firemen was that they had gotten there early enough to at least save part of it.

By the time the police showed up to relieve Mary of the body, she had already questioned the entire cast, the stagehands, and the artistic director. None of them had seen their lead actress attacked or had been able to shed much light on the events of the evening. They were too caught up in the excitement of opening night. The one who provided the most information was Robert Davies. He managed to keep his tears under control long enough to verify that he had known the deceased for years, and that her name was indeed Abigail Corday, not Emily Worsham. He was stunned and seemed very much confused, repeating over and over that there was a thin line between insanity and genius. He was of little use to Mary, and when she left, he burst into tears again.

They had another hour until the play was scheduled to be over, but George knew how to locate his driver. He asked one of the policemen the whereabouts of the closest saloon, and that's where they found him. As they were riding off in the carriage, Mary couldn't help commenting.

"I see my detective tutelage is rubbing off on you."

"It is, indeed, but I doubt whether I could ever match your cool thinking and brave actions in such a stressful situation. I'm more than impressed. I'm in awe."

"Don't tell me you actually believe a woman can do a man's job?"

"No, of course not. Whatever gave you that insane idea?" George quipped, and it allowed them something they both needed: a good laugh. Then George got serious again. "I've always thought women were more than equal, superior really. My mother faces adversity every day with more grace and fortitude than any man I know."

"Is that your attraction for me, George?" Mary joked. "Am I your mother figure?"

He leaned in and kissed her more ardently than ever. "Does that answer your question?"

"Quite sufficiently, thank you."

She wrapped her arms around him, and he more than welcomed her. They became so consumed with one another that they almost forgot they were in his carriage. Almost. It dawned on both of them that besides it being too soon, they didn't want the memory of their first time making love to be awkward groping inside George's carriage.

George dropped her off at her tenement apartment on Elizabeth Street. After walking her to the door, he kissed her good night and left. Elated, Mary entered her apartment and suddenly felt something she had never felt before: an overwhelming disgust of her surroundings.

Mary wasn't delusional. She had never been the least bit

enamored with her living conditions. She had always viewed residing in her tiny, one-room apartment with shoddy secondhand furniture as a means to an end and nothing more. It was merely a place to live until her detective career took her to something better. That made it possible for her to look past what others might have seen as the depressing drabness and near squalor that was her apartment. Yet, all of a sudden, even she was beginning to also view it in that light.

She wondered about the cause of this. Could it be that weeks with George, regularly experiencing the life of the privileged, had somehow seeped into her bones and made her dissatisfied with her situation? She had never consciously sought wealth, and she wasn't seeing George because of his largesse, but she still felt guilty that she enjoyed it. Mary had always prided herself in being more concerned with the inner person and had thought she was immune to that type of allure. But maybe the comforts of riches really were addictive, and she was getting hooked.

More importantly, considering the circumstances, she thought, *Is that such a bad thing?*

12

M ARY HAD SPENT the past few weeks unsuccessfully trying to answer one question: where was John Worsham's
body? Then, in one night, her list of the unanswered had
grown exponentially. She had now added: who killed Abigail
Corday, why did she impersonate Emily Worsham, and why
had she wanted John Worsham's death investigated? No matter what name she used, were Abigail and John even related?
Had someone hired her to act a part, and if so, who? With the
current unexpected turn of events, she was confident more
dilemmas would arise before she found solutions to any of
these.

Mary needed information. With that pursuit in mind and
in spite of Huntington's threat the night before, she wrote a
letter to Leland Stanford. It was public knowledge that there
was no love lost between Huntington and Stanford even
though they had been business partners for decades. Huntington had recently forced him out of the presidency of
their railroad, and conversely, Stanford had double-crossed

Huntington in 1885 when he had promised to support Aaron Sargent, Huntington's candidate for the US Senate. Instead, Stanford had decided to throw his hat into the ring and had won. Considering his vast knowledge of Huntington and also their animosity toward each other, Mary thought that if Stanford had some information about the Huntingtons and Worsham, he might be willing to disclose it. But presently it was a moot point, because Stanford had yet to write her back.

Mary hadn't slept well. Her reaction to her poor circumstances when she had returned home the night before didn't disappear when she climbed into bed. The noise of her neighbors and the street below had kept her up for the first time in a long while. Smells that had never bothered her before—the ones emanating from the other apartments, the musty hallway, the garbage outside—were somehow magnified and made her restless. She was embarrassed that she had responded that way, but she did nevertheless.

Mary decided to return to the scene of the crime in broad daylight to see if she could find any clues that might give her answers or at least lead her toward them. George needed to assess a work of art he was considering purchasing, so Mary was on her own. She was impatient, uncomfortable, and annoyed with public transportation that day. She chided herself for it, but there was no denying that she was. She hated the thought of seeming pampered, and it made her cranky. Then the dark humor of it hit her. How pathetic her existence must have been that a few weeks of carriage rides and nice dinners made her feel spoiled! She began to laugh.

When she arrived at the Thalia Theatre, firemen were doing a last inspection of the scene as workers hired by the German owners to cart the debris away waited for them to finish. Mary already knew it would be too much of a coincidence for the fire to have accidentally started immediately after Abigail Corday stumbled onto the stage and died. She reasoned the two events must be connected in some way. She found the firemen to be very cooperative and forthcoming. Apparently, the police had scoured the theater in the early morning hours after the fire was extinguished, and Mary was right. It was arson, the fire having been started in Abigail Corday's dressing room. She conjectured that, most likely, the dressing room was also where the stabbing took place, and since the police had already been there, she felt she wouldn't be interfering in their investigation if she went to examine it, or rather what was left of it.

As she had expected, there wasn't much. Most of the room was charred. The heat from the fire had even melted the mirror on the wall. After searching for a while, she had just come to the conclusion that continuing was fruitless when she spotted something through a hole in what had once been the seat of a club chair. It was a partially melted metal buckle with a small piece of burned material attached to it. The material had obviously been much longer and thicker before the fire, and Mary thought it might have been leather. It didn't look like part of any woman's clothing, or at least any of which she was aware. It could have been a male shoe buckle, but it didn't look decorative enough. She wasn't sure if it meant anything, but in case it did, she placed it in her pocketbook.

❧

SHORTY WAS ANNOYED. As he sat in the store, he reviewed what had happened. He hadn't wanted to use a blade. That wasn't his style. He preferred strangling, especially with women. It wasn't as messy, and it was more enjoyable. But that actress was wild. She had fought with more strength than many of his male assignments. He had scratches on his face and arms to prove it. *The crazy bitch,* he thought as he touched his bandaged right hand.

She had screamed out, "You can't stop fate! I am the future of the American theater!" That's when he had put his hand over her mouth and she had bitten a chunk out of it. Right then and there he'd decided to stop fooling around. Two quick thrusts with his knife, and she was on the floor, quiet as can be. It was then that he started the fire and quickly made his exit, thankful that the stage door was close to her dressing room. He was sure no one had seen him.

He had to be honest with himself. He should've been better prepared. Shorty knew the assignment was a woman, so he had taken it for granted that she'd be weak. As a result, he had increased his risk of being caught, had suffered wounds, and more importantly, he hadn't enjoyed himself. He vowed never to underestimate an assignment again. At that point in his thinking, the same ten-year-old boy who had delivered his payoff in the bar several weeks back entered the store, holding an envelope.

"Here, mister, this is for you." The boy handed Shorty the envelope. He took a quick peek at the cash inside and smiled. He liked being paid on time.

"Hey, kid," he said. "What's your name?"

"They call me Killer."

"Really, huh? You're that tough?"

Embarrassed, the boy shuffled his feet and then admitted, "Nah, wish I was. Everyone calls me Peewee."

"Hey, nothin' to be ashamed of, lad. Work hard and no reason why ya can't grow up to be a killer."

The boy shrugged, heartened by Shorty's advice. Shorty pulled a letter out of his pocket that had been there for a while. When he had been hired for this past assignment, he had cursed himself afterward for not having a note ready for his mysterious employer. He knew he could take care of Sean Handley on his own, but he needed to know exactly what his client wanted him to do. He definitely didn't want to upset someone who paid him so well.

"Kid, do me a favor and give this note to whoever gave ya the envelope and tell 'em to pass it up until it gets to the person this money comes from. Okay?" The boy nodded, and Shorty peeled off one of the bills in the stack he'd just gotten. "This is for yer trouble."

The boy's eyes lit up. "Sure, mister!" He grabbed the bill and ran out. Shorty was fully aware that the kid could just take off with the money, but he didn't think it was likely. He was from the neighborhood, and he was sure the boy would be afraid he might run into Shorty again.

The owner of the store made his way to Shorty, indicating the now-absent kid. "Was that little rat botherin' you?" he said in a thick Italian accent.

"Nah, he was fine."

"Good ta hear. Today you don't know what you gonna run into." He showed Shorty the front page of the *Brooklyn Daily Eagle*. "You see this?"

In big, thick letters, the headline read, ACTRESS DIES ON-STAGE. Below it was an artist's drawing of Abigail Corday lying on the stage floor, surrounded by the set of *A Doll's House*.

"Can you believe that? On opening night," the owner continued. "The world is a crazy place, no?"

Shorty wasn't listening. He was trying to figure out how she had gotten to the stage. He had poked her twice and set a fire. She must have somehow picked herself up after he left. *That was one determined bitch,* he thought. But he needed to find out more, and Shorty didn't read that well. He handed the newspaper back to the owner.

"Do they say if they found the guy who did it or they know who he is?"

"They know nothin'. They don't even know if it's a man or woman. Stupid police!"

Shorty breathed a sigh of relief. "Yeah, stupid police."

"Anyhow," the owner said, "I got somethin' I think'll work."

The owner held up a new buckle attached to a leather strap. He had been a master cobbler in Italy and had continued practicing his trade in the United States. A leg brace was a little out of his area of expertise, but not by that much. He put it up to Shorty's leg brace, where he was missing a strap.

"Will be simple to attach. *Perfetto,* no?"

"Yeah, *perfetto,*" Shorty answered, and he smiled.

∽✑∽

GEORGE AND HIS brother Cornelius were leaving an art auction. Cornelius was not happy with him.

"You're insane, George!"

"Thank you, dear brother, and a very happy day to you, too."

"The man's been discredited by every major art critic

around the world." Cornelius was referring to a Paul Cézanne still life George had just purchased. He felt that George had severely overpaid for it.

"Maybe, but what about the minor critics?"

"That's not funny!"

"My brother doesn't find humor in something. I'm shocked, simply apoplectic."

"You're being irresponsible. Father's left you a nice sum of money, and paying a ridiculous amount for a piece of . . . whatever from a no-name and never-will-be-a-name painter is—"

"It wasn't that much, and besides, it pleases my eye. Can't I just enjoy something? Must everything be an investment?"

Cornelius took a breath, trying to calm himself. "Let's talk about something else."

"Excellent idea. I always knew my brother was a wise and intelligent man."

Cornelius looked at George, about to respond with a retort in kind, when their eyes met. Then, in true brotherly fashion, they both burst out laughing.

"George, you are a severe pain in the ol' derrière."

"Well, at least it's in a fleshy part of the anatomy."

They were still laughing when they entered Cornelius's carriage. After Cornelius signaled his driver to take off, he turned to his brother.

"So, I see you're quite smitten with this Mary Handley."

"She's positively charming, incredibly bright, and we have much in common."

"Really, George," he said while emitting a slight chortle.

"Go ahead, big brother, express your opinion, not that I could ever stop you."

"Much in common?" he said, scoffing, then rattled off a litany of questions. "Did you meet her parents? Where do they live? Where did she go to school? Who are her friends—"

"I will find all that out in due time."

"Then you know absolutely nothing about her. After all these years, do you really not know that it's breeding that counts?"

"So we human beings are no different than racehorses?"

"You're being snide, but there are similarities, more than we all care to admit."

"Cornelius, you're my brother and I love you, but you also happen to be an insufferable snob and a complete—sans the French—ass."

"Really? What am I in Italian?"

George shook his head and smiled briefly. They sat in silence for a while and then went on to other subjects, as if nothing had happened.

∾

IT WAS EARLY afternoon when Mary arrived at Lazlo's Books, already beginning to feel the fatigue from her poor night's sleep. The store was more crowded than normal, and Lazlo greeted her in grand style as if wanting others to hear.

"Mary, there are quite a few people here who would like to speak with you."

"About what?"

"Why, your book recommendations, of course." He smiled toward the customers, then gleefully whispered to Mary, "Word has gotten out that you have another case."

"I wonder how that could have happened." She gave Lazlo an accusatory glance.

"I didn't say a word, not that anyone would heed me."

"Lazlo, you know what Mr. Franklin said about honesty."

"That it's the best policy, and it always has been for me. I assume this is just gossip trickling down from the event with Mr. Worsham's body a few weeks back."

"It wouldn't surprise me. I've learned of the upper class's fondness for worthless blather. They cloak it in fine wine and expensive dress, labeling it as sport rather than the idiocy that it indubitably is."

"My, you are in a mood this afternoon."

"Have you seen today's newspaper yet?"

"No, I've been too busy."

"When you do, you'll see why." She sighed. "Lazlo, I'm sorry this case is taking more than the original two weeks. My presence here has only been intermittent, and I'll understand if you want to replace me."

"Replace you? I wish I had ten more of you!" He pointed to the many customers. "Please, take as much time as you need. There will always be a position for you here."

"Thank you for being so understanding."

"I'm merely employing good business sense. Here, maybe this will cheer you up." He took a letter out of his coat pocket and handed it to her. "Your first letter at Lazlo's Books addressed to 'Mary Handley—Consulting Detective.'"

The return address caught her eye. It was from Emily Worsham.

13

AFTER MARY HAD fulfilled her obligation to Lazlo and had spoken with the customers who were, for lack of a better word, her fans, she retreated to her makeshift office to read the letter.

Indeed, it was from the real Emily Worsham in Richmond, Virginia, if one could believe anyone was real anymore. Mary had written to her about her uncle back when she thought Abigail Corday really was Emily Worsham. Having interviewed the director of *A Doll's House,* Mary knew of Abigail Corday's obsession with "living the part." She reasoned that Abigail had plagued whoever employed her to impersonate Emily for all the information about the real Emily he or she had. Whether that was a lot or a little, it most likely included Emily Worsham's actual address in Richmond.

In her response to Mary, Emily Worsham naturally expressed much confusion. She had never asked her to look into her uncle's death and never would have. "My uncle died of heart failure," she had written, "and there was nothing fishy about it." This Emily Worsham was concerned that perhaps Mary would seek money for her services and was very explicit that no such money would be forthcoming.

"It makes absolutely no sense that I would ask you to exhume my uncle's body in New York," she had written, "when he is buried down here in Richmond."

Needless to say, that got Mary's attention.

❧

SEAN AND PATTI were wildly happy and madly in love. It hadn't been long since Sean had decided to yield every so often on their minor disputes, and it had led to benefits far beyond any expectations he might have had. Patti had become much more understanding and loving, and both of them had realized how many of their arguments had been about inconsequential claptrap. Patti even conceded that Sean's desire to work for free on his day off was perfectly fine with her. She had noticed his growing enthusiasm for police work and didn't want to put a damper on it.

"Don't worry, Patti. It won't take me long to go through the list I've compiled."

"Take as much time as you need. I know how much it means to you, Sean."

It was a world of difference to both of them, and Sean had decided that, after over a year of dating, it was time. He had never been so sure about anything. He took a good portion of his meager savings and on the same night that the fire burned most of the Thalia Theatre, throwing Mary's case into total confusion, Sean did something that had nothing to do with his career. He bought Patti a ring. On Thursday of that week, after work, he went to her apartment and got down on one knee. Patti immediately got excited.

"Sean, what are you doing?!"

"What I should have done a long time ago. I've loved you from the moment we met, but it wasn't until this last week that I realized how far it extends. It goes beyond life." As Sean took out the ring case and opened it, he quoted Patti's favorite excerpt from Walt Whitman's *Leaves of Grass*. "'I bequeath myself to the dirt to grow from the grass I love. If you want me again, look for me under your boot-soles.'" He then took a breath and asked, "Patricia Cassidy, will you marry me?"

Even though that particular quote had more to do with a love of nature than human love, the fact that Sean had tried to fit her favorite Whitman quote into his proposal touched Patti deeply. She took his hands in hers, signaling him to rise.

"Of course, Sean, I would love to be your wife."

Sean happily started to slip the ring on her finger when a thought occurred to him. "Did I get it wrong, Patti—the quote?"

"You were letter perfect."

He breathed a sigh of relief. "Good, I was afraid that—"

"Sean, we don't need poetry. We have each other."

Sean wasn't an emotional being. At least, if he was, he rarely showed it. But Patti's words struck a chord in him. He had never really had a partner or anyone on whom he could always count. He and Mary had gotten along better lately, but they still weren't close. And his male friends—well, most of them thought any emotion besides anger and laughter indicated weakness. Sean hadn't realized until that moment how much he longed for someone who would always be his ally. A warm, content feeling ran through his body as she spoke. He had heard about the power of words and had wondered what that meant. Now he knew, and somehow he also knew he would remember this moment for the rest of his life.

∼✑∼

MARY'S CASE HAD taken a weird turn. Now there were two possible stories about John Worsham's death and two graves. The Emily whose letter she'd received, if indeed she was the real Emily Worsham, had written that he had died of natural causes. Whoever hired Abigail Corday wanted to imply Worsham was murdered. It was hard to believe anything anyone said, and given Mary's naturally inquisitive mind, she would not be able to rest until she found out the truth about John Worsham, his niece Emily, and the mystery surrounding Abigail Corday and her death. These thoughts were running through Mary's mind as she asked George to wait for her, stepped out of his carriage, and walked toward her parents' house. But her pensive state immediately vanished when she heard her mother scream. Alarmed, she lifted her dress, ran as fast as she could toward the entrance, and charged inside.

"Mother, what's going on? Are you—"

Mary stopped, because what she saw was highly unusual. Her mother was hugging Sean, actually squeezing him tightly. And then there was something even rarer. She had a huge smile on her face, truly from cheek to cheek. Her father shook Sean's hand as Elizabeth proceeded to hug Patti, who was also there. It was only then that her mother acknowledged Mary.

"Mary darling, Sean and Patti are getting married. Isn't

that wonderful?" It took a second for Mary to react. Her mother had rarely, if ever, called her darling, and she struggled to process it. After a moment, Mary rushed to Patti and hugged her, then shook Sean's hand with both of hers.

"I am so happy for the two of you," she said, then continued in a loving but humorous tone. "This is my good friend, Sean, so you better take excellent care of her, and that includes plenty of Walt Whitman."

"Don't worry, sis. Walt won't get in our way. You see," he said, "we don't need poetry. We have each other." The way Sean and Patti looked at each other, it was obvious that phrase had a special meaning for them.

Of course, as always, the little bit of sunshine that had entered the Handleys' lives didn't last. According to Elizabeth's twisted philosophy, Sean's happiness meant Mary was surely unhappy, and she needed an extra shove.

"So, Mary, you know what this means. You're next."

"Not now, Elizabeth," Jeffrey implored.

"At least give Mary a certain moratorium," Patti pitched in.

"Yes, of course," Sean agreed, "though it does sound a little ghoulish, Patti."

"I believe you're thinking of 'crematorium,' Sean," Patti replied, "and I don't think Mary's quite ready for that yet."

Everyone laughed except Elizabeth, who had no intention of relenting.

"Now is as good a time as any. As they say, there's no time like the present."

"Speaking of the present," Mary quickly interjected, "George is *presently* waiting for me in the carriage outside and—"

Elizabeth's eyes widened, filled with anxiety. "George as in George Vanderbilt?"

"Yes, Mother," Mary casually responded. "We're on our way down to Richmond, Virginia. We're in a rush to catch our train, and I wanted to inform you that I wouldn't be here for dinner tomorrow night."

Elizabeth became unnerved. As she glanced around the house, she chided Mary. "How could you do this to me? The house is a mess. He'll think we're boors, and slovenly ones at that."

"Calm down, Mother. George isn't like that. Besides, your house is spotless as usual, and he's not going to see it anyway."

"I'm sure you think this is funny, Mary, but it's not."

"It is, Mother, very much so," Sean said, then he and Mary looked at each other and laughed. By now Elizabeth was fuming, and Jeffrey felt he needed to intercede.

"No need to get upset, dear. Like Mary said, he's out in the—"

A knock stopped Jeffrey. It threw Mary a bit, too. She knew it was probably George, but she had been hoping this meeting would take place at a later date when they had more time and, hopefully, when their relationship had progressed further. Still, that didn't stop her from opening the door right away.

"Sorry to interrupt, Mary, but I heard the scream and I wanted to make sure everything was all right."

"Everything is fine, George. The scream was one of joy. This is my brother, Sean, and his fiancée, Patti. They just informed us of their engagement."

George shook their hands. "Ah yes, Sean, the policeman. Mary's told me a lot about you. And Patti, Mary's good friend from Lazlo's Books. My, this is a happy day."

Elizabeth could stay silent no longer. She put on her best "company" visage and tried to exude as much charm as possible. "Please excuse the mess, Mr. Vanderbilt. Our maid came down with a case of the flu, and as you can see from my dress, I wasn't expecting company."

Mary and Sean looked at each other as if their mother had gone batty. But they had no desire to embarrass her, so they kept quiet.

"You must be Mrs. Handley," George said. "Well, it's quite clear where Mary got her considerable beauty."

"Thank you, Mr. Vanderbilt. That's very kind of you."

Jeffrey stepped forward, shook George's hand, and introduced himself.

"So pleased to make your acquaintance, Mr. Handley," George responded. "I understand I have you to thank for Mary's stellar education."

Jeffrey almost blushed, another first. "I played a very minor role. It's really Mary who's responsible for that. She was a driven girl."

"Maybe, but as I'm sure you know, it all starts with parenting, and you were the one who fed her curiosity with books."

It was clear to all that Mary had told George quite a bit about her family. This sparked Elizabeth's curiosity. She couldn't help wondering if her daughter had lambasted her to a Vanderbilt. She put on as pleasant a face as she could muster and asked the question that was troubling her.

"And what, pray tell, Mr. Vanderbilt, has my lovely daughter told you about me? Nothing scandalous, I hope." Then she laughed, as if "scandalous" were the absolute last word that would come to mind when anyone spoke of her, especially her daughter.

At this point, Mary interceded. She knew that George was

too much of a gentleman to repeat what was told to him in confidence, but she also didn't want to make him lie.

"George, we better be going or we'll miss our train."

George picked up his cue like a veteran actor onstage and checked his pocket watch. "Mary, you're right as usual. Mr. and Mrs. Handley, I want you to know that though I am quite taken with your daughter, there is nothing untoward about this trip. It's strictly business."

"Business, what business?" Elizabeth hadn't meant to voice her thoughts out loud but somehow the words sprung from her mouth.

"Oh, didn't I tell you, Mother? I've hired George as my assistant."

After a few quick good-byes, Mary and George were out the door. "Confusion" was too mild a word to describe Elizabeth's state. She was completely nonplussed.

"My daughter hires a Vanderbilt as her assistant. The sky might as well be green and the grass blue. Nothing makes sense anymore."

She walked off, shaking her head and muttering to herself.

14

MARY HAD NOT done much traveling. Growing up, there was just one short journey: the infamous and also fortuitous sojourn she had taken with her family and their neighbors the McNishes from Brooklyn to Long Island when she was twelve. It was infamous because on the way home she had discovered the body of a dead Frenchman whose murder she had eventually solved years later while on the Goodrich case. It was fortuitous because that was when and how she discovered her passion for detective work.

As far as other trips were concerned, the recent one she had taken to Chicago had been beyond unpleasant. Since Mary was paying for it, she had purchased a third-class ticket. It would be an understatement to describe the excursion as crowded and uncomfortable. It was brutal. There was a basic wooden bench where she was squeezed together with other passengers, almost unable to move, and their car was so close to the engine that they were on the receiving end of every bit of noise and smoke it emitted. The only convenience provided was a single filthy toilet. To avoid it, Mary had waited for a stop and had risked missing the train by running into the depot for her bathroom needs.

Her only other significant travel was during the Goodrich case. The Brooklyn Police Department had sent Mary to Philadelphia in search of the killer. They had paid for a ticket in second class, which was much roomier than third class, and in addition to that, her wooden seat had the ability to re-cline. It was certainly a reasonable way to travel and pleasant enough, if you hadn't experienced first class.

When traveling, dining, or really doing anything with a Vanderbilt, there was generally only one class—the best and the finest. The train they took to Richmond had comfortable sleeping quarters and porters to serve one's every need. It was equipped with a car from the Pullman Palace Car Company called the Delmonico, which served food that rivaled in quality the famed restaurant of the same name. During their waking hours, George had suggested their non-dining time be spent in the Ladies' Car. It wasn't strictly for women. Male companions could be present, but the logic behind it was that it would spare ladies from the gruff language and the smoke emanating from cigars, cigarettes, and pipes in a male-dominated car. Mary didn't mind those things. In fact, she was guilty of tossing out a very unladylike obscen-ity every now and then herself. The Ladies' Car was a little too feminine for her, but there was absolutely no chance Mary would object. With its upholstered, cushy chairs and excellent amenities, it was infinitely better than anything she had ever experienced. Besides, George was being incredibly generous and gracious. It was unthinkable for her to respond with anything but gratitude. Unlike some men, his behavior was genuine and not a sleazy attempt to buy a woman's affections. He continually impressed Mary.

When it came to sleeping, George had arranged for separate quarters. As she lay down in her extremely comfortable bed, it occurred to her how easy it would be to get used to this lifestyle. Then thoughts of guilt washed over her consciousness, and she had trouble falling asleep. She couldn't help wondering about the people in third class and the tortuous ride they were no doubt experiencing. There seemed such a vast contrast between rich and poor. She realized that not everyone could be rich, but it would be nice if the poor were less poor and could experience a bit more comfort in their lives. *Maybe the burgeoning union movement will do that,* she thought. That seemed to give her some peace, and she fell asleep. The next morning she met George for breakfast, and they had just finished eating when they arrived at the Richmond train station.

They hired a carriage and set out to meet Emily Worsham. As they traveled, it struck them how quickly Richmond was growing. There was building going on everywhere.

"Look, George," Mary said. "That trolley is running on electricity."

"Impressive. We don't have anything like that in Manhattan."

"I had read that they have the first electric trolley system in the United States. Poor Manhattan, so behind the times."

"I must admit that many of our residents are apelike in their behavior. But they're mostly bankers, industrialists, and politicians, so that doesn't take up a large section of the population."

"I certainly hope you're not including the Vanderbilts in that group."

"Mary, I know you grew up poor—"

"Not just grew up, still am."

"True, but look what you've made of yourself, and I'm not referring to money."

"Thank you, George, though I do feel I have a long way to go."

"And that's exactly how people who achieve greatness feel, or they wouldn't achieve it."

Embarrassed by George's implication, Mary attempted to lighten the conversation. "I'm at a complete loss for words, so cherish this moment. It occurs as often as Halley's Comet."

George stayed serious. "Mary, I'd never be presumptuous enough to say I wish I had an upbringing like yours."

"I hope not for your sake. If so, five more minutes with my mother would make you dearly regret you ever had that thought."

What Mary didn't understand was that George had something he had to get off his chest. He turned to face her, and it was apparent how earnest he was. "I grew up in a family where my grandfather did the achieving, and the rest of us are either living off his spoils or trying to add to his accomplishments. I hope to do something different. If I succeed, people will point to the money I had at my disposal. If I fail, they'll call me the idiot rich boy who squandered his inheritance."

Mary put her hand on his. "Maybe there is something I can impart to you from my painfully torturous and challenging childhood."

"You forgot 'disadvantaged.'"

"Yes, that too. And there is one simple fact of which I've had to keep reminding myself. It doesn't matter what people think, George. It's what you think that counts."

George digested her words. "Thank you, Mary Handley. You always make me feel better." He leaned over and kissed her on the cheek.

❧

EMILY WORSHAM LIVED in a section of Richmond called Shockoe Bottom. It was a mostly commercial area on the James River near the docks where ships regularly came and went. Since sailors frequented the neighborhood, many of the businesses catered to one's basest needs. There were a multitude of bars and gambling establishments, and several houses of ill repute. As their carriage rode along, Mary was transfixed by the surroundings.

"Can you imagine, George? Arabella Huntington grew up here. The woman has more than transformed herself. Her behavior suggests she has a self-induced amnesia of her past."

"From what I've seen so far, I don't blame her."

Emily Worsham's house was painted gray and was small but well cared for. It had a recently mowed green lawn and a flower box across the front devoted to Virginia bluebells. It even had a white picket fence. When Emily Worsham greeted them at her door, Mary was first struck by her appearance. She was far more slight and feminine looking than Abigail Corday ever was. However, she looked to be in her late twenties, about the same age, and her accent and her mannerisms were almost identical. It occurred to Mary that Abigail Corday must have been a very fine actress, and she couldn't help wondering what she might have accomplished if she hadn't been murdered.

"Thank you so much for informing me of your visit, Miss Handley and Mr. Vanderbilt. I appreciated the notice, but what I really enjoyed was getting a telegram. It was my first, and I must say it provided me with some excitement."

Mary had sent her a telegram stating when they were going to arrive, that they had a few questions, and making it perfectly clear that she expected no compensation.

"I hope it didn't cause you any concern, Miss Worsham—"

"My name is Lancaster now. I've been married for almost ten years. I have no trouble getting mail under my maiden name because the postman—well, he and I have known each other since we were children. That boy gave me my first kiss."

Apparently, Abigail Corday had either by accident or design in her portrayal landed on a personality trait of the real Emily Worsham: wandering conversation. Mary realized she would have to keep her on track or she and George were going to learn facts about her life that they had no desire to ever know.

"What I meant, Mrs. Lancaster—"

"Oh please, call me Emily. I hate bein' that formal, don't you, Mary? It's okay if I call you Mary, isn't it?"

Mary decided to abandon the topic of the telegram and get to the reason they came as soon as possible or they might never get there.

"Yes, Mary's perfectly fine, Emily."

"And please call me George," George added to avoid any discussion about his name.

"That's nice. It feels so much friendlier now, doesn't it?"

"Much more," Mary hastily replied. "So, Emily, about your uncle—"

"Oh, you two must think I'm an awful hostess. Would you like some lemonade or perhaps something a bit more potent?"

"That's very kind, but no, thank you," Mary quickly responded. "Now, your uncle. You said he was buried down here?"

"Yes, the poor man died in '78," Emily replied. "I was a mere teenager then. You know what they say. Time flies."

"'Seventy-eight?" Mary asked. "Are you sure it was that year, 1878?" She pronounced it slowly and clearly so there could be no mistake. After all, it was eight years later than what any of the Huntingtons had told her, and 1870 was engraved on the headstone in New York.

"I'm one hundred percent, positively certain. It was the year of my Sweet Sixteen, only I never had a party because we couldn't afford it. I was devastated, simply crushed, and . . ."

As Emily Worsham rambled on, Mary and George caught each other's eye. The new date was yet another wrinkle in the case. Every new piece of information radically changed the situation. Now John Worsham not only had two different graves in two different states but also two different dates on which he had died. The confusion was multiplying. It was hard to believe what anyone said at this point, and that made Mary even more determined to get at the truth.

Several minutes later, Mary and George left with only one more pertinent fact other than the time of John Worsham's death: he was buried in Hollywood Cemetery on Cherry Street. According to Emily, her parents, who were deceased, had never told her much about Uncle John except that he owned a faro gambling house. That was something the fake Emily Worsham had already told Mary.

Their next stop was Hollywood Cemetery, where they were directed to John Worsham's grave. On the tombstone it read, J. A. WORSHAM, BORN 1821, DIED 5/27/78, AGED 57 YEARS.

"This is it," Mary said.

"What does the 'A' stand for?"

"Archer. He named his son after him."

"And yet he never knew him. That's sad."

"At least we may be able to provide Archer with a certain amount of closure as to how his father died."

"What now, boss?" George asked with a combination of wryness and genuine curiosity.

"We don't know anything about him after 1870, but I do know this isn't the end. After what happened in New York, there's no question that having him exhumed down here is a must. If his body is there, maybe there will be enough preserved to determine when he really did die, and whether his death was due to heart failure or something more sinister."

Mary had very cleverly thought ahead and had brought a notarized letter from Archer Worsham Huntington granting permission to exhume his father's body. It wasn't easy working through the complicated bureaucracy that was put in place to discourage people from accomplishing something out of the norm, but by the end of the day, they had achieved what they had wanted: John Worsham's body was due to be exhumed at ten o'clock the next morning.

George had gotten them two rooms at the Ballard House, a hotel on Franklin and Fourteenth Streets, and of course, they were the best two rooms available. The Ballard House wasn't terribly luxurious, but it was certainly more so than what Mary had ever experienced in her pre-Vanderbilt days and she was still feeling pangs of guilt.

"George, maybe we should get rooms that are a little . . . less elaborate."

"Why?"

He had a good point, and Mary didn't have an answer. The rooms were there, George had the money, and the gesture wouldn't correct any of the world's wrongs. So she decided to drop the subject altogether.

It had always been a mystery to Mary how some restaurants stayed afloat while employing some of the worst business practices known to man. Such was the case with the restaurant at the Ballard House. That evening she and George were standing at the entrance waiting to be seated for almost ten minutes while more than half of the tables were empty.

"Is this what they call Southern hospitality?" Mary quipped.

"It's just good old-fashioned incompetence." George explained that he had been to the South many times and assured Mary that this restaurant was the exception rather than the norm.

It was at this point that a middle-aged, obsequious-looking man approached them.

"Excuse me for intruding, madam, but are you Mary Handley?"

"Yes, and to whom do I have the pleasure of speaking?"

"I understand you've been inquiring about John Worsham. I have some information that I believe would interest you."

"Really?"

The man looked around uncomfortably but said nothing.

"All right," said Mary, "I will formally ask then. What sort of information do you have, sir?"

"Sorry, I misspoke. I personally don't have the information, but I know someone who does and I was asked to arrange a meeting. He's just a short walk from here."

"The way things are going here," said George as he nodded toward the dining room, "we could go meet this man and be back before they even think about seating us for dinner."

"I don't mean any offense, sir," interjected the man, "but I was asked to retrieve only Miss Handley."

"Then fortune has smiled upon you," responded George. "You've lucked into a twofer."

Mary chimed in. "Mr. Vanderbilt is my trusty assistant. I go everywhere with him."

"Yes, and I'm sure Mr. Vanderbilt is extremely competent. By the way, are you—"

"Yes, I'm one of those Vanderbilts."

"How positively fortunate," the man responded while laughing self-consciously. "For you, that is. I mean, why would it be fortunate for me?"

"Well then," said George, "let's go see your friend or associate or whoever the purveyor of this information is."

"I'm afraid I'm going to have to insist—only Miss Handley."

George was about to protest when Mary stepped in. "Excuse us for a moment, will you?" The man nodded; Mary took George aside and spoke in a low voice.

"I can handle this. He's harmless." They glanced at the man, who shrugged nervously.

"I'm not worried about him. I'm more concerned with whomever engaged him."

"Have I told you how schooled I am in the arts of self-defense?"

"Yes, ad nauseam."

"Why, George, has the bloom come off the rose? Have I been boring you?"

"Never, but you must admit it's a bit off-putting to discover that your lady friend has the ability to thump you at her will."

His comment made Mary laugh, and he joined in. Then she put her hand to his cheek. "Do me a favor and stay here. If they do indeed seat you, have a glass of wine. I'll be back shortly."

George was concerned, but he also knew how bullheaded Mary was. He was watching her leave with the man when he felt a tap on his shoulder. Their table was ready.

Mary and the man walked in silence. A little more than a block from the hotel she broke it. "You said it was a short walk. How much farther are we going?"

"Not far, another block or two."

"Don't you think it's about time you told me your name?"

"Oh, didn't I? I'm awfully sorry. Jeremy. We turn here on Twelfth Street, and it's about halfway up."

They hadn't gone far up the block when a man jumped out of a doorway, surprising Mary and grabbing her from behind. He was average height but lean and sinewy. Mary could feel the hardness of his bicep as he wrapped his arm around her neck and squeezed.

Jeremy screamed, "Oh, my God!"

"Forget about John Worsham and go home," the man whispered intensely to Mary.

"Worsham?" Mary asked in a cracked voice, the pressure to her neck showing.

"Yes."

"I don't know a John Worsham. I'm looking into the death of John Gorsham."

"Gorsham?"

"Yes, the plumber."

Surely Mary's ruse would have been quickly found out, but it gave her attacker just enough pause to slightly loosen his grip on her neck. That was all she needed. She gave him a quick, hard shot to the ribs with her elbow that caused him to grunt and allowed her to get free. Then, using her considerable jujitsu skills, she grabbed his right arm and flipped him over her shoulder, sending him crashing to the pavement. He looked stunned.

Jeremy looked even more stunned, and he backed away a bit.

"Congratulations," Mary said to her attacker. "All by yourself you've lowered the average intelligence level of the everyday hoodlum."

"Huh?" he replied, still recovering from her nasty surprise.

"Translation: you're an idiot."

He charged at her again. She flipped him again, slamming him against the pavement even harder and clearly giving him the message that the first time was no fluke. It was time to try a different tack. The man jumped to his feet, pulling out a small pistol.

Mary wasn't surprised. She was ready. Before he could even straighten his hand and shoot, she elbowed him in the stomach and grabbed his gun hand, twisting until the gun dropped. She then quickly picked it up and pressed it hard into his crotch area. He immediately stopped resisting and stood absolutely still.

"I'll give you one chance to tell me who hired you, or your privates will be blown into little pieces. Of course, judging from the probe of this pistol, that would be a very tiny loss."

The man wasted no time in pointing to Jeremy. "He said it would be an easy job." He then addressed Jeremy. "Does this look easy, you prick?"

Mary looked toward Jeremy, whose eyes were filled with fear. He had just seen Mary pummel a man who could easily pound him. Mary turned to her attacker.

"Get out of here," she ordered him, and she kept the gun as he scrambled off, grateful all his body parts were still intact.

Jeremy turned and ran too, clearly panicked. Mary kicked off her shoes and took off after him.

Jeremy wasn't the least bit athletic. She caught up to him in seconds and, still holding the pistol, leapt onto his back. The two of them crashed to the cement, Jeremy taking the brunt of the fall. Mary pressed the pistol to his head.

"I need to know why you did this, and I need to know now."

Jeremy instantly capitulated and agreed to take her to a man who would explain everything. Mary had a choice. She could go with him alone or march him back to the hotel to get George. George was very protective, and he might insist on calling the police, which would only delay the process and possibly scare off Jeremy's partner when he didn't return immediately. Besides, having George with her would constantly divert her attention, because she'd be concerned about his getting hurt. After all, even by his own admission, he wasn't as skilled at combat as she was. Mary now had a gun, and she had easily dispatched Jeremy's professional hire, so she felt confident she could handle anything that might arise. Jeremy had a small horse and buggy, and she left with him.

Mary had her pistol trained on Jeremy as they drove a short distance out of town. It was just a precaution. There was little chance of his trying anything since he knew she could easily take him. Soon, they arrived at a little cottage with a sizable front porch on the edge of a wooded area surrounded by mulberry and black walnut trees. They dismounted from the buggy, and with Jeremy hesitantly leading the way and Mary following with her recently acquired pistol, they entered the cottage.

It was a comfortably furnished place, not flashy but substantial, and consisted of a living room, a dining room, a kitchen, and two bedrooms. Jeremy led her to one of the bedrooms. Inside was an elderly man under the covers of his bed, propped up against pillows and reading a newspaper by the light of a kerosene lamp. He immediately tensed.

"Jeremy, what is the meaning of this?"

"I apologize, Father, but I had no choice. I'd like you to meet Mary Handley."

The old man looked at Mary and suddenly the tension drained from his body, replaced by a combination of wiliness and gamesmanship. "So this is the infamous Mary Handley."

"Maybe not infamous," responded Mary, "but at least known. Who are you?"

"I thought you'd know by now. I, my dear young lady, am John Worsham."

Mary was taken aback. He looked awfully good for a man who'd been dead for over a decade, and possibly two.

15

THE MAN WHO said he was John Worsham was very unhappy with his son Jeremy.

"I told you to discourage her, not to kill her!"

"But, Father—"

"You're forty-three years old, Jeremy. When will you learn to think properly? You have absolutely no common sense. Zero."

"I was thinking properly, but the man I hired wasn't."

"I should have known. Incompetents hire incompetents."

"Father—"

"Go! And pray that this lovely lady doesn't press charges."

With a pained look on his face Jeremy turned toward Mary, as if asking for a reprieve. He received none and left the room moping like a wounded puppy, a forty-three-year-old wounded puppy. Alone with Mary, John Worsham's demeanor changed to that of the ultimate Southern gentleman.

"I'm sorry, Miss Handley. The world is full of morons, but it's especially disheartening when one of them is your son."

"Then you'll understand that in order to avoid also being

one, I need proof that you are indeed John Worsham. I've gone to a lot of trouble and experienced too much misinformation to just take your word for it."

He smiled. It was a somewhat crafty look. "I'm impressed. I wouldn't trust me either." He opened a drawer of his night table, removed a piece of paper, and held it out for Mary to inspect. "I always keep this handy in case I have to make a quick exit." It was John Worsham's birth certificate.

"That doesn't prove anything," Mary informed him. "Birth certificates didn't become part of government records until many years after you were born, and this could easily have been forged."

"Good point," he said, strangely enjoying himself. He got out of bed and walked over to his dresser, opened the top drawer, and started digging inside. Mary made sure she had her pistol ready in case what he removed was a weapon. Instead, he pulled out a photograph, gave it to her, and got back into bed. Mary looked at it. It was a twenty-year-old photograph of Arabella Huntington, whose married name was Worsham at that time, holding a baby who was most probably Archer. Next to them, with his arm around Arabella, was a man who looked very much like a younger version of the man lying on the bed before her at that moment. Mary was convinced.

"How is Archer, by the way?" John Worsham asked. "He was an adorable baby boy, you know."

"He'd be much better off if he knew his father was alive, and he could have his first conversation with him."

"Unfortunately, I won't be around for much longer. Advancing age has finally caught up with this ol' warrior. I'm sixty-nine, and the doctors say I won't make it to seventy. Weak heart."

If he was looking for sympathy, he wasn't going to get it from Mary. This man had abandoned his paternal responsibility and, intentionally or not, almost had her killed.

"You were already buried twice for a weak heart. You know what they say—third time's a charm."

Instead of being upset or insulted, John Worsham let out a loud laugh. It was a roar. "God, I wish I was younger! I'd have had so much fun flirting with you." Then he started to wheeze and seemed short of breath.

"Are you all right, Mr. Worsham?"

It was a brief episode. The wheezing passed, and he started breathing normally.

"I apologize. I periodically get these infernal bouts. They're so terribly inconvenient."

"Maybe we need to go at an easier pace. I've been trying to autopsy your body for a while now, but I prefer not to do it here, alone."

"An excellent idea. Let restraint rule the day."

"Good. Now maybe you can explain calmly why you faked your death twice over the past twenty years."

"Ah hell, why not?" he said, then shrugged. "I'm not long for this world anyway."

And John Worsham started telling Mary his story. It was essentially two separate stories, but he started with the first. He had been friendly with the Yarrington family. In fact, he had sent many customers from his faro parlor to their boardinghouse.

"I'm not sure if you know what went on at the Yarringtons'—"

"I've been apprised."

He nodded, then continued. They had a business arrangement where he received a percentage for his referrals. He was married with children, a son and a daughter, not that it would have made a difference to Arabella, but she was never really interested in him.

"She was focused on landing a bigger fish, and the one she reeled in was a whopper."

The whopper was Collis Huntington, who had often come to Richmond on business and whom Worsham had referred to the Yarringtons. One day, back in 1869, Worsham was called to the boardinghouse and was shuttled into a room with Huntington and Arabella. They informed him that Arabella was pregnant with Huntington's child. They had already planned their move to New York, and this provided a new complication. Huntington was married and refused to subject his wife to the type of scandal this situation would most certainly bring. Though he didn't love her anymore, his wife had staked him to his start and he felt a strong loyalty to her. Besides, she was sickly, and he didn't expect her to be around much longer.

"I heard she hung on for another fourteen years. That must've driven ol' Collis and Arabella insane." He laughed but stifled it before he experienced another coughing bout, then continued his story.

They had decided that Arabella would give birth in Richmond before relocating to New York. Huntington offered to pay Worsham a very generous sum of money to go to New York with them for a year. He'd parade around as Arabella's husband and the father of their child, establishing Arabella as a married woman, and even more importantly, making Archer seem legitimate and not a bastard.

"It makes sense," Mary reasoned. "Having a bastard or being one can make you a social pariah, and that's the exact opposite of what Arabella desires for herself and her son."

"From prostitute to New York royalty; that ascent was

always in Arabella's mind," Worsham said. "Anyhow, after a year, they faked my death and I was free to return to Richmond and to my family. Of course, I had to promise to stay quiet about the arrangement." Worsham looked up at Mary and smiled. "It was too good of an offer to refuse."

"What about your family? Surely, they—"

"Back then it was normal for me to disappear on business trips for months at a time. So this one was a little longer, and I returned with a lot of money. They had no complaints."

"It sounds like it made everyone happy."

"I certainly was. So were Arabella and Collis. They even named their son after me, and I'm sure Archer is much quicker than my hopeless offspring." He gestured to the door, obviously meaning Jeremy.

As far as the second death was concerned, he had gotten into trouble with some riverboat gangsters and needed to avoid them.

"It wasn't so bad being isolated here when I was healthy. My wife died back in '73. She was a big admirer of Henry David Thoreau. I finally took the time to read *Walden* and began to appreciate nature."

If Worsham craved the activity of a town, Richmond was out of the question, but Ashland was reasonably close. His son and daughter had alternated bringing him supplies until his daughter moved to Georgia with her family and he was left with just Jeremy. For the last year, he had been mostly bedridden but still occasionally felt well enough to get out of the house.

While he spoke, Mary studied his face carefully. It had a long, full life written all over it. In his day, he must have been the type of man for whom the phrase "he could charm the skin off a snake" had been invented.

"Do you have any idea," she asked, "why someone would hire a woman to impersonate your niece Emily and suggest you were murdered in 1870?"

"Not a clue. But I'm a small fish and I've been hiding out in the woods for twelve years. Can you imagine how many enemies Mr. Big Fish Collis Huntington has accumulated during his rise to the top? They're probably standing in line to take him down."

That was the part of the puzzle that Mary still had to figure out, along with who killed Abigail Corday and why. She was contemplating this as she bade John Worsham farewell, then found Jeremy sitting on the porch licking his wounds.

"Your father said for you to drive me back to the Ballard House."

"Did he tell you everything?"

"It's a secret, but it's safe with me. Let's go. I'm tired and George is waiting for me. He must be frantic by now."

She stepped off the porch and headed for the buggy. Jeremy stood.

"He wouldn't have divulged anything if he was feeling better. He's not well, you know."

"I know."

Mary waved at him to follow her and kept walking. She was indeed tired, so tired that she missed catching the wild look Jeremy had in his eyes. He pulled a large pistol out of his coat, took aim, and fired.

The power of the bullet entering Mary's back instantly propelled her forward and then down. She fell face-first, but by the time she hit the ground she didn't feel a thing. She was already unconscious.

16

MARY AWOKE IN the Richmond hospital with a concerned George at her side. She was in a private room, of course, but the luxury of it didn't help the burning sensation she felt in her back.

She sighed loudly and turned restlessly in her bed. "What's that in my back?"

"It was a bullet. You were shot."

"It feels like I'm being prodded with a hot poker." She started to move some more, and George stopped her.

"You need to rest, Mary. Luckily, it didn't hit any vital organs, and they were able to extract it without doing any further damage. But you've lost a lot of blood, and you had to have a transfusion."

Mary looked alarmed, and George quickly continued. "Yes, I know it was risky, but it was the only way to save you, and it seems to have worked." Blood transfusions were something science hadn't perfected yet, and only about fifty percent of them were successful.

"Did you choose an appropriate bull to be my donor?" Though Mary was joking about her bullheadedness, her question wasn't that outrageous. Scientists had been experimenting for years with transfusing animal blood to humans.

"They couldn't find one stubborn enough. Instead, they took mine." He showed Mary his arm, which had a bandage on it.

"I've always wanted blue blood. Does this mean we're related?"

"I certainly hope not. I despise most of my relatives."

Mary started to laugh, but it soon turned into a cough. She was still very weak and this short conversation had sapped her energy. George called the doctor in to check her, and when he was assured she was fine, he left. Mary needed to rest.

Later, George gave Mary the details of what had transpired. After Jeremy shot her, he went inside. He told his father that he was weak and not in his right mind, so Jeremy had to take action to protect him and his secret. Instead of getting the congratulations he was expecting, John Worsham had been irate.

"In my sixty-nine years, I have bamboozled, cheated, even robbed, but never once," he shouted, "not once did I physically harm anyone. And I never ever killed a soul!"

"She couldn't be trusted, Father. I did it for you." Jeremy was at a complete loss. He thought he had finally done something to satisfy a father he could never seem to please.

"Then do this for me. Help me put that girl's body in the buggy."

Worsham quickly threw on some clothes, and when Mary's body was in the buggy and he was at the reins, he turned to his son.

"I've tried for forty-three years to turn you into a man and failed. You're on your own now. Good luck." He felt adrenaline flowing through his veins. It reminded him of old times, and he was oddly enthused as he galloped off in the buggy with Mary.

Jeremy knew his father was going to tell the authorities what had happened. Since he had also taken the only transportation, Jeremy packed some supplies and headed off into the woods, where he figured he could get lost for a while until he could come up with a plan. Unfortunately for him, the next day he wandered too close to a black bear and her cubs, and she attacked, killing him in seconds.

John Worsham got Mary to the hospital just in time. It was almost a relief that the people of Richmond would find out he was alive. He figured his heart would probably get him before any riverboat men would at this point. Besides, he was warming to the idea of spending his last days in the town where he had lived most of his life and raised more than his share of hell.

While Mary's adventure was unfolding, George was back at the hotel awaiting her return. His worry increased, and he eventually went outside and randomly searched the streets of Richmond, looking for her. Quickly realizing the low possibility of success, he went to the police station. They had no information about Mary. His next stop was the hospital, and he was inquiring about her at the front desk when two orderlies carried her in. Having been to hospitals many times because of his mother's bouts with malaria, George was in very familiar territory, and he knew exactly what to do in order to assure Mary received the best care possible.

Just a few days later, while Mary was still recuperating in

the hospital, she got a surprise visit from Emily Worsham. Apparently, John Worsham had notified what family he had left in Richmond of his return and the circumstances.

"My family and I want to thank you for bringing my uncle back to us. We are very grateful and have much catching up to do. And we're all simply devastated that one of us caused your condition. Jeremy was always trouble. I remember when I was eight years old . . ."

Mary didn't feel well enough yet to endure listening to Emily Worsham's wandering conversation. She very courteously thanked Emily for visiting her and for the information that led to discovering her uncle. Mary suggested they correspond after she returned to Brooklyn.

A week later, when Mary was well enough to travel, George convinced her to go farther south with him to Asheville and see his dream being built. Mary still needed to recuperate further, but she could do it there, at his burgeoning estate, which he had decided to call Biltmore after his family's ancestral home in Bildt, Holland. Then they would return to New York, and she could continue her detective work once she had fully healed. He knew that Mary still wanted to find out who hired Abigail Corday and, of course, who killed her. Judging from what they had just learned in Richmond, certainly Collis and Arabella Huntington were high on the list of suspects.

∼∽

LELAND STANFORD WAS in Manhattan for both pleasure and business, after having promised to help Republican senator William Evarts plot his reelection campaign. He was staying at the renowned Fifth Avenue Hotel and had just been informed of an unexpected visitor: Collis Huntington. An assistant showed him into the living room of Stanford's suite, then left. Stanford stood by the window overlooking Fifth Avenue. He had no desire to sit or to invite Huntington to do so. That would suggest Huntington was welcome.

"So, Collis, what brings you here?" bellowed Stanford, putting on his best jovial tone. "You're not contemplating a run for the senate, are you?"

"You know me better than that, Leland."

Hearing Huntington's dark tone, Stanford rolled up the welcome mat and revealed his true, hostile feelings. "Yes, I do. Make it quick. What is it you want?"

"Just the answer to one question, then you'll be free to pursue your politics or university business or whatever it is you're doing in New York."

"And that question is?"

"Someone is prying into my private affairs, affairs that concern my family. If they have the slightest bit of intelligence, they may have contacted you, hoping that you might want to divulge information due to our differences over the years."

"I'm well aware of our sad little story, Collis. Will I be getting your question sometime in the near future?"

"Have you been contacted about such matters?"

Stanford succinctly answered, "Yes." He strategically paused, then continued. "Now that I've answered your one question, I can get back to my own affairs. A pleasure as always, Collis."

Huntington saw how much enjoyment Stanford was getting from dangling the information in front of him. He refused to give Stanford the satisfaction of begging him for more, no matter how much he may have wanted to know the details. As Huntington headed for the door, Stanford softened. It was a family matter, and family meant a lot to him. Stanford had lost his only child to typhoid when the boy was just a teenager, and not a day passed where he didn't think of him. He had named Leland Stanford Junior University after him and was put out that it was becoming better known as just Stanford University.

"I don't like gossip. . . . I didn't respond."

Huntington stopped and turned. "Thank you, Leland."

"The person who wrote to me was a detective. A woman. Her name was . . ." Stanford paused, trying to remember.

"Not necessary. I know who she is."

As Huntington opened the door to leave, Stanford said, "God help her for committing the cardinal sin: incurring the wrath of Collis Huntington."

As Huntington entered the hallway and closed the door, he was already planning Mary Handley's fate. Whatever it was, he didn't want it to be quick. He wanted her to suffer.

∽◎∽

ROBERT DAVIES HEARD the words the lawyer was telling him, but his mind was on Abigail. He smiled when he thought of her. There was no doubt that she had been crazy, but it was mostly a fun crazy, except, of course, for the fact that it had gotten her killed. Robert felt no guilt about it. He had warned her, but she was too far gone. Yet, she *had* left him something very significant, something of great value.

Upon her death, on that very night, he felt a sadness, a

depth of emotion of which he had never thought himself capable. He embraced it and cultivated it. No one doubted what he was feeling, not even the police or that lady detective. He had always secretly felt that Hamlet—the role he had always wanted to play—was beyond his abilities as an actor, and that he would never emotionally understand the scene where Hamlet grieves over Ophelia. Now he did, thanks to Abigail.

"Did you hear me?" the lawyer asked, bringing Robert back to the conversation.

"Yes, I did, sir, every word. Thank you. Thank you very much."

"You're a lucky man, Mr. Davies. Few receive such a generous inheritance."

They shook hands and Robert had started to leave when something occurred to him. "I won't be receiving it for a while, but could I take this information to the bank and get a loan?"

"I don't see why not. With this kind of money, a lot of people will want to do business with you. If you can wait, I'll prepare the proper papers."

As Robert left the lawyer's office, his head was soaring, feeling an energy he had never felt before. He could quit his job and start his own theater company: the Robert Davies Players. He liked that name. He liked it very much. And their first production would be *Hamlet*. Too bad Abigail wouldn't be around to play Ophelia, but again, he reminded himself, he had warned her about getting too lost in her role.

Still, he knew he would be brilliant. Abigail had done that for him. It was her parting gift.

ANDREW HASWELL GREEN was in demand, and rightfully so. He was at a benefit for the New York Metropolitan Museum of Art, given on the twentieth anniversary of its founding. Since Green was the driving force behind the establishment of the museum, everyone wanted to speak with him, and conversely, he needed to speak with them. His consolidation project for New York and Brooklyn had stalled with the Huntington fiasco, and the Brooklyn propaganda machines were working overtime. He needed help.

The elite of New York were out in force: the Rockefellers, the Carnegies, the Vanderbilts, the Morgans, and many more. Thomas Edison had called in his regrets from New Jersey earlier that day. He said he would be working well into the night. His absence didn't matter to Green. The turnout was large, and there were plenty of opportunities to garner support.

Green had been pressured not to invite the Huntingtons because of the scandalous speculation around the missing body of Arabella's former husband. The gossip consensus was that Arabella had John Worsham killed and had disposed of the body in case evidence might arise later that would require an autopsy. There were other less popular theories, one involving bigamy and an even more outrageous one about John Worsham being a foreign spy who was called back to his country. The possibility of Archer's illegitimacy had been bandied about, but it was far down on the list. Still, Green was adamant about inviting the Huntingtons. Asking Collis Huntington to step back from the consolidation project because of rumor and innuendo was hard enough to do. He found that aspect of politics distasteful but unfortunately necessary. He had observed that the Huntingtons were getting a polite but chilly reception, and it couldn't have been comfortable for them. Of course, his own conversation with them was a bit awkward, but as far as he could tell, there didn't seem to be any antagonism.

He had just completed a whirlwind of conversations, one right after another, and decided he was in dire need of a walk to clear his head. He excused himself from his current group and put his champagne glass on a passing waiter's tray. He walked the length of the room, smiling and waving to others as he went, then turned down a corridor that headed toward the bathrooms. The bathrooms weren't his destination; rather, it was the deserted corridor with its dim lighting and shadows, which he hoped would provide the solitude he needed to gather his thoughts.

Once safely away from the crowd, he stopped and leaned against a nearby wall. He felt some moisture dripping down his face. Was it sweat? *My goodness,* he thought, *I can't let these people see me sweat or I won't be able to raise a nickel.* He reached into the right outside pocket of his tuxedo jacket, where he always kept a handkerchief for such purposes. When he pulled it out, a small piece of paper floated to the floor. He didn't remember having put the paper in his pocket, but maybe he had forgotten. He picked it up.

The paper read, "I know what you are, and I'm going to divulge it unless . . ." Green quickly turned the paper over, then back again, but there were no more words. His head was swimming, his heart pounding.

Questions shot through his mind. *What does this person know, who is he going to tell, and what does he want me to do?* Green knew a follow-up note with demands was surely forthcoming. This one was likely just a device to taunt him, and it was doing its job.

Green patted his forehead with his handkerchief, then returned it to the same pocket. He walked back down the corridor to the brink of the room where the benefit was being held, stopped, and surveyed the crowd. Everyone had something in his or her life that they didn't want exposed, no matter how cleanly they had conducted themselves. Green was no exception. He had infinitely fewer demons than any of the people in that room, but he still had them.

He looked over the many faces, trying to figure out who could have had the opportunity to plant the slip of paper in his pocket. He quickly dismissed that as useless. He was so busy working the crowd there was no way he would have noticed a slight bump or rustling of his jacket.

While he was perusing the room, his gaze fell on Collis Huntington, and their eyes locked. Perfunctory waves and smiles followed, but before Huntington had turned away, Green could have sworn he had detected a knowing, almost sadistic smile on his face. Of course, Green realized it could have been his imagination playing tricks on him after receiving such a note, but it was certainly possible that Huntington wasn't genuinely feeling as gracious as he had behaved when he so magnanimously ceded his involvement in the consolidation project. Green had heard about some of Huntington's business methods and had witnessed him in action with McLaughlin. The idea that he might want to exact revenge wasn't at all farfetched.

Nevertheless, Green was a lawyer, and he had spent his life dealing with hard facts. There were none yet. Nothing was certain except that he wasn't going to sleep that night, or any other night, until he found out what the note was all about.

ABIGAIL CORDAY WAS Shorty's last job. It had been many weeks since, and he felt stale. This wasn't a new occurrence. He had been through slow periods before and had learned how to stay sharp. The key had been in finding a way to keep his senses alive. It wasn't easy. Picking random fights accomplished what he wanted for a while, but that had lost its luster. The problem was his work was the only thing that excited him, until one day he discovered something that was almost as stimulating.

Prostitutes made him feel alive. He didn't exactly know why. It could have been the despair that drove them, or their total indifference. All he knew was that they solved his problem. And they didn't have to be pretty. His one physical requirement was weight. He liked them heavy.

He found what he was looking for down by the Brooklyn docks in front of a pawnshop, ironically standing directly under the shop's identifying sign, the one with three balls. She wasn't as big as he liked them, but she was plump, heavily made up, and eager. They haggled over price briefly. The amount didn't bother him. He just wanted to test her level of desperation. She passed.

She took Shorty to a flophouse nearby where rooms could be rented by the hour and where the management never questioned her "guests," allowing them to be anonymous. Shorty waited in the shadows as she got the key. The room had an old rickety bed, a sink that had rusted, and a couple of thin towels, but it would do. The woman looked at Shorty.

"What do you like, darlin'?"

"Get undressed and lie down on your back."

"Ooo, I love a man who knows what he wants."

That excited Shorty, not because he was falling for her

act, but rather because she was trying hard to please. As she undressed and plopped down on the bed, Shorty took off his shirt.

"Big muscles," she said. "Sexy."

Shorty was getting hard. He had been concerned about his choice because of her lack of girth, but she was more than making up for it.

He was the type of man who liked working from the bottom up. He started at her thighs, caressing and kissing. She began moaning with pleasure on the first caress. It was so outrageously phony he got harder.

"Oh, darlin', I need you inside me. Take off those pants, I need you now."

But Shorty wasn't going to change his routine. In fact, with his mouth in her nether regions and his hands on her large breasts, he was wondering about something that had always perplexed him. *Would the size of her breasts shrink if she lost weight or would they stay the same?* He let it go and worked his mouth up to her breasts. When he got to her face and they were looking at each other eye to eye, she instantly stopped her moans of ecstasy.

"Kissing on the mouth is extra," she said, businesslike.

"Sure. Anything you want."

He slowly bent to kiss her, and just as she opened her mouth to receive him, he wrapped his hands around her neck and started to squeeze. Her surprised expression raised his desire to a new level. She began struggling, hitting at him and kicking her feet, which made him even more eager. He was a fan of Cuban habanera music, and he heard that repeated beat in his head as he pressed harder and she eventually succumbed to her inevitable death.

He rose from her body and looked down at his crotch, where he could feel the moisture from his ejaculation. *This was a good one,* he thought. His senses were pulsating, and he felt razor sharp. *I'm ready for what I have to do.*

As he put his shirt back on, he sneered at her dead, rotund body on the bed with her bulging eyes reflecting the shock of her last seconds on earth. He had made sure the manager didn't see him, and he felt safe when he grabbed the two raggedy towels and took out some matches. He set the towels on fire, then threw them on the bed. Shorty watched as the flames grew, catching onto the dirty blanket and sheets. He waited until he could smell burning flesh, then hustled out as quickly as he could.

17

IT WOULD BE an understatement to say that Biltmore was impressive. It was truly magnificent. For a dream, it was developing into a wondrous reality. The main house was still being constructed, and George apologized that they had to stay in the guest quarters. As far as Mary was concerned, there was absolutely no need for an apology. The house that he called the "guest quarters" was three times larger than her parents' abode and had infinitely more amenities. With its comfortable, tasteful furniture, its fine art and modern conveniences, Mary would have felt blessed to be able to live in such a place.

Because of her condition and the train ride, Mary needed a couple of days' rest until they could start touring the property. And considering what she was about to see, Mary may have asked for more time. It was overwhelming.

The main house had been under construction for a year and was designed in the style of a French Renaissance château. George had hired famed architect Richard Morris Hunt and landscape designer Frederick Law Olmstead to make his dream a reality, and he told Mary it probably wouldn't be completed for another five years. The plans called for thirty-five bedrooms, forty-three bathrooms, three kitchens, and sixty-five fireplaces. There were countless other areas, including a bowling alley, a gym, and an indoor swimming pool. The château would eventually cover over four full acres of floor space. He had even had three miles of railroad track constructed leading to his house from the main railroad line so that it would be easier to transport materials for its construction. The magnitude of it took Mary's breath away.

In order to view the land, they needed a horse and buggy. George had already bought over eight thousand acres, and he intended to own over fifteen times that amount.

"Are you planning to create your own state?" Mary quipped.

"I had thought of that, but the name Georgia was already taken."

"How about the District of Vanderbilt?"

"Ah, that has a nice sound. I'm already warming to it. And I think my first act as—"

"King?"

"I prefer governor."

"Oh, how very democratic of you."

"Yes, I thought so. Anyhow, my first act will be to pass a law. At Biltmore, there will be no hypocrisy and no snobbery."

"Here, here," said Mary, playing along.

"And there will be no prejudice against anyone because of race, creed, color, religion, *gender*"—he faced Mary, who nodded her approval—"or poverty. People will be free to choose how they live their lives as long as they're not harming anyone."

"What about the rich?"

"Doesn't that last section cover it?"

"Hypothetically, but you may need some protection after the workers see how you're living." She pointed to the elaborate châteaus he was having built. Suddenly, George got serious.

"Mary, I'm painfully aware that the source of my wealth is my grandfather, who didn't use the most ethical methods. And frankly, neither have his offspring. Here, I am trying to accomplish something that will benefit the land, the animals, *and* the workers, whom I am paying handsomely. That's a far cry from my father, who is best remembered for his statement 'The public be damned.' "

Mary could see he was hurt and immediately sought to remedy that. "I'm sorry, George. I was joking. I didn't mean to—"

"My one vice is that I love beauty of all kinds and want to immerse myself in it. I'm fortunate to have the money for it, and that's what I'm trying to do here. Does that violate the first law of Biltmore? Am I a hypocrite?" He looked at her, desperately wanting her respect.

"No," Mary said as she gently put her hand to his cheek. "It makes you honest, and generous, and incredibly human." She then kissed him tenderly on the lips.

As they toured the estate, the scope and beauty of what George was trying to accomplish took over. Mary found it awe inspiring.

He showed her the dairy, which was already working and where there were close to two hundred cows. Next was the horse barn, and there were further plans for poultry, swine, and sheep. What was probably most impressive to Mary was that all the animals seemed to be well taken care of and thriving. There were also gardens and nurseries. Olmstead had already designed an area for a forest where the trees would be well preserved. As they traveled over the property, a combination of flat land and rolling hills with spectacular views and a seemingly perfect climate, it occurred to Mary that George was building his own little Garden of Eden. Correction: not so little.

Because of Mary's condition, George didn't want to take a chance of tiring her out, so they took two days to see everything. He really wanted to do it in three days, but by the second day, Mary was feeling much better and prodded him to continue. That night, as they were sipping wine after finishing their sumptuous candlelit meal, she lowered her glass and looked straight at him.

"George, I think you're marvelous."

"That's fortunate, because I think you're marvelous, too."

She rose, went to him, and sat on his lap as she kissed him more fervently than she had ever before. He put his arms around her and returned her ardor. She had untied his cravat and started to unbutton his shirt when George stopped her.

"I see where this is going, Mary, and I'm concerned."

George was a true gentleman, and he was worried about her reputation. She found it touching.

"I'm the one who should be concerned, and I'm not. As a matter of fact, I've never been more certain about anything in my life."

They made their way to her bedroom, which was, of course, the larger one. George had seen to that. As they undressed each other, he was careful of her wound, which endeared him to her even more.

Making love that night was a bit awkward at first, as it often can be when two people are feeling out each other's preferences for the first time. Then it progressed to an ecstasy Mary had never felt before. She only had one person with whom to compare this experience, and that was Charles. He was possibly more experienced than George at lovemaking, but he was also more like a lost boy than he was a man. There was something fulfilling about being with a man who had purpose and a sense of self. George knew who he was. Most importantly, Mary adored who he was.

They spent three more blissful days enjoying Biltmore and each other. On the morning of the fourth day, Mary and George were still in bed when she turned to him.

"George," she started, but he already knew what she was thinking.

"It's time to go back. You need to find out who killed Abigail Corday and why."

"I hope you don't mind. I know she's not really my client, but—"

"You're you, and I love every part of you, even the part that's going to drag us away from the happiest days of my life."

"Really? I've felt the same way."

"Good, then I will proceed." He turned, and now they were both on their sides facing each other. She thought he wanted to make love again, which was perfectly fine with her. Instead, he got very serious.

"Mary Handley, will you do me the supreme honor of becoming my wife?"

Mary took a moment to process his words, then replied, "If this is some misguided, gentlemanly attempt to make an honest woman out of me, it's not necessary."

"I know that."

His words sent Mary's head spinning. She found it hard to accept his proposal at face value. It might just have been that happiness had eluded her for so long that she couldn't recognize it when it was in front of her.

"George, we've only known each other for a relatively short time, and what you think is love may just be a temporary infatuation. So I suggest—"

He gently put his two fingers on her lips to quiet her. "As a celebrated lady detective once told me, I've never been more certain about anything in my life."

Mary studied his face. There was no doubt he was being earnest. She was convinced. And ecstatic.

She sat up in bed. "George Vanderbilt, I want you to know that I am now officially consenting to your proposal, but only under the condition that you agree to one caveat. You must accept"—she interrupted her speech to lie down next to him again, warmly looking into his eyes—"that I am simply mad about you."

The two of them kissed, and, naturally, made love again, which they found to be an infinitely more satisfying way to complete a deal than signing a contract. They spent the rest of the day enjoying Biltmore and each other before leaving the next day for New York.

When they arrived at Grand Central Depot and were disembarking the train, Mary spotted her mother waiting for them. Before they left, she had sent Elizabeth a telegram to explain that they had gone to Biltmore and were on their way home, so that she wouldn't worry about her being gone so long. She had conveniently omitted that she had been shot but did mention that she had a surprise for her.

"Mother," Mary exclaimed, "you didn't have to meet our train. The surprise could have waited until I came to the house."

Elizabeth was desperately trying to put up a good front, but her face betrayed her. This had nothing to do with her surprise. Whatever it was, it was grim.

"We need your help, Mary," she said, quivering. "Sean's been arrested. They say he murdered Patti."

Abandoning any attempt at pretense, she crumpled into Mary's arms, crying.

18

Sean was in a holding cell at Second Street Station. As fate would have it, it was the same cell in which they had put the Goodrich killer after Mary's famous arrest.

George hired a carriage and they dropped a distraught Elizabeth off at her house. She had been so consumed with her tragedy that it hadn't seemed to faze her at all that she was in a carriage with a Vanderbilt. Given the circumstances, Mary decided not to tell her about their engagement just yet. Instead, she would wait until her mother could fully enjoy it. She and George then proceeded on to Second Street Station, where she stopped George from following her out of the carriage.

"It's better that I go in alone. Sean could reveal certain things to me that he might be hesitant to say in front of you."

"You're right, Mary. I'm just concerned. When will I see you again?"

Mary's mind was on Sean. "I don't know. How about dinner tonight?"

"I'll pick you up at seven."

George scooted back into his seat and closed the carriage door. Mary had already started ascending the very familiar steps of Second Street Station when she abruptly did an about-face, returned to the carriage, and stuck her head in the window.

"George, you need to know something. Sean was a bit of an ass growing up, but there is one thing of which I am certain. My brother is not a murderer."

"How could he be? Look who he has for a sister."

"I love you."

"Love you, too."

They kissed, George's carriage took off, and Mary entered Second Street Station.

Billy O'Brien escorted Mary to the holding cell area. He had known Mary and Sean since they were little and had been on the police force even longer. That didn't matter. The two of them walked in silence. The shock of Sean's being arrested hadn't worn off, but that wasn't why Mary was silent. The horror of her friend Patti, a woman whose love of life was evident in every breath she took, being brutally killed began to also affect her. She knew that she had to suppress that feeling and never let it show if she was to be of any use to Sean.

Billy ushered her into the anteroom before the holding cells where the guard would take over.

"Watch out after the lad, Mary. I've never seen him so depressed."

"Wouldn't you be? The love of his life was murdered, and they're blaming him for it."

Billy shrugged. He looked as if he wanted to tell her

something but decided not to. The guard escorted her to Sean's cell. He was sitting on a cot. The second he saw her he jumped up.

"Mary!"

"Well, well, Sean Handley, fancy meeting you here." Mary was purposely being flip. She wanted to cool down as much emotion as possible so she could glean the facts. She turned to the guard.

"Open the door, please."

The guard looked at her with incredulity. "The man's a murderer."

"I'm a private detective, he's my client, and he also happens to be my brother. So like I said, open the door."

The guard reluctantly obeyed Mary's wishes, and as he closed it with her inside, she turned to him once more.

"By the way, we're innocent until proven guilty in this country. Until a jury of his peers convicts him, I suggest you exhibit your poor judgment elsewhere."

Having received this verbal lashing, the guard moped off, muttering to himself. Sean looked at his sister in awe.

"God, it's good to see you!"

"I bet those are words you never expected to utter in this lifetime."

Sean smiled wistfully. "Yeah, probably not." Then adrenaline shot through his body and took over as he started pacing. "Mary, I didn't do this! I would never harm Patti! Never!"

"I know that, Sean. You need to calm down."

"Easy for you to say!"

"No, it's not easy. My big brother is in jail for murder, my good friend is dead, and it's all killing me. But I need the facts as you know them, and the only way I'm going to get them, all of them, is if you're thinking properly. For God's sake, Sean, you're a policeman. You know what I'm talking about."

Mary's words accomplished what she wanted. Sean took a few deep breaths and slowly gained his composure. He was far from calm, but this was as good as he was going to get.

"Thanks, sis, you're right. I'm ready."

The problem was that Sean didn't have much to tell. Two nights before, he and Patti had gone to dinner and then he had walked her back to her apartment. Unfortunately, they had gotten into one of those silly squabbles they had recently been avoiding.

"It was stupid. She had fixed her hair differently. My mind was somewhere else, on my case, and I hadn't mentioned her hair all evening. She called me on it, and instead of just apologizing, which I should have done, I told her I had more important things to think about."

Mary didn't have to speak, her incredulity apparent.

"I know, stupid. Anyhow, we wound up yelling at each other for a few seconds, maybe as much as a minute, and I stormed off, down the stairs and out of the building. One of her neighbors found her about thirty minutes later. She had been strangled."

Sean sat on his cot, upset. "If I hadn't started that dumb argument, I'd have stayed with her and she'd still be here. It's my fault she's dead!" He buried his head in his hands.

Mary wanted to comfort Sean, but she needed information. "Did any of the neighbors hear your argument?"

"You know how we were, Mary. When we got that way, we were pretty loud."

"What about later? Did anyone see you leave?"

"I doubt that, or I wouldn't be here."

"Did you note the time?"

"When I left? Exactly eight oh two P.M. I don't know why, but I glanced at the pocket watch Patti had given me for my birthday . . . so I'd always be on time."

Sadness was once again beginning to consume Sean. But Mary wanted to focus on the facts, the most important one being that she now knew Patti had been killed between 8:02 P.M. and 8:32 P.M.

Sean looked up, pained, full of remorse. "The last words I said to her were 'I hate you.'"

"Patti and I were close. Believe me, Sean. She knew you didn't mean that."

He stared at her, helpless, tears dripping down his cheeks. "I loved her, Mary."

"So did I. We're going to find out who did this to her."

Mary patted her brother on the shoulder, then called for the guard. She had a case to solve.

                        ∾

SUPERINTENDENT CAMPBELL WAS actually working when Mary burst into his office. It was paperwork, drudgery as far as he was concerned, but he had to do it.

"Sean? Are you insane?" she screamed. "You know he's not a murderer."

Superintendent Campbell didn't take Mary's bait. He calmly rose and gestured toward a chair, "Have a seat, Mary." As she reluctantly sat, crossing her legs indignantly, he slowly closed his office door. "What happened? I was expecting you a couple of days ago."

"I was out of town," Mary responded quickly in short, clipped tones.

"So that explains it," he said as he sat back down at his desk.

"Chief—"

"The answer to your questions are, no, I'm not insane, and also no, I don't think Sean's a murderer."

"Good, then release him."

"Unfortunately, even I don't have that kind of power."

"Of course you do. The evidence you have against him is completely circumstantial."

"People are convicted on circumstantial evidence every day, and what they have against Sean is . . . well, it's not good."

By now, Mary had abandoned her attack and was beginning to really listen and observe. She remembered the look on Billy's face, and Superintendent Campbell now had the same look.

"Okay, Chief, tell me about it."

His story was similar to Sean's in that it included Sean and Patti's long history of very loud and antagonistic arguments. This particular spat was the same. He mentioned the name of the next-door neighbor, a Mrs. Schmidt, who heard the argument and found Patti's body.

"Sean's told me all of that already, and though it's suspicious, it's hardly damning."

"I agree with you, but I'm not finished. It doesn't help that Sean announced to the world that he was going to kill her."

Mary was taken aback but still skeptical. "Sean really said that?"

"Indeed."

"When? It wasn't that night, was it?"

"No, but that doesn't make a difference."

"How could it not? Are you trying to tell me Sean, in the

heat of an argument, screamed that he was going to commit murder, then, over the next month or two, proceeded to date his potential victim, even get engaged to her, while all the time he was plotting to kill her? That's absurd! It sounds like a bizarre concoction devised by Edgar Allan Poe."

"That's not how James Ridgeway feels."

"Ridgeway, the chief prosecutor? Why in God's name would he—"

"Mary, it's Brooklyn and it's murder. He jumps at the big ones, not at some kid who steals from a pushcart."

"Still, these types of murders happen in Brooklyn every day. Sean is a relative nobody."

"I take it you haven't seen the newspapers yet. Here's to-day's. Yesterday's was worse."

He handed Mary a copy of the *Brooklyn Daily Eagle;* on the front page was a huge headline that read, MARY HANDLEY'S BROTHER ARRESTED FOR MURDER.

All of Mary's cockiness was knocked out of her. She sat motionless as the realization sunk in that her notoriety could send her brother to the electric chair.

19

Lazlo's Books was swarming with newspaper reporters and curiosity seekers. Mary turned the corner, spotted a group milling about outside the bookstore, and immediately knew what was waiting for her. Running as far from them as possible seemed like a good idea at first. Nevertheless, she decided to press on. Her reasoning was that she would have to deal with them sooner or later, and she might as well do it at Lazlo's, where possibly some good would come from the free publicity he would get.

As Mary braced herself for the onslaught of reporters, she couldn't help being reminded of her first day on the Goodrich case, when she was swarmed by the press. Except there was a noteworthy difference. Before, it was a fun event where they were probing to see who this lady detective might be, hoping to discover a new media darling. Now they were hoping for Mary to get testy, deny her brother or implicate him. She was determined to avoid all of that.

Lazlo watched from the doorway as the reporters surrounded Mary and tossed questions at her rapid-fire.

"Miss Handley, what is your reaction to your brother's arrest?"

"Clear and simple, it's a miscarriage of justice that will soon be rectified. Sean is innocent."

"But he threatened to kill her, and she was murdered," another reporter chimed in.

"*She* was Patricia Cassidy. Please give her the dignity of remembering her name. Patti was a wonderful person and a good friend. Sean and Patti were very much in love."

"Then how do you explain what happened?"

"We've all had experiences with someone close to us where we've gotten into arguments and said things we didn't mean. The difference in Sean's situation is that sadly Patti was murdered. But that doesn't mean that he acted on those words any more than any of you have."

More questions were thrown at her, and she chose the first one she could ascertain. "How is your brother holding up under all this pressure?"

"Sean's a brilliant police officer and a Handley, which makes him sturdy and resilient."

"So he's okay?"

"About as okay as anyone could be who's been accused of killing the one true love of his life. He's feeling a whole range of emotions from sadness to anger to guilt. It's only natural. Now, if you gentlemen will excuse me—"

Mary began to make her way through the throng of reporters. Lazlo saw it, and he tried to burrow a path from him to her. She didn't see him until they met in the middle, and the look in her eyes screamed, *Get me out of here!* Lazlo immediately turned around and helped her tunnel her way into the store as he shouted to the reporters.

"Thank you, everyone. Miss Handley has much work to do."

He closed the door on the reporters. Lazlo shielded Mary from any curiosity seekers inside as he led her to her office, where she sat down with a deep sigh.

"Thank you, Lazlo." She took a moment to collect herself. "How is Sean really doing?"

A serious concern crept into her voice. "He's scared, Lazlo, really scared, and I don't blame him."

Mary wasn't even sure why she had shown up at her office. There was nothing there that she needed to do. But Lazlo knew why. She needed a safe haven in which to rest and a friendly shoulder on which to lean. Lazlo was more than happy to provide that shoulder for this young lady who was the epitome of what he would have wished for in a daughter if he had ever wanted children.

⤞⤝

WHEN GEORGE PICKED Mary up for dinner that night, he informed her that they would be having a surprise guest at their table: William Jay Gaynor.

"The name sounds familiar," she said, "but I can't place it."

"He's a lawyer. I've asked him to take a look at Sean's case."

"Sean doesn't need a lawyer yet. Hopefully, his case will never go to trial."

"Trust me, Mary. He should have had one two days ago when he was arrested."

"I do trust you, George, but honestly, none of us have the money for a lawyer, and especially not a good one."

"I've already taken care of it."

"No, I can't allow you to pay for our problems."

"I'm only going to say this once, Mary. I love you. . . . Well, I'm going to say it many times again and again over eternity."

"Good, because I love you, too, but—"

"No buts. We're going to be married and your family is going to be my family. And the Vanderbilts have not had a jailbird in the family yet . . . at least, I don't think so." He stopped and looked at her. "Ah, Mary, don't make it so hard. I want to help."

"I wouldn't take on my family so quickly. You're bound to regret it."

"And along those lines . . ."

George took a ring box out of his coat and opened it to reveal a magnificent diamond engagement ring. It had a simple platinum band with a five-carat round diamond resting on it. It was perfect. Suddenly, Mary couldn't breathe.

"Oh, George . . . I don't know much about jewelry, but I do know that is . . . simply beautiful."

"You like it then?"

"*Like* it? I . . . I . . . I can't speak."

"I'll take that as a yes. We'll have it sized to your finger as soon as you have time."

"Time? Are there any jewelers open tonight?"

They both laughed as they began traveling over the Brooklyn Bridge into Manhattan.

William Jay Gaynor was not a typical lawyer. In fact, there was nothing typical about him. He was a devout Roman Catholic who had studied to be a priest but decided on the law instead. Unlike most lawyers, he believed in always speaking the truth. He repeatedly attacked politicians and journalists, labeling them a shady lot who didn't hesitate to use lies to forward their causes and line their wallets. Surprisingly enough, he was also very successful and one of the top lawyers in Brooklyn. Mary and George were on their way to the Lower East Side of Manhattan to meet him at a place owned by the Iceland brothers on Ludlow Street. Following his unconventional style, Gaynor was an Irish Catholic who simply loved kosher deli food.

The Iceland Brothers Deli was a small restaurant with limited table space. There was a long counter on the right side of the entrance with meats like corned beef, pastrami, and roast beef clearly in view but with glass shielding them from the customers' touch. Large kosher salamis and bolognas hung on the walls, and there was a counterman making sandwiches in plain sight with doors to a kitchen behind him. As Mary and George entered, they were greeted by the counterman, who smiled broadly.

"Welcome to Iceland Brothers Deli," he said, betraying his Russian Jewish origins.

They smiled back and thanked him, then looked around for Gaynor. The dining room was about three-quarters full, and George spotted Gaynor sitting alone at a table for four, eating a large bowl of matzo ball soup. Gaynor was heavy-set, and at only forty-one, he already had a gray beard and had lost a great deal of hair.

"Good evening, Mr. Gaynor. May I present to you my fiancée, Mary Handley."

"Pleased to meet you, Miss Handley," said Gaynor, rising briefly and nodding to Mary.

As they all sat, Gaynor indicated his soup. "I apologize for ordering before you, but I can't resist the smells." He took a deep breath through his nose, inhaling the atmosphere.

A waiter arrived to take their order.

"I'll have lean corned beef on rye bread with a glass of seltzer," Mary said.

"That was awfully fast, Mary," George said. "Have you eaten in a kosher deli before?"

"Not here, but my first boyfriend was Jewish."

"Really? Should I be jealous?"

"We were fourteen, and I was attracted to him because he appeared to be deep and moody, one of those mysterious, tortured souls. Then I found out the source of his torture was that he was orthodox and loved pork. That ended the magic."

They all laughed then ordered three lean corned beef sandwiches.

"So," said Gaynor, "here we are, three Christians, soon to be eating kosher food. I wonder what Jesus would have to say about that."

"I don't pretend to have had the seminary education that you've had, Mr. Gaynor," Mary responded. "But I do remember that Jesus was Jewish. So, I don't believe he would object."

Gaynor looked at George and pointed to Mary. "I like her, George. Excellent choice."

"I'm a very lucky man." George looked at Mary, they exchanged loving glances, and then he turned back to Gaynor. "So, William, will you take Sean's case?"

"Before I do, you must tell me everything you know. I don't believe what I read in the newspapers."

Mary divulged every detail she could remember, including her brief interaction with Billy and her visit to Superintendent Campbell. Every once in a while, George would add a comment, but mostly she spoke. She stressed that even though Sean and Patti had a history of loud, sometimes explosive arguments, not once did it ever get physical between them.

"Even if the jury believes that," Gaynor responded, "you realize what they might be thinking and what the prosecutor, especially one like Ridgeway, will no doubt verbalize."

Mary reluctantly responded, "There's always a first time."

An agonizing silence filled the atmosphere around the table as Mary processed yet another piece of information that confirmed just how much trouble Sean was in.

"I like you, Miss Handley," Gaynor started.

"Please, call me Mary."

"I believe you to be an honest person, Mary. I have no reason to think that anything you've told me is incorrect. More facts may surface later, but that's to be expected."

"Does that mean you'll defend Sean?"

"Yes, but with one condition: you may not under any circumstance speak with the press."

Mary was taken aback by this request. She had always handled the press quite well during the Goodrich case, and she told Gaynor so.

"That was the Goodrich case. This is the Handley case." And Gaynor lifted a newspaper that he had kept folded on the floor next to his chair. It was the late edition of the *Brooklyn Daily Eagle*. He opened it, revealing the headline: HANDLEY SAYS BROTHER IS GUILTY.

"I never said that!"

"In your conversation with the press earlier today, did you ever use the word 'guilt'?"

"Not in that context. I was referring to the wide range of emotions Sean was feeling—"

"It doesn't matter. From now on, all you say is 'no comment.' Are we agreed?"

"Agreed." But all Mary had in her mind was that she had just put a nail in Sean's coffin.

"Good. Since I left the seminary, I've latched on to Ben Franklin as a guiding light for my behavior," he said, then pointed to the headline. "You need to keep in mind one of his sayings—'A slip of the foot you may soon recover, but a slip of the tongue you may never get over.'"

It wasn't lost on Mary that possibly Gaynor and Lazlo had something in common and should meet. But she was in no mood to make introductions. All she could think of was how the reporters had twisted her words and used them against Sean. Gaynor was right. She was no longer the darling of the press. Rather, like Sean, she had a target on her back.

20

HUGH McLAUGHLIN WALKED into a saloon near Clinton Hill in Brooklyn looking for Alfred Chapin. He found him sitting alone at a booth in the back as far away from any other human being as possible. His nerves evident, Chapin was nursing a drink with his hands wrapped firmly around the glass. He didn't look at McLaughlin but stared straight ahead, almost as if someone were sitting across from him.

"Sit down," Chapin whispered.

McLaughlin was amused. "Ya talking to me, Yer Honor?"

"Shush. No names."

"I didn't say yer name unless ya changed yers to—"

"Will you please just sit?"

McLaughlin finally gave way and sat. "Is it possible ya don't know? Huntington's out of the consolidation project. That oughta cheer ya up." It clearly didn't. "Okay, what has yer knickers in an uproar this fine evenin'?"

"We need to talk about . . . the thing."

"What thing?" McLaughlin knew perfectly well what Chapin meant, but he couldn't resist toying with him.

"You know . . . *it*."

"It? Sorry, but I'm not catchin' yer drift. What exactly—?"

"The deal, damn it! The deal! Think *water*. . . ."

"Oh, right, the deal . . . What deal again?"

McLaughlin saw that Chapin's veins were about to pop out of his forehead, so he decided to stop fooling with him before the mayor had a stroke.

"I was just havin' some fun. I know what deal."

"I'm glad you're so smug, but you wouldn't be if you knew what's happened."

"Tell me then. What happened?"

"Someone upped the bid on the company. I don't know who. I'll have to pay three times what we discussed."

"Three times?" McLaughlin was genuinely surprised.

"Ah, all of a sudden you're not so smug."

McLaughlin's face slowly spread to accommodate a wide grin. "Well, looks like I have an anonymous benefactor."

"You're not Pip in *Great Expectations*. This is serious."

"Who? In what?"

"It's a Charles Dickens novel."

"Who the bloody hell is he?"

"Forget it. What are we going to do?"

"I dunno what yer gonna do, but I'm gonna celebrate." He reached over, took Chapin's drink, and downed it.

"Are you out of your mind?"

"I'm gonna make three times more than I thought I was gonna make. So are my friends. I could kiss ya. We all could kiss ya"—he lowered his voice to a whisper—"my beautiful mayor."

"This is going to get out, and when it does—"

"All that's gonna get out is that our wonderful mayor got

Brooklyn water, savin' our dear city from those New York bastards."

"But the price."

"Do the deal. Nobody knows and nobody cares. Companies, contracts, kickbacks, they're all the same. It's been goin' on for years and will continue long after we're gone."

"Well, I've never done this," Chapin pronounced emphatically, beginning to perspire.

"What do ya know? The college lad is about to pop his cherry." He turned toward the bar. "Bring me a bottle of yer finest Irish whiskey. My friend and I got some celebratin' to do!"

Chapin could stand it no longer. He rose and whisked out of there as fast as he could.

Completely unfazed, McLaughlin shrugged and chuckled. *Oh well, more for me then,* he mused as he got ready to get rip-roaring drunk.

❧

GEORGE HAD TAKEN Mary home. He hadn't wanted to risk her staying at his house in Manhattan on the off chance that someone might spot them, thus compromising her reputation. Mary didn't care about flighty things like reputations, especially when she rejected the criteria on which they were based. George did care, and his reasoning wasn't entirely misguided. He knew there would be enough speculation about a Vanderbilt marrying someone from a lower social class, and he didn't want Mary to be subjected to further gossip about her being a loose woman who'd trapped him with her sexual wares. He realized the absurdity of altering their behavior to suit those of smaller minds, but he wanted Mary's transition to marriage to be easy and painless.

"I'll have to take a short sabbatical from being your assistant the next few days. I have some business about Biltmore. It's here in town, but I'll still be busy."

"I can't have my assistant run willy-nilly, attending to less important work. I just may have to hire a new one."

"I'd be devastated if you did, and even more so if he performed some of the same duties I have."

He leaned over and kissed her. When they broke, she said, "Since we won't be seeing each other for the next few days, why don't you spend the night at my apartment? I guarantee that no one there knows anyone from your neck of the woods."

He agreed as long as they didn't make a habit of it. He truly was concerned about her reputation. After they had entered her apartment and she had turned on a couple of kerosene lamps, Mary curtsied mockingly.

"Welcome to my humble abode, extremely humble—that is, bordering on pathetic."

He looked around the one-room apartment with its used furniture, rusty sink, and ancient Franklin stove, trying to be as positive as possible.

"You do this place a disservice. It's a bit cozy but really quite nice. I like what you've done with it."

"Oh yes, I do have a decorator's touch," Mary said, and started giving a mock tour. She first pointed to her small dining table. "Reclaimed from a garbage heap on the street." Then she indicated her bed. "Early Handley, very early. It was my bed growing up and before that it was my grandmother's."

George played along. "Ah, an antique piece then."

"Most definitely, if age is the only requirement to be one." Then she went to the sink. "And did you know that rust is fashionable this year?"

"Of course. I have relatives who, though still alive, are gathering quite a bit of rust."

They shared a laugh.

"No, this really is . . . fine. One minor point. I don't see a bathroom."

"Not minor, I'm afraid. More major . . . Down the hall, two doors to your right."

George opened the door, looked, then shut it. For the first time he seemed nonplussed. "There's a line in front of it."

"There often is at this time of night." She went to him. "Now you have a larger grasp of the life from which you are rescuing me."

"It is you who is rescuing me, from a life of humdrum, loveless relationships."

They kissed, and the talk was over.

The next morning George dropped Mary off at Patti's apartment building, and he continued back into Manhattan. Whatever happiness Mary had experienced the night before with George had been more than countered by the direness of Sean's situation. She figured her first move should be to speak with Mrs. Schmidt, the woman who had heard Sean and Patti arguing and had found her body. It had crossed her mind to ask Gaynor for permission to investigate, but she'd rejected the idea. Wealthy people hired private investigators when they were in trouble. Why shouldn't Sean have one? Besides, Mary couldn't imagine sitting still while Sean was in this kind of trouble.

Mrs. Schmidt was a stout, kindly German in her early fifties. A widow, she lived alone. She had emigrated to the United States a couple of years after her husband's death, hoping for new beginnings, but those new beginnings only led her to Brooklyn, a small tenement apartment, and a job in a sweatshop. Having once slaved away at the Lowry Hat Factory, Mary could easily sympathize with her, but she had questions that needed answering.

"Did you see Sean and Patti arguing?" Mary asked her after her arrival and an exchange of pleasantries.

"Ach, many times, but that day, just hear. I work two shifts. I was tired."

"In all those times, did you ever see Sean hit her?"

"No, never. He is nice boy. I never thought he would until . . ." Mrs. Schmidt shrugged, seemingly not wanting to verbalize what had happened.

"What made you go to Patti's apartment?"

"The voices quiet. I think it is over. Then, twenty, thirty minutes later, I hear horrible screams, shrieks, and then silence, an awful silence."

"Did you hear or see Sean?"

"No, just some footsteps clanging down the stairs. I go to check on Patti. The door is open and . . . it was terrible, such a beautiful young girl."

"Very beautiful. It was a tragedy. We all loved Patti." Mary stopped and took a moment, trying to overcome the strong emotion she was feeling of having lost her close friend. But Sean needed her and she had to press on. "Is there anything else that you can remember, maybe in her apartment, things moved around, something different?"

"In fight, they knock over many of Patti's beautiful plants. Dirt everywhere. It is lucky I go there."

Mary was confused. "Why, to save the plants?"

"No. They also knock over garbage and it catch fire right by her bed. I put it out or whole building burn down."

The fire was new information, and it sounded all too familiar to Mary. "Did you tell the police?"

She shook her head. "They don't care about plants like you. They never ask."

"How do you know the fire started because of their fight? Did you see a candle or a broken kerosene lamp?"

Mrs. Schmidt took time to think. "No, but if I don't put it out, whole building goes. For sure."

Mary thanked Mrs. Schmidt for being so helpful. She offered Mary a pickle, but Mary was in no mood to eat. On her way out, she was contemplating the striking similarities of two crimes: the killings of Abigail Corday and Patricia Cassidy. Patti was strangled, and Mary had seen strangulation marks on Abigail Corday's neck. It was very possible the killer had tried to strangle her but found a knife more effective. In both cases, a fire was started afterward. The question was: Why would the same person want to kill both Abigail Corday and Patti? What was the common link?

No matter how many ways Mary examined it—and she tried every conceivable one—logic kept telling her that *she* was the only link.

It was a devastating thought.

21

"OH NO, MARY, not again!" moaned Superintendent Campbell, his mouth full of home-fried potatoes. Mary had just told him everything she had found out in Richmond. "Tell me you're not really going after Collis Huntington."

"I'm not."

"Why am I not convinced?" he asked as he cut a piece of his rare steak, popped it into his mouth, and started chewing away. They were in O'Brian's, Superintendent Campbell's favorite luncheon spot just a few blocks from police headquarters, where the quantity of the food, not the quality, was their specialty. Superintendent Campbell had started planning his day around his meals ever since he left the field and his work had become less interesting. His huge porterhouse steak hung out over the plate's edges with home-fried potatoes piled on top and crammed into what little plate space was left. Mary's lunch was much lighter. She was having O'Brian's "Salad of Chicken" with some fresh fruit.

"I just have some questions to ask him."

"Please, we all know what that means."

"So the rich should be able to do whatever they want without being questioned?"

Superintendent Campbell stopped chewing and stared at her for a moment. "I just figured out what your problem is. You're prejudiced." And he continued eating.

"Me?"

"Yes, you . . . against the rich."

"Oh, the poor rich. They're so disadvantaged, so picked upon."

He pointed with his fork. "That's exactly what I'm talking about."

"And what I'm talking about is that Arabella Huntington was irate that I was looking into her past, and then all of a sudden the client who hired me to do so was killed. Then Collis Huntington threatens my family and in no time at all, my brother is accused of murder, a murder oddly similar to my client's at the theater. Could they all be coincidences? Possibly, but considering my discovery in Richmond, they certainly need investigation."

"Of course they do. No one can question your analytical skills, Mary. It's just the way you go about things. It's like you're venting anger on them."

"What anger?"

"That they're privileged and that you're not. Especially now, when you're so emotionally involved." He cut another big piece of steak and pointed his fork at her. "You can't bull your way over Collis Huntington, because he's a much bigger bull than you."

Superintendent Campbell's words gave her pause. She remembered when he had suggested a mode of behavior to get the most out of Thomas Edison, and it had worked perfectly. She decided she needed a more subtle approach with Huntington.

"You're right, Chief. I do need to set my emotions aside and be more tactical."

"Of course I'm right, and I'm also right that you're prejudiced against the rich."

"That's where you're wrong."

"No, I am one hundred percent—"

"I can't be prejudiced against the rich. I'm marrying one of them."

Superintendent Campbell was caught so completely off guard he almost choked on his food. He stopped and patted his mouth with a napkin before asking, "What's this?"

It was then that Mary realized she had been so consumed with Sean she hadn't told any of her friends the happy news yet. It made her feel good that she finally had.

"George Vanderbilt and I are engaged."

"That certainly qualifies as rich." Suddenly perturbed, he put down his fork. "How do I not know this?"

"It's very recent, Chief, and I haven't really told anyone—"

"Not the engagement. I didn't even know you had a relationship with George Vanderbilt."

"Well, I'm sure you would have, but you're hidden away in an office all day and—"

"Not necessary to explain, Mary," he said, quickly cutting her off. "I understand."

Knowing that this was yet another painful reminder to Superintendent Campbell that he had been separated from the action he loved, she decided not to pursue it further.

After devouring a forkful of home-fried potatoes, Superintendent Campbell had gotten over his brief consternation. He looked Mary in the eyes. "The important thing is, are you happy?"

Mary smiled. "Beyond anything I ever imagined."

"Good, then *I'm* happy. You deserve it, Mary."

A period of time passed—it could have been a minute, maybe longer—where they both sat there smiling, basking in Mary's glow. Then she broke it and glanced at his plate.

"Of course, I'd be a lot happier, Chief, if you'd limit your food intake."

He stared at her as if he had discovered a traitor in his midst. "Did my wife put you up to this?"

"No, but I'm thrilled she's aware. Chief, please excuse me for saying this—"

"But you're going to anyway."

"As much as you would like to blame your recent . . . growth on your sedentary job, we both know it has more to do with your fondness for cuisine, all types of cuisine, and in significant portions."

Superintendent Campbell started to contest this but stopped. He knew she was right.

"It's one of the few pleasures I have left."

"Think of dieting this way, Chief. You may be eating smaller portions on a daily basis, but you'll probably live longer to enjoy many more meals. So in the end, you'll come out ahead."

"That's a great way to look at it, Mary."

"But it doesn't help?"

"Not in the least."

As Mary chewed on a strawberry, Superintendent Campbell cut into his steak with the fervor of a man who was having his last meal.

❧

MARY CONTEMPLATED HOW she was going to deal with Collis Huntington. When she had met Thomas Edison, Superintendent Campbell (Chief Campbell at the time) had advised her to behave as the cliché of how men of the day viewed females: unknowledgeable and helpless. That wouldn't work in this case. Huntington had already met her and knew that she didn't fit that stereotype. Besides, any man who was married to Arabella Huntington had to be apprised of a female's abilities. She had decided that she shouldn't alter her true investigative nature but was also fully aware she had to control one thing. She had to make sure her distress over Sean's situation didn't interfere with her business, and that wouldn't be easy.

Her first challenge was somehow getting to speak with Huntington. She'd had trouble trying to interview Edison and J. P. Morgan during the Goodrich case, and she was representing the Brooklyn Police Department then. She didn't even have that much leverage now with Huntington. Mary had decided against attempting to arrange a meeting in advance. It might be too easy for Huntington to refuse her or delay. Instead, she had opted to knock on the front door of the Huntingtons' Park Avenue home, hoping that she might catch him in a generous enough mood to grant her a few minutes.

Mary looked around the outside of the Huntington mansion and, bracing herself, knocked on the door.

A butler answered. He immediately left to check with Collis Huntington, who happened to be at home. He returned shortly, beckoned Mary to come in, and escorted her to the drawing room. This seemed all too easy. Mary couldn't help wondering if this was pure luck or if Collis Huntington had plans to toy with her. If he chose the latter, she was ready. *Let the games begin,* she thought as she entered the Huntington drawing room.

Arabella was on the telephone. Also present besides Collis Huntington was his nephew Henry. At forty, Henry was closer to Arabella's age, and they both had similar interests in the arts. After the butler escorted Mary in and left, Arabella raised her right pointer finger in the air, smiling, as if to say, *Wait a minute,* as she continued her telephone conversation.

"Why, of course, Louise, I completely understand. These things do happen. . . . Yes, well, thank you for giving proper notice. Good-bye." She hung up the telephone and turned to her husband. "Louise Carnegie. There seems to have been some horrendous snafu, a nightmare she called it, and the caterer can't accommodate half of the people they have invited to their benefit. She's so, so sorry, but . . ." Arabella stopped, her sarcasm evident.

"I'm sure they had to cut down their list," Huntington replied, "by two."

Arabella nodded her agreement, then turned to Mary, assuming a relatively convivial tone. "Miss Handley, sorry to keep you waiting. May I present to you Collis's nephew Henry Huntington." Henry nodded, which Mary returned. "We were about to have afternoon tea. Would you like to join us?"

"That's very kind of you," Mary replied, "but if you don't mind the interruption, I just desire a few words with your husband."

"I suppose that's fine," said Arabella. "Isn't it, dear?"

"Of course."

"Splendid," she exclaimed, then turned to the other Huntington in the room. "Henry, I believe you've heard us speak of Miss Handley."

"Yes," Henry responded, narrowing his eyes. "The nemesis."

"I wouldn't go that far. In order to be a nemesis, one has to be a formidable opponent. I doubt whether even Miss Handley's impression of herself is that grandiose."

Arabella was trying to bait her, but Mary would have no part of it. "You're right. Nemesis is far beyond my reach. I think of myself merely as an impartial fact collector."

"Really? I'd have thought you had greater ambitions now that you're marrying a Vanderbilt."

Apparently, the upper-crust gossip pipeline had been working overtime. It occurred to Mary that in all probability the only reason she had been admitted to the Huntington mansion was that she was soon to become "one of them." With the social snubs they had suffered lately, they couldn't afford to turn away a Vanderbilt, even if Mary was only a Vanderbilt-to-be. Of course, none of that guaranteed Mary would find complete cordiality and cooperation. After all, she was viewed as the source of their troubles.

"Oh, you've heard," Mary said, trying to sound as innocent as possible so as not to seem bothered by Arabella's words. "George is an incredible man. I'm absolutely thrilled."

"Yes, I bet you are," Arabella replied, her words full of disdain.

This exchange was followed by a silent but brief war of looks as Arabella's expression implied *Gold digger* and Mary's response said, *Me? You invented the term.*

Arabella broke the silence when she turned to Henry. "Let's adjourn to the dining room for our tea. Collis can join us after his little chat."

"You and I in the dining room," Henry said, flirting. "Imagine what could happen."

"Don't be naughty, Henry. I keep a baseball bat by my seat."

They both laughed and were soon gone. Huntington turned to Mary.

"I'm afraid my nephew has an incurable crush on Arabella. Thankfully, they both know my claim supersedes all others and that there will be plenty of time after I'm gone."

"That's very . . . understanding of you."

"And practical."

Mary thought differently. His statement sounded more territorial than anything else.

"Have a seat, Miss Handley."

They both sat on two love seats adjacent to each other.

"I don't want to waste your valuable time, so I'll try to be brief."

"You're here about your brother."

"Why do you think—"

"Why else would you be here? Certainly not because of your deceased client, whatever her name was."

"Abigail Corday, though to be frank, she presented herself as John Worsham's niece Emily." That was as close as Mary was going to get to an apology until she was absolutely sure the Huntingtons had nothing to do with Patti's death and Sean's arrest.

"The point is, I didn't frame your brother. I assume that's what you are working toward, so we might as well get to it right away."

Superintendent Campbell was right again, and his words kept repeating in Mary's mind. It indeed appeared that Huntington could be a bigger bull than she was. Mary realized if she wanted to get anywhere with him, she'd have to be more sly.

"I want you to remember, Mr. Huntington, that you said that and not I."

"Duly noted."

"I don't make accusations lightly. I would need considerable evidence before ever considering those words."

"Yes, I know how professional and ladylike you are," he said, his impatience growing.

"I hope I didn't offend you in some way."

"What offends me is this little cat and mouse game you're playing, so let me end it. I don't have people killed when they cross me. I don't have to. I make their lives so miserable that they want to kill themselves."

"I see."

"It's a fine distinction. In fact, I prefer they suffer for the rest of their lives rather than die and be relieved of their misery. That makes them an everyday reminder to others who might contemplate similar action."

"The machinations of a mogul. Interesting."

"Hopefully educational, too. Now, if you'll excuse me," Huntington said as he began to rise, but Mary stopped him.

"So, using your premise, wouldn't killing Patricia Cassidy and framing my brother for murder be a way of making me suffer for the rest of my life? That is, if you were angered by my actions. You couldn't have been by theirs. You didn't know them."

He slowly sat down again. "You're a bright woman, Miss Handley. Have you ever considered a career in business?"

"This is my business."

"I mean real business: building industries, creating an empire. I can always use smart people."

"It's astonishing how quickly one can go from the enemy to the employed. In this case, it only took one little theory."

"A sound theory, too, possibly even compelling, except for one crucial fact. I don't commit murder or have people killed. I don't have to."

"It sounds plausible, but I am curious what your theory of the situation is."

"I'm not a detective, Miss Handley."

"Modesty, all of a sudden? I'm not asking you to hand me the killer, but you are obviously a great observer of human behavior or you wouldn't be as successful as you are." Mary thought that complimenting him seemed like a reasonable plan. She hoped his feeling of superiority would make him slip.

Huntington leaned forward. "If it were me, I'd try to find out who hired this actress to impersonate Emily in the first place. Whoever it was wanted to embarrass me, but why? I believe the word you detectives use is 'motive.' What was theirs?"

"That's it?"

"What else do you want?"

"What you suggested might perfectly well solve your questions, but what about mine and my brother's?"

"Isn't it all a game of dominoes?"

The look on his face told Mary that he knew something, but as far as he was concerned, he was through. Huntington stood up.

"Well, this has been a perfectly nice little chat. Now I must tend to the others."

Mary quickly rose. "It appears you're aware of a connection between the two murders."

"Only two? Why not three, four, or five?"

He was being flippant. Or maybe he wasn't. Either way, he was good at keeping her off-balance. "This is no joking matter."

"It couldn't be," he said. "I have no sense of humor."

As he strolled toward the dining room, Mary asked, "I know you've planned some sort of retribution for me. If it isn't my brother, what is it?"

"As luck would have it, your brother's misfortune is my fortune: it has caused your family pain as your actions have done to mine, and it has tarnished your credibility. I no longer have to plot anything and can concentrate my efforts on more important matters. Good afternoon, Miss Handley." And with that he disappeared into the dining room.

On her way back to Brooklyn, Mary kept reviewing her meeting with Huntington. He was a tough person to read. Was he trying to lead her astray or was he attempting to help? Why was he so cryptic in his supposed clues? More importantly, why in the world would he want to help her, a woman who, no matter how inadvertently, had put such stress on his family?

Mary had no absolute conclusions about Huntington. For the moment, she had decided to keep her knowledge of Archer's being a bastard to herself, saving it for a time when she might need to use it as a device to combat Huntington or to squeeze information out of him. Right now, his involvement in Sean's dilemma was ambiguous at best. She considered taking at face value his statement about Sean's misfortune being his fortune. And it was very possible his suggestion that more murders were involved could be an attempt to send her off in more directions to make her agonize even further over her brother's predicament. Or he may have done that for more personal reasons than just sport. Maybe he really did frame Sean.

In any case, Sean was her brother and she couldn't afford to play a game of odds. She had to speak with him immediately about this. His life was at stake.

22

WILLIAM GAYNOR WAS in Sean's cell when Mary arrived. He had been advising him on how he should answer questions from District Attorney Ridgeway and other prosecutors. It was a simple approach and easy to follow: stay mute unless Gaynor was there.

"Technically, they shouldn't deny you counsel," Gaynor had said, "but it's a gray area. One thing that isn't gray though is the Fifth Amendment of the United States Constitution. Keep pleading that until they get sick of it and agree to send for me."

Sean was sitting on his cot, his right leg nervously fidgeting up and down. "I'm afraid we're too late on that. I've already made the mistake of talking to them."

"What did you tell them?"

"What I told you—the truth."

Gaynor was not pleased with this news, but there was no point in making Sean more nervous than he was. "Okay, well, don't worry about it. From now on, that's what you do."

Mary was begrudgingly escorted by the same guard who'd been convinced of Sean's guilt and who was unhappy that he now had high-priced counsel. He grunted his displeasure but didn't speak as he opened the cell for Mary to enter, then slammed the door and left.

"Pleasant fellow. Sorry I'm late. I had to make my way through the reporters outside." She quickly turned to Gaynor. "Don't worry. I stayed completely mum."

"Thanks for getting me a lawyer, sis, and congratulations."

She looked at Gaynor again and he shrugged. "I thought he knew."

"Which makes you happier: the engagement or getting Mother off your back?"

Mary laughed. "George is fabulous. I can't wait for you two to spend time together. You'll really like him."

"I know I will." Sean's smile suddenly disappeared as he thought of Patti and as the reality of his situation settled back in, both filling him with sadness.

"Sean—"

"Don't mind this, Mary," he said as he turned away, his voice cracking. "It happens every once in a while."

Mary's instinct was to go to him, but Gaynor signaled her to give him a moment. It was strange, but she couldn't help noting that Sean's tragedy had made her feel closer to him than she had ever been. His masculine façade of having to be the big, superior brother had been stripped away, leaving him vulnerable and accessible.

It didn't take long for Sean to gather himself. He turned back toward Mary and said, "I'm happy for you, sis. I really am."

Mary needed to get back to business or both of them

might fall apart, and that would do no good at all. "Well, you might not be," she replied, "after you hear what I have to say."

Mary told Sean and Gaynor about her meeting with Huntington. Gaynor sat pensively listening as Sean got angrier with every word. Finally, Sean exploded.

"That bastard killed Patti just to get back at you! What kind of ass—"

"It's just a theory, Sean. He may have had nothing to do with it."

Gaynor spoke softly, "But it may explain what happened earlier today."

"What happened?"

"Judge Moore denied Sean bail."

"That doesn't make sense. He has no record, he's a policeman, the evidence is circumstantial—"

"An influential man like Huntington can make that happen with one phone call. It's also not uncommon when the prosecution really wants a conviction."

Mary shook her head. "That means we have to examine every possibility. I need to know more about the murder case you were working on, Sean."

"What does that have to do with Patti?"

"Possibly nothing, but Huntington alluded to other murders. He may have been trying to throw me off, but if it's true, your case, just because it was your case, would probably have the greatest chance of having something to do with Patti's death."

Sean nodded solemnly, not saying a word. It would be some time before the mention of Patti's death would stop having an effect on him. He took a moment to gather himself and then told Mary everything he remembered about Gabrielle Evans, the old lady who was murdered in her Clinton Hill house. He told her how messy the house was and how he had found the button, which seemed like a clue despite everyone's doubts. He also mentioned how he had discovered which coat that button would fit and had gotten a list of local stores that carried it.

"I went on my day off every week, first to stores and then to interview the people who bought the coat. Sometimes Patti would go with me, and we'd make a day out of it."

"Patti went with you?"

"Sometimes. Then we'd picnic in the park. She loved doing that."

Sean started to drift off again, but Mary needed to keep him focused. "Where's the button and the list, Sean?"

"It's in the top drawer of my dresser. I put them under my socks. I visited all the names with the exception of the last four and hadn't found anything yet. I thought I was onto something but maybe it was just wishful thinking."

The guard appeared outside the cell. "Okay, Handley, time to go."

Mary looked at him. "You can't force me to leave."

"I'm not talking to you. I'm talking to your killer brother. This is just a holding cell. We're moving him to the Raymond Street Jail."

The Raymond Street Jail was known as the Brooklyn Bastille for its deplorable conditions and the depravity of its inmates.

"You can't do that. He hasn't been convicted yet. And besides, the convicts there will tear him apart. He's a policeman."

"Not anymore." He motioned to Sean. "Hands behind your back."

Sean did as he was told, and the guard opened the cell. As he put handcuffs on Sean, Mary looked to Gaynor, who grabbed his attaché case.

"This stinks of sleazy politics. I'm going to find Judge Moore. If you don't hear from me, Mary, I'll meet you at your office in the morning." And he was gone.

As the guard led Sean out of the cell, he looked at Mary, his desperation palpable. Mary watched as the guard walked him down the hall. Sean turned his head briefly, his voice pleading.

"You have to find the killer, Mary. Please find Patti's killer."

"Don't worry, Sean. I'll get him, whoever it is."

Mary wasn't sure Huntington was the culprit, and any number of people had that kind of political clout. Fighting the unknown was extremely frustrating. Mary ducked back into the empty cell. She didn't want Sean to see her—his only hope—break down into tears.

23

I T WAS ONLY four thirty P.M. and Superintendent Campbell was sneaking out of work early. As he stepped outside, he turned to his left and was soon taken aback by the sight of a very irate Mary marching down the street in his direction.

"What the hell is going on, Chief?"

"Mary, what—"

"They just transferred Sean to Raymond Street. You know perfectly well what will happen to him there!"

"I'm sorry to hear that. No one told me—"

"You've got to stop it. Do something, Chief. Please."

"I'll try, but Ridgeway is intent on making an example out of a policeman gone wrong."

"In order for him to make an example, Sean has to be alive when they put him on trial, and he won't be if he stays at Raymond Street. You know that and that ambitious bastard Ridgeway should know it, too."

"You need to go home, Mary."

"How can you suggest that? Sean could be dead by morning."

"Mary—"

"You're the superintendent of police. Can't you do anything?"

"I will do everything I can, but you know who the real decision makers are. If any one of them sees you in this state, you'll do Sean more harm than good."

"I've got to do something. I can't just . . ." Mary was frustrated and angry. Still, she saw the logic in his words and knew he was right. "Okay, Chief."

Mary left as quickly as she had arrived. She was a detective, and even though Superintendent Campbell was her friend, she didn't want him to see her cry, which was happening too frequently as of late.

∽

ANDREW HASWELL GREEN looked into the mirror above the dresser in his bedroom as he unsuccessfully tried to comb his hair with his left hand. He put down the comb and felt the plaster of Paris cast that ran from his fist to his elbow on his right arm. He had punched a wall, and the wall had won. Green had lived a life of restraint, refusing to let negative emotions like anger influence his actions. What had caused his uncharacteristic outburst was a second note, which he had found in his coat pocket after he'd been to the market.

The note read, "Back away from public life or your perversions will be revealed."

Green was almost seventy years old and had never married. He had shared his house with former New York governor Samuel Tilden, another confirmed bachelor, until Tilden's death in 1886. It was easy to arrive at conclusions about two confirmed bachelors living together, which made it almost impossible to avoid the truth. Green was gay. Nineteenth-century mores allowed for confirmed bachelors as long as they kept their sexual activity discreet. Now it appeared someone was threatening to raise Green's profile.

Green's body of work had always overridden any concern about his sex life. He had made substantial improvements in cleaning up New York City politics and helping the city grow both physically and culturally. It seemed a comical irony that at his age, when sex was virtually nonexistent in his life, someone was extorting him about it.

He was worried—not for himself but rather for what he still wanted to accomplish and couldn't if these extortionists had their way. He felt the anger surge through him again.

Screw them, he thought. *Let those bastards come at me.*

He quickly gained control of himself. He had to avoid punching another wall.

∽

Friday-night dinner at the Handleys' wasn't the same. The absence of Sean and his awful situation made Mary wish for the old days when her mother would randomly attack her for no apparent reason. At least that would signal some semblance of normalcy.

Only the mild clanging sounds of forks and knives occasionally hitting plates could be heard as the three Handleys silently worked their way through their meal. Finally, Mary could take it no longer.

"Sean is going to be all right. I promise you both I'm going to find Patti's true killer."

"We know that, Mary," Jeffrey replied. "It's just that until then . . . it's hard."

Elizabeth didn't acknowledge Mary's proclamation. She kept attending to the business of eating her dinner without picking her head up.

"Mother, I *will* free him. You know I will."

Elizabeth continued eating in silence, once again not reacting to Mary's words. After a few moments, she put down her utensils, patted her mouth with her napkin, and turned to Mary.

"I appreciate your attempt to provide us with some comfort, Mary. I really do. But you need to have a look at it from our perspective. My unmarried daughter, whose experience is a drop in the ocean compared to the prosecutors gunning for my son, says she's gonna work wonders. Pardon me if I don't jump up and start callin' for champagne."

"I'm good at what I do."

"I'm sure you think you are."

"Why is it that you never believe in me?"

"Because you never do what a girl should do."

"I see. And a girl's supposed to clean the house, tend to children, and make Irish stew as she waits for her husband to come home."

Elizabeth stood up. "Don't you dare make a mockery of my life!"

Mary stood to face her. "Why not? You always make one of mine!"

It was now Jeffrey's turn to stand. As he did, he also extended his hands out toward each of them with his palms up, indicating for them to stop. "That's enough. Our problems are big enough without you two going head-to-head!"

"This is entirely your fault, Jeffrey. I told you not to coddle the girl, but ever since she was a baby—"

"You're right. I'm guilty of loving my daughter. Please forgive me."

"I love her too, but children need direction. Look what you did with all those books. She's almost twenty-six and an old maid, for God's sake!"

Mary shook her head in amazement. "So, once again that's the crux of the matter, what everything always boils down to: my not being married."

"Family and children, they're the most important thing in life for a woman. If you don't have that, you have nothing."

"Then rest easy, Mother. I have something." Mary realized this was as good a time as any to reveal her good news.

"What's that supposed to mean?"

"What you've been nagging me about for years. I'm engaged."

"Stop it, Mary! I hate it when you fool with me like that."

"I'm not fooling with you. George Vanderbilt and I are engaged."

Elizabeth paused for a few seconds, taking it in.

Jeffrey immediately ran over to hug her. "Mary, darling, that's wonderful! Congratulations!"

Elizabeth stayed put and emitted an emphatic, "Hah!"

"What's that supposed to mean?"

"Rich men like that make a habit of promising poor girls the world in order to take advantage of them. I hope you didn't let him touch you."

"Elizabeth!" Jeffrey quickly jumped in. "What kind of thing is that to say?"

"It's the truth. That's what everyone in this house always avoids, except for me. If he wanted to marry Mary so badly, he'd have given her a ring. I'm sorry, but that's the truth."

"Really, Mother, is that the truth?" Mary opened her pocketbook, pulled out the ring box George had given her, and opened it. "Is this the kind of ring you had in mind?"

Elizabeth gasped, unable to speak. Jeffrey bent down to get a closer look.

"That's worth more money than I'd make in two lifetimes."

Confused, overwhelmed, Elizabeth managed to get out, "Why isn't it on your finger?"

"George and I haven't found time to get it sized yet."

"It's . . . it's exquisite."

As Mary put the ring and ring box back in her pocketbook, she said, "I'm glad you like it, Mother, because when I'm home making up the wedding list, that might help you get an invite. Right now I'm on the fence about you."

As Mary stormed out of the house, something she was all too used to doing, Elizabeth called to her. "You shouldn't keep a ring like that in your pocketbook. It isn't safe." But before Elizabeth could finish, the door had slammed.

Elizabeth and Jeffrey slowly sat down, absorbing what had just transpired. After a while, Elizabeth turned to Jeffrey.

"Our daughter's engaged," she said, still somewhat in shock. Then, with even more incredulity, she continued: "To a Vanderbilt."

She looked at Jeffrey. They rarely imbibed, but he got out a bottle of scotch and poured them each a drink. They downed the scotch in a silent toast as if speaking it out loud would jinx it. Then they reached out and squeezed each other's hands tightly, trying to revel in the good news and ward off the bad.

24

MARY WAS IMPRESSED. Sean's list of names and addresses was extremely detailed, and all in geographical order, so traveling from one suspect to the next would be most efficient. But the list would have to wait. She first had to meet with Gaynor at her office. Mary had to admit that, even though it was just one room in the back of Lazlo's Books, calling it her office gave her a strong sense of pride.

When she arrived at Lazlo's Books, Mary found Gaynor had beaten her there and was engaged in a conversation with Lazlo. She knew the two of them would get along famously, and apparently they had already hit it off. They were discussing politics and their mutual disdain for the prevalent corruption of their elected officials.

"Everyone complains about Boss Tweed and how corrupt he was, as if his downfall ended those shenanigans," Gaynor postulated. "The fact is that right here in Brooklyn we have a political machine that is possibly more venal than anything Tweed could have imagined."

"Politicians are like cockroaches," Lazlo added. "As soon as you get rid of one, two more pop up who are even worse."

"I like that, Lazlo. Can I use it?"

"Feel free. I find that to be an extreme compliment from someone who follows the directives of Ben Franklin as closely as you do."

"Yes, indeed."

"To Ben," Lazlo announced as if they were toasting. Instead, they stood for a few seconds with their hands over their hearts in serene remembrance.

"Lazlo," Mary interjected, "I hate to interrupt your meeting of the Benjamin Franklin Admiration Society, but I do have some business to discuss with Mr. Gaynor."

"Oh, yes. Sorry, Mary. Nice meeting you, Mr. Gaynor."

"Call me William."

"Be delighted." They shook hands and Lazlo returned to store business.

Mary showed Gaynor to her office. She was anxious to find out what had happened, so before they had even sat down, she began asking.

"Did Judge Moore provide any help?"

"The short answer to that is no."

"And the long answer?"

"It's not very long. I have a meeting at ten this morning with Ridgeway. I want to find out why he's being so hard on Sean. If he is getting pressure from above, maybe I'll be able to discern its origin."

"Ten? We should be on our way."

"Mary, I don't think Ridgeway will allow—"

"I'm going, Mr. Gaynor."

Gaynor saw Mary's resolute look and realized that any argument would be useless. "Well then, we might as well go together. My carriage is outside."

In the carriage on the way to Ridgeway's office, Gaynor waxed on about corrupt politicians and how it was his dream to overturn the political machines and put honest people in office. Mary listened halfheartedly. She was mostly thinking about Sean, not only about proving his innocence but also wondering whether he was avoiding danger at the Raymond Street Jail.

District Attorney James W. Ridgeway had neatly groomed dark brown hair and was dressed in a medium-gray three-piece suit. Everything about him screamed conservative—perfect for a district attorney. He spoke in precise tones, carefully enunciating every word—all words Mary didn't want to hear.

"I'm sorry, Miss Handley, but my appointment is with Sean's lawyer, and that is the only person with whom I'll speak."

"Surely you don't mind—"

"But I do. Make yourself comfortable. I doubt whether Mr. Gaynor and I will be long."

Mary could tell from his attitude that there was no point in arguing. Gaynor gave Mary an *I told you so* look as he disappeared with Ridgeway into his office.

Mary looked around the outer office. It was fairly large, especially since its only occupant was Ridgeway's secretary, Mrs. Donovan. She was a pleasant-looking woman in her midthirties who would pause periodically between the avalanche of calls she was fielding for Ridgeway to give Mary a welcoming smile, then log the calls into a book of loose paper held together by a ring binder. Mary sat nearby on a wood-framed couch with comfortable cushions, wondering, of course, about the conversation in Ridgeway's office.

After a short while, Ridgeway came out of his office and beckoned to his secretary. "Mrs. Donovan, could you please come and bring some paper? I need your shorthand skills." She quickly obliged, and Mary was left alone.

They all emerged a few minutes later, Mrs. Donovan returning to her desk and Gaynor heading toward Mary. Ridgeway gave a cursory nod to Mary and went back inside.

"What happened?" Mary asked.

"I'll tell you in the carriage."

The news wasn't good. Ridgeway wouldn't budge on any level, not on sending Sean back to Second Street Station or even isolating him from the population at the Raymond Street Jail.

"He's adamant about making an example of what he calls a 'bad apple.'"

"So he's decided to kill Sean before he even has a trial?"

"That's not how Ridgeway views it. He says he wants to treat him like any other criminal. And before you say anything, Mary, I did inform him that because of his job, Sean can't be treated like any other criminal and that I understood that kind of treatment *after* he was convicted, but certainly not before. He still didn't budge. This type of appalling intransigence is maddening."

Mary thought for a moment, then, despite the panic she felt within, she calmly responded, "It doesn't make any sense. There must be other factors involved, political pressure or some other kind."

"I agree."

"Good, I'm glad you do, because . . ." Mary then proceeded to open her pocketbook and take out a bunch of papers.

"What's that?" Gaynor asked.

"Mrs. Donovan's call sheets. I saw her logging calls and I ripped out the pages starting from yesterday and dating back until the week before."

Gaynor was shocked. "You stole from the district attorney?"

"I knew he wasn't going to help us. I had no choice."

"No matter. As Benjamin Franklin so aptly put it—"

"I'm sorry, but in this case, I'm taking my cues from Dudley Bradstreet in his book *The Life and Uncommon Adventures of Captain Dudley Bradstreet,* where Mr. Bradley clearly stated that turnabout is fair play."

"That's where that phrase came from, Dudley Bradstreet?" Gaynor's brow crinkled, indicating his surprise. "George had told me you were bright, but I had mistakenly taken that lightly."

"The question is, do I inspect these papers by myself or do you want to be included?"

"By all means, include me."

The two of them went over the call sheets page by page and Mary very quickly noticed a pattern. They examined the calls on the day that Sean was arrested, the day that he was arraigned, and the day that he was transferred to the Raymond Street Jail, and there was only one name besides assistant district attorneys that called on all three of those days: Hugh McLaughlin.

❧

SHORTY WAS DRINKING his lunchtime ale in his favorite neighborhood saloon. It wasn't a coincidence that he was on one side of the bar alone and the twelve or so others were crowded on the other side. No one really wanted to risk an interaction with him. Shorty didn't feel slighted. He enjoyed his reputation.

After taking a long sip of his ale, Shorty noticed every eye in the place had turned toward the door. He also turned and saw that a woman had entered. It was a rare sight in this place, extremely rare, especially since this was one of the many saloons where women were not allowed.

"Hello, I'm looking for Kieran Kilpatrick," the woman said.

Not used to hearing Shorty's given name, one of the men at the bar laughed, spitting out his beer. Shorty shot him a quick glance, and all humor instantly drained from the man's being. The bartender was about to tell the woman to leave when Shorty raised his hand, signaling him to back off.

"What do you want with him?" Shorty asked her.

"Can I assume you're Mr. Kilpatrick?"

"Yeah, sure, you can assume," Shorty said, taking a mocking tone as he watched the woman step forward and extend her hand.

"Your landlady from across the street said you might be here. How do you do? I'm Mary Handley, and I'd like to ask you a few questions."

Shorty studied her, then slowly shook her hand. He had heard a lot about Sean Handley's sister. *A real uppity bitch,* he thought. *I'd love to play with her. She won't be so cocky when I'm through.*

25

GAYNOR, WHO WAS obsessed with Brooklyn politics and its dirty machinations, had told Mary that both Judge Moore and District Attorney Ridgeway were part of the Brooklyn Ring and owed their jobs to Hugh McLaughlin. That made a meeting with McLaughlin essential, but when Mary tried to get one, he wasn't in his office. The Ridgeway meeting had been at ten A.M. and it was only noon, so instead of wasting time, she'd decided to visit the last four names on Sean's list. If they didn't pan out, she was determined to start back at the top of the list in case Sean had missed something.

Mary had already interviewed the first two of the four and found nothing unusual. One was a thin old man with a bad case of asthma who looked physically incapable of overpowering anyone. The other one was a man who had left the city to care for his ill mother. His wife confirmed he had been gone long enough that he couldn't possibly be involved in any of the murders.

"He gave up his job and here I am stuck with the rent," his

wife lamented, then shook her head. "Take it from me. Never marry a mama's boy."

Kieran Kilpatrick was the third on the list, and Mary had noticed straight off that he possessed an innate snarl and brooding anger that made him seem like a sure candidate. However, there were a lot of angry, unhappy people in this world, her mother being one of them, and those qualities alone would never help narrow the list.

Shorty's swagger was evident. "A pretty one like you, I'll answer any question you have."

"Thank you, Mr. Kilpatrick. Would you prefer to go someplace a bit more private?"

"Whoa, you work fast, lady. I haven't even met your parents yet." He glanced toward the others in the saloon, who, as if on cue, broke out into laughter.

"I was referring to our conversation, nothing else."

"It's okay. They can hear anything we have to say. Right, boys?" He glanced once again at the other men, who responded with murmurs of "Right," "Sure," and "Yeah."

"As you wish. I'm curious about your coat."

"You like it, huh?" Shorty was wearing an oilcloth duster with an oilskin hood hanging down the back. The coat came all the way down to his shoes. "Are you looking to hire me for one of those gentlemen's fashion magazines?"

"Frankly—"

"I've been practicing. See?" Sporting a smug smirk, he opened the coat and gingerly turned around in model-like fashion while the men hooted their approval.

That was when his leg brace caught her attention. The brace had leather straps with buckles on them that held it securely in place. One of the straps was considerably less worn than the others and looked almost new. It immediately re-minded her of the strap and buckle she had recovered from Abigail Corday's dressing room. At this point, she had a very strong feeling he was Abigail's killer and was probably in-volved in the two other murders, but she had to learn more.

"Though your style is superb, I was referring to a coat you bought at Johnson's Clothing Store on Fulton Street. It was in the style of a navy peacoat, but it was brown."

"Let me see, a brown navy peacoat?" Shorty mused aloud as if he were straining his brain to remember it. He was not a good actor, and Mary saw right through his ruse.

"The salesman remembered you buying it."

"Oh yeah, right, Johnson's. I hated that coat and got rid of it."

"Really? He said you bought it three months ago. It was practically brand-new."

Shorty saw that she was pinning him down, and he didn't like it. And when Shorty didn't like something, he got angry. "I said I hated it. I burned the damn thing!"

He didn't realize it, but in mentioning fire, Shorty had convinced Mary he was the one. She hoped she could goad him into making more slips.

"I'm sorry if I offended you. I do the same thing. If I don't like a piece of clothing, I get rid of it. And your new coat is so attractive."

Thinking he'd averted disaster, Shorty beamed, admiring his coat. "Yes, it is."

"Do you ride?"

"Huh?"

"Your coat is usually worn by people who ride horses."

"Not me. I'm saving up to buy one of those horseless carriages when they start makin' 'em for us common folk. This will protect my clothes from the dust and mud on Brooklyn streets."

"You are quite the sartorial splendor." Mary saw the blank look on Shorty's face, and she decided to explain. "You dress well, Mr. Kilpatrick."

"Thanks. You look pretty good yourself."

"But isn't that a little like putting the cart before the horse?"

"The what?"

"The cart before the horse. It's a phrase from Lucian's *Dialogues of the Dead*. It means—"

Shorty felt he had lost control, so of course, he got angry. "You don't have to explain nothin'. I'm not stupid!"

Mary already knew that he was stupid. Now she knew that he was insecure about it, too. She decided that if there was a master plan behind the murders, he certainly didn't have the wherewithal to devise it. He could have easily been hired to perform the deeds. He was clearly mean-spirited enough. That, coupled with his fragile sense of self, made him an excellent candidate as a killer. Of course, there was also the possibility he was one of those maniacs who committed multiple murders for fun. The fact that the three murders were all connected to either her or Sean made that unlikely, though none of it mattered. She didn't have enough evidence to convict him of anything yet.

"I didn't mean to imply any such thing. You are clearly a very astute individual, and it would be a travesty for anyone to suggest otherwise."

"Yeah, that's me all right: astute." He turned toward his admirers with his chest puffed out, and they all hollered their approval.

"Well, thank you for your time, Mr. Kilpatrick."

"Call me Shorty. Everyone does."

"Why, that's lovely of you, Shorty. I consider that a compliment." She had started to leave when Shorty, now overconfident, called out to her.

"Aren't you forgetting something? You wanted to ask me about my jacket."

"Yes, well, there's no point now, is there? You don't have it anymore." She was thinking, *You got rid of it because you killed that old lady, you son of a bitch.*

As Shorty watched her go, he started to get excited. He was imagining his hands around Mary's neck.

26

"ALL I WANT is to look at the crime scene," Mary said later that afternoon back at Second Street Station as she gazed sweetly into Billy's eyes. She was trying to convince him to leave his post at the sergeant's desk in order to show her Gabrielle Evans's house.

"You can't fool me with your blarney, Mary girl. I'm more Irish than you'll ever be," responded Billy.

"I won't touch a thing there. I promise."

"I seem to remember a young lass sweet-talkin' her way into the Goodrich brownstone. I got in a load of hot water for that." Billy had been guarding the door of Charles Goodrich's brownstone while Chief Campbell and others were inside. Mary had convinced Billy to let her into the crime scene.

"That didn't turn out so badly, did it, Billy?" Mary had, after all, solved the case.

"For you, no, but I'm the one the chief yelled at."

"Come and watch over me then." Mary examined Billy's

face as he paused to think. She was pretty sure she had him but decided he needed one more gentle shove. "I just want to help Sean. Come on, Billy, admit it. Deep down, you know he didn't do it."

Billy sighed. Both he and Mary had known from the start that she would get to him. It was just a matter of time, and it didn't take very long. He shook his head.

"Mary Handley, I don't know why I'm such a sucker for you and your brother." He called to a policeman walking by. "Flannigan, take over. I've got some business." As Flannigan headed for the sergeant's desk, Billy stood and strode off, leaving Mary behind. Without looking back, he called out, "What are you waitin' for, lass? I can't take all day."

Mary didn't have Shorty's jacket, so the button was useless and she had no proof he was at Gabrielle Evans's house when she was killed, or at any time for that matter. On the way over to Clinton Hill, Mary asked Billy what he knew about Kieran Kilpatrick.

"Shorty? He's a bad one, that fella. We've had him in a few times, drunk and disorderly, fightin'. But we could never hold him too long. Maybe thirty days was the most."

"I'm hoping you'll get him for a lot longer . . . or possibly a brief stay, just long enough to sample the new electric chair."

"You think he's our man?"

"I know it. All I have to do is prove it."

When they got to the house, Mary noticed some scratches on the limestone in the front entry but paid little attention to it. Billy opened the door. The police had left all the drapes open, so it was easy to see. Mary paused to take it in. No matter how much she had read or had been told about Gabrielle Evans and her lifestyle, it was still shocking to personally see how she had lived, changing a once-beautiful house into a junkyard. The amount of garbage was staggering and the stench unbearable. She wondered what sick twist of the mind made a person live like this.

"What's that smell, Billy?"

"Which one, lass? The house is full of 'em."

"An animal of some kind."

"Ah, yes. The ol' bat was one of those crazy cat ladies. Had two of 'em, who are in the care of some woman now. She'd let 'em roam free, do whatever the little darlins' hearts desired. She even used to *talk* to 'em."

"Lots of people talk to their animals, Billy."

"How many make up voices for 'em, so they can talk back? They'd chatter on about the weather, politics. But she was really talkin' to herself." Billy shuddered. "Gives ya the creeps."

"Sounds like a very lonely old woman." Mary shook her head, feeling sorry for Gabrielle Evans, but not for long. Sean was her primary concern. "Where did you find the body, Billy?"

He pointed. "Over there, bent over that stack of newspapers."

Mary went to the stack of newspapers, inspected that area, then turned toward the open door. Billy was blocking the light that was shining in from it.

"Billy, could you step to the side, please?"

He did as she asked, being careful to avoid putting his foot into a wooden crate filled with ashtrays.

With a clear line of sight to the entrance, Mary could see a series of scratches on the wooden floor leading to the stack of newspapers, where they abruptly ended. She carefully and judiciously followed the scratches to the entrance, then stepped outside to the scrapes she had seen on the limestone.

"Billy, was there anything out here?"

"Yes, a statue. It had fallen. The head was broken off."

"Thanks, Billy. I have to go. You can close up now."

"That's it?"

"I now know Shorty did it." Mary was in a hurry and was rushing off.

Billy called to her. "How is that possible? We've been investigating for weeks and you've only been here a minute."

"You have to know what you're looking for," she yelled back as she turned the corner.

Billy scratched his head. He didn't have a clue.

∽◦◦

SUPERINTENDENT CAMPBELL WAS feeling something he hadn't experienced in a long time: frustration. When he was a chief detective, frustration came with the job, and it was part of what propelled him to solve problems. This was different. It came with a feeling of helplessness. Needless to say, he was not in a good mood when, carrying an extreme sense of urgency, Mary burst into his office talking faster than an auctioneer who worked on commission.

"Chief, a man named Kieran Kilpatrick who's also known as Shorty killed Patti. And not only her. I'm pretty sure he killed Gabrielle Evans, the victim from Sean's case, as well as Abigail Corday, the actress who was stabbed at the Thalia Theatre just before it burned down. And there are probably more. Just check any unsolved murders over the past five or ten years, and if fire was involved, it was probably him."

"Mary—"

"He's not the brains behind it, but he did the killings. And I have to find out why there was no fire at Gabrielle Evans's house, but he did that, all right. The metal from his leg brace left scratches on the wood floor and on the limestone outside, probably while she was fighting him off. And Sean was onto him. He was three interviews away from catching him when—"

"Mary, I just got a phone call."

"Let me finish. Mrs. Schmidt said she heard clanging down the stairs after Patti was killed. Sean wouldn't clang, but a man with a leg brace—"

"Sean's been stabbed."

Mary froze. All of the adrenaline instantly drained out of her body. She was practically numb when she asked the question she did not want to ask. "Is he dead, Chief?

Superintendent Campbell rose but didn't answer.

"Tell me, Chief. Is Sean dead?"

"I don't know."

He went to Mary and gently ushered her out with him. They were going to the Raymond Street Jail to find out. A strange thought occurred to Mary. Was it possible her mother's absurd theory about the balance of happiness and sadness in the world was indeed true? Mary was hoping that her joy hadn't resulted in Sean's troubles. She was praying it didn't result in his death.

27

W̲HEN A CRIME was committed, especially a high-profile one (and Sean's case qualified as high profile, because he was a policeman accused of murder), there were often conflicting reports. And the stabbing at Raymond Street—since it involved Sean—was no different. Several people at the Raymond Street Jail had called Superintendent Campbell immediately after the attack, hoping to curry favor with the boss. It only resulted in confusion. Their stories varied from "Sean was wounded, but he's okay," to "He's seriously hurt," to "I heard he's dead." Superintendent Campbell and Mary had to find out where the truth lay in all of that.

They were met at the jail by Warden John J. Wilson, who had survived many political appointments and regimes at Raymond Street. Needless to say, the warden was worried about Superintendent Campbell's reaction to one of his men, even if he was accused of murder, being stabbed on the warden's watch. As he approached Superintendent Campbell, he launched into his long-winded excuse about how devastated he was that it had happened, that he had often checked on the prisoner personally and had alerted the guards.

"To my deep, deep regret and disgust," Wilson droned on, "one of the guards somehow got distracted and that's when it happened. I personally think this man should be fired—"

"Enough, Wilson," said Superintendent Campbell. "Just tell me how and where he is. We'll deal with everything else later."

"The doctor's with him now. I'm not a medical man, so I'll let him tell you the details."

As Wilson led them to the prison infirmary, he informed Superintendent Campbell and Mary of what had happened. Sean was attacked by two men, one who was a cousin of someone he had arrested. He fended off one of them successfully, but while he was doing that, the other stabbed him in his leg.

"The wound is awfully . . . well, like I said, I'll let the doctor tell you."

Mary was incredibly relieved that Sean was still alive. Of course, she wouldn't know if that would last or what state he was in until they had spoken with the doctor. As they walked through the dungeonlike halls of the Raymond Street Jail, she saw why it had earned the nickname of the Brooklyn Bastille. Regardless of its having been rebuilt eleven years before, it was a decrepit place: dark, dreary, and falling apart. And her reason for being there made it even more depressing.

When they entered the small infirmary, Mary immediately spotted Sean lying on a bed in the middle as a doctor stood over him shaking his head. More importantly, Sean wasn't moving. She ran to his bedside.

"How is he, doctor?"

"Who are you?"

"Dr. Lansing," Wilson replied, "I'd like to introduce Superintendent Campbell and Mary Handley."

"Pleased to meet you, both of you." He extended his hand to shake Superintendent Campbell's but Campbell had no time for formalities and got right to the point.

"What's the prognosis, Dr. Lansing?"

"I'm not sure if I'll be able to save the leg, but regardless, he's lost a lot of blood."

"Why is he still here?" Mary asked, trying to hide her outrage. "Brooklyn Hospital isn't that far away, and they have ambulance service now."

"It's too dangerous to move him. He's presently sedated with morphine, and I thought maybe we could get an inmate to donate blood if we promised him an extra privilege or two."

"No inmates. Take mine."

"Mary," said Superintendent Campbell, "I'm not sure you realize—"

"I know how risky blood transfusions are for both of us, but I'm Sean's sister, and there's a greater likelihood my blood will work for him rather than some stranger's."

"Don't be bullheaded about this, Mary."

"Being bullheaded is my specialty."

Mary returned to Sean's bedside and started preparing by rolling up the sleeve of her blouse. The doctor looked at Superintendent Campbell, shrugged, and went to her.

Two hours later, Sean awoke to see Mary lying in the bed next to him. He was still groggy from the morphine.

"Mary? Are you all right?"

She had been sleeping, and Sean's words aroused her. She quickly sat up. "Sean, you're awake. How are you?"

"A little dizzy," Sean replied, then glanced down at his injured leg, "and in pain, but otherwise, I guess okay . . . What are you doing here?"

"You needed a transfusion, and I insisted on Handley blood."

"I understand. We wouldn't want to soil our name with some stranger's blood."

"To be honest, it's a long story, but you may have gotten some Vanderbilt blood, too."

"That explains it then."

"What?"

"I awoke with an irresistible urge to build a mansion."

Mary laughed. "You get some of my blood, and all of a sudden you're witty."

She filled Sean in on her investigation with the button and everything she had found out about Shorty. As Sean listened to the details, his grogginess faded away and energy seeped back into his body.

"I knew that button meant something," he said.

"It did, but I think Shorty's just hired help, and we don't really have anything to get him, especially on Patti's murder. We have to find out the common thread that links these crimes." Mary shrugged. "It could be Huntington, McLaughlin, or any number of others."

Sean sighed. "Great."

Dr. Lansing came in to check on his two patients. "How are we doing, Sean?"

"Terrific. I'm thinking of playing outfield for the Brooklyn Bridegrooms."

"You can wait on that. They're in first place and doing just fine without you."

Mary stood up. A dizziness came over her, but she ignored it. "I've got to be going."

"We took a decent amount of blood from you," said Dr. Lansing. "I suggest you rest a while longer."

"That's not possible."

"I suppose no amount of words will change your mind."

"It appears you know my sister, doc."

"Yes, and she should know that stubbornness can be lethal." Dr. Lansing looked at Mary, then back at Sean. "Superintendent Campbell has placed a guard at the door. You should be safe from any more attacks. I'll check in on you later. Mary, two words that you'll never heed: be careful." He nodded and walked out.

"You really charmed him, sis."

"I've got the magic touch, all right. Be careful, Sean."

Mary started to leave but Sean stopped her. "Wait." She turned. "I apologize, Mary."

"For what? You were the one who was stabbed."

"Not that . . . chess. You never cheated. You were just really good at it."

Sean was referring to their longtime rivalry. No matter how minor it might have seemed to someone who didn't know them, it was a big concession for him.

"That's all right, Sean. I really wasn't that good. It's just that you were that bad."

They both shared a smile. It was a warm one, and she left.

28

"JUDGE MOORE MIGHT be in on it, too," said Gaynor as he and Mary sat in his office. It was a large square-shaped one with an expansive bay window. Gaynor sat at an oversized oak desk, and bookcases adorned his walls, filled with law books, treatises on philosophy, and of course, the writings of Benjamin Franklin. It was dusk. Mary had gone straight to his office from the Raymond Street Jail to report what had happened to Sean and all the information she had gathered during that very long day. Her hope was that, at the very least, she could finally get Sean out on bail.

"In on what?" Mary asked.

"That's an excellent question. We haven't figured out the what, but we know that there definitely is one. I went to see Judge Moore again after I heard about Sean being stabbed."

"How did you find out?"

"I am not without resources, Mary. There are people all over Brooklyn, good people, who believe in honest government that serves its citizens instead of itself."

"And?"

"Moore wouldn't budge. I had a feeling he wouldn't, and I was prepared." He opened the top desk drawer, pulled out several sheets of paper, and handed them to Mary, who sat across from him. "These are the telephone call sheets for Judge Moore's office over the last week."

"Why, Mr. Gaynor, don't tell me you stole from Judge Moore's office? What would Ben say?" she asked with her tongue firmly planted in her cheek.

"It's unfortunate, but you're right. When you're dealing with rascals, there are times you also have to be one."

Mary quickly perused the papers, then pointed to a spot halfway down the second sheet. "Here it is. On the day Sean was refused bail, Judge Moore had gotten a call from Hugh McLaughlin. The same as the Ridgeway calls." Mary rose. "We need to see McLaughlin and find out what he has against Sean."

"Sit down, Mary. I called McLaughlin's office. He's out of town and won't be in until tomorrow."

"Then we go first thing in the morning."

"Not we, only you. He is well aware that I'm an adversary of his brand of politics, and my presence might hinder your mission."

"It's still a fishing expedition. I have no idea why he'd have a vendetta against Sean."

They stared blankly at each other. Neither of them had a clue.

❧

HUGH McLAUGHLIN WAS feeling chipper, much more so than he had in a long time. It wasn't surprising. He had just achieved one of his life's goals: buying a summer home on the

North Shore of Long Island. As he got off the train at Grand Central Depot, he was met by Liam Riley.

"Liam, my boy, there was no need to meet me here."

Liam knew otherwise. "I wouldn't think of letting you arrive without a reception. How's your new house?"

"Ah, Liam, I can't tell ya how gratifyin' it is. Imagine me, a McLaughlin from the wrong side of the street—and the wrong side of the street in Brooklyn is as wrong as it can be—havin' a home next to all those highfalutin society fellas. I feel like stickin' my head out the window and thumbin' my nose at 'em, and I just might do that."

"That's terrific, sir. I'm happy for you."

"It shows what a man can accomplish with determination and hard work. Let that be a lesson to ya, lad."

"There aren't many Hugh McLaughlins around. I can't imagine ever coming close to your success."

"Don't sell yerself short. Ya done some fine work for me, Liam. Very fine. I'm gettin' old and it won't be long until yer steppin' into my shoes. How does 'Boss Riley' sound?"

"It sounds wonderful, but—"

"Don't doubt yerself, son. I've told ya this a thousand times and I'll tell ya a thousand more. What ya need ta do is dream big, Liam. Dream big and the world is yers."

With that, McLaughlin handed his suitcase to Liam. No matter what he had said, McLaughlin had no intention of relinquishing a scintilla of his position. He had been driven his whole life by a lust for power. Now that he had it, they'd have to put him in his coffin and seal it tight before he ever let it go.

This exact thought was going through McLaughlin's mind as he stepped out onto the street outside with Liam trailing behind, lugging his bag.

29

Mary was returning home from Gaynor's office when she spotted George sitting outside her tenement building in his carriage.

"Hello, darling," he greeted her.

"George, what a nice surprise." She gave him a kiss hello through the carriage window. "How are your business dealings progressing?"

"They're long and boring without you but almost done. . . . You're back in the nick of time, you know."

"In the nick for what?"

"My brother Cornelius is giving us an intimate dinner party in celebration of our engagement."

Mary paused, then asked, "Tonight?"

"I realize it's the last minute, but I thought, why not?"

"Did you ever consider what I might think?"

George could see that Mary was a bit testy. It was unlike her, especially with him. "I suspect you had a particularly trying day."

"I'm sorry, George. I didn't mean to snap at you." She got

into his carriage and as she sat, she began to rattle off all that had transpired since they had last spoken. He was truly upset when she told him that Sean had been stabbed and relieved when he learned he had survived. It was then that he decided to postpone the dinner. Mary had gone through enough.

"No, George, as a matter of fact, seeing you now makes me feel much better. I've missed you."

They kissed.

"Well," he said, "maybe I need to go off on private business more often."

"Don't you dare. . . . I would need to borrow a dress though. Time is short, and my wardrobe is quite limited. Correction: threadbare."

"I anticipated that might be a problem, and I have a solution." He reached to the side and returned with a wire hanger, a white cloth covering what was on it.

"You bought a dress for me?"

"Yes, I hope you don't—"

"Don't you think that's a little presumptuous? How do you know I will like it? How do you know it will fit? How—" A bit flustered, she stopped.

"Are you finished, Mary?"

"For now, but I reserve the right to revisit this."

"Of course, but now I need to speak. . . . First of all, if you don't like the dress or don't want to attend this dinner, it's perfectly fine with me. But you must understand this. I have traveled the globe and have met all kinds of people from all walks of life. And you, Mary Handley, are the dearest, most precious person I have ever encountered. I would never consciously do anything to harm you, and my every waking thought is to honor you in the best way I know how."

Mary melted. "God, you always know the perfect thing to say." She kissed him. When they broke, she declared, "I'm going to wear it. I don't care if it doesn't fit."

"But it will, Mary. I know it will."

And it did. Naturally, George was current on all the latest fashions and knew what would suit her. It was a slim-fitting, full-length red velvet dress that was cinched at the waist to show off Mary's lovely figure. The only part of the dress that was not red velvet was a piece of very light beige silk that extended from just above the breast and looped over her left shoulder. Of course, George had also brought a diamond necklace and bracelet that he had borrowed from his mother, who wasn't feeling well and had passed along her regrets. They went perfectly with her outfit.

Cornelius Vanderbilt II lived on Fifth Avenue and Fifty-Seventh Street, just five blocks from George's abode on Fifth and Fifty-Second. It was the largest private residence ever built in New York City, a multifloored mansion with many rooms for every occasion imaginable and adorned with the finest furniture and art from all over the world. Cornelius had a competitive mindset about his home. He always had to have the biggest and the most prestigious.

As George had described, it was indeed an intimate party, a total of eight—the Rockefellers; the Carnegies; and Cornelius Vanderbilt and his wife, Alice, along with George and Mary—and they were sitting in the drawing room, sipping aperitifs of dry champagne, except for the Rockefellers, of course, who clung to their glasses of club soda as if they were beacons in the dark. Rockefeller was a devout churchgoer who disapproved of drinking, smoking, card playing, dancing, the theater, and many other activities.

Mary had quipped to George earlier that evening, "If it involves fun, Mr. Rockefeller is clearly against it."

"That's not so," George had replied. "He truly enjoys counting his money."

As always, the men were discussing business, and Mary made the mistake of feeling comfortable enough to express her opinions, which were decidedly sympathetic to the worker and the small business man. Rockefeller had an immediate, knee-jerk reaction.

"Surely you do believe in the rights of the individual, don't you, Miss Handley?" Rockefeller said as he sipped his club soda, mistakenly thinking he would trap her with his savvy.

Mary paused before answering him. She wanted to make sure she didn't begin her relationship with her future in-laws by offending their guest, but she also was not one to back down from her views. She had to word her response carefully.

"I most certainly believe in the rights of the individual, as long as those rights do not include denying other individuals their rights."

"I couldn't agree with you more," responded Rockefeller. "Every person should have a chance to compete. Survival of the fittest will take care of the rest."

Mary could see this conversation might lead her into making disagreeable statements, at least in this crowd, and decided not to respond. She felt she wasn't being rude, because Rockefeller had made a statement and wasn't asking a question. George instantly picked up on Mary's discomfort and decided to come to her rescue by changing the subject.

"Have any of you been following the Brooklyn Bridegrooms? They switch leagues and they're still in first place. Quite a team, eh?"

There was a brief lull in the conversation. The second the words were out of George's mouth he knew it was a mistake. This was certainly not a baseball group. Mary appreciated George's effort to divert the conversation, but even she had to stifle a chuckle. George was one of the least likely people to be a baseball fan.

"No," replied Cornelius drily, "but thank you for the update, George."

"So, Miss Handley," Rockefeller said, continuing, "do you believe in survival of the fittest?"

Mary started to feel a bit light-headed. "I believe Mr. Darwin's Theory of Evolution on the animal kingdom is a brilliant treatise."

Cornelius jumped in. "I don't think Mr. Rockefeller was referencing animals."

"Well then, if you mean the human race, one must consider advancements in medical science. People who might not have survived in a different time are still alive and leading fruitful lives. I suspect that will only continue to improve."

"I hope you don't mind if I put in my two cents," Carnegie interjected.

"Go ahead, Andy," interrupted Rockefeller. "You always do, and it's usually four."

They all laughed at Rockefeller's attempt at humor. In a way they were encouraging him, because he was usually so dour. Mary tried her best to force a reaction approximating laughter. George was better at it. He had had more practice.

"If I may be so presumptuous," Carnegie interjected, then looked at Rockefeller, who held off on another witticism at Carnegie's expense—his words had made it too easy—"I think my good friend John was referring to the business world, though why he would ask a delightful young lady like you about such matters is beyond me."

Carnegie's comment exhibited a total disrespect for and disregard of women's abilities, as if they were pretty things to be seen and not heard, or at least not heard about anything consequential. Needless to say, it took significant biting of her lip for Mary not to respond.

"I agree wholeheartedly with you," said Alice Vanderbilt, addressing Carnegie. "Business is such a boring topic, but feel free to discuss it all you like after dinner when you gentlemen retreat with your cigars and cognac"—she turned to Rockefeller—"or whatever your preference. That's when we women can return to more pleasant conversation."

Her comment made Mary dig deeper into her lip, but in a way it was a relief. She hoped it had ended this discussion. She also wasn't feeling 100 percent and was afraid she might say something she would regret. Mary reasoned that the cause of her upset might be drinking champagne on an empty stomach, so she stopped, holding the champagne glass as if it were a theater prop. But Carnegie and Rockefeller were not going to let it go.

"Actually, Andy," Rockefeller said, "I would like to hear Miss Handley's response."

"Of what consequence could any of my words be? There are captains of industry present here, and I am but a mere lady detective."

"I am always interested in the opinions of the God-fearing, churchgoing public."

Although Mary believed in God, she would never consider herself part of the category in which Rockefeller had placed her. Too often it was associated with blind belief, a lack of logic, and intolerance. She caught George's eye, and he ever so discreetly nodded for her to go ahead.

"All right, if you insist. I think that survival of the fittest could and should be applied to business. The person who builds the most efficient enterprise with the best product should always prevail, but there should be certain restrictions."

"Restrictions?" Rockefeller asked. "Do you not believe in laissez-faire capitalism?"

"Oh please, John," Alice Vanderbilt interrupted. "How can you expect we women to know about laissez-faire capitalism? You'd have much better luck asking us about the latest fashions."

That was it. Mary was no longer going to hold back her opinions or intellect. She couldn't swallow what these people were serving.

"If by 'laissez-faire' you mean fair competition to determine the market, I'd say yes. However, if that practice means that large companies can, with impunity, artificially lower prices, receive special rebates from other companies, and engage in ruthless and illegal practices to limit competition, I'd say no."

Mary knew she was in for a fight. Both Carnegie and Rockefeller were known for their questionable business practices. In fact, rumors abounded about Rockefeller's minions forcing people to sell their oil land at gunpoint for less than the market price.

"And where did you get such foolish notions about business?" Carnegie asked.

"Oh, those aren't my notions. I was quoting Senator John Sherman of Ohio. I expect you know he's proposed a bill called the Sherman Antitrust Act that is before Congress now and is expected to pass in the next month or so."

A silent pause followed. Rockefeller and Carnegie hadn't expected her to be so knowledgeable on the subject. Rockefeller harrumphed his displeasure but Carnegie spoke up.

"I'm sure you think you're being clever, but your notions of business are merely the chatter of a naïve and silly young woman."

Mary was feeling even weaker, and she no longer had the strength to filter her words. "Oh, am I no longer delightful?" she quipped.

George jumped in. "Actually, I think Mary's being quite clever, Mr. Carnegie, or you would have responded with something more substantive than name-calling."

Cornelius saw that his party was turning into a disaster and came to the defense of his more successful guests. "It's easy to be judgmental, Mary, but we are more than one aspect of our lives. Are you aware of what these men are doing for the world now?"

She tried to fight it but Mary's speech was getting slower and faces were becoming blurry. "Yes . . . I've read Mr. Carnegie's treatise . . . *The Gospel of* . . ."

"*Wealth. The Gospel of Wealth.*"

"That's it. Spend your life making it, and at the end, give it away."

"Then you know that he and Mr. Rockefeller are engaged in donating a sizable portion of their fortune to charity, educational institutions, and helping the less fortunate."

"I . . . think it's incredibly commendable . . . generous, and . . . selfless. I . . . applaud them." Mary started clapping her hands in a slow, offbeat motion. After three claps, one hand missed the other. George became concerned.

"Mary, are you all right?"

By now the room was spinning. Faces and furniture flew by her like a merry-go-round at a fair. "I also think that . . . guilt is a great motivator."

Then Mary passed out and collapsed to the floor.

30

THE DOCTOR HAD no idea what had caused Mary to faint. The Carnegies and Rockefellers had left and George had carried her upstairs to put her on a bed in one of the guest rooms. She was awake but still groggy when the doctor decided that she might benefit from bloodletting. Fortunately, that jogged George's memory, and before the doctor could start the process, George informed him that she had given a good deal of blood to her brother that day.

"I'm glad you told me that," said the doctor. "We could have had a catastrophe on our hands, and we wouldn't want that." George wholeheartedly agreed as the doctor prescribed a simple cure.

"Make sure she gets a healthy meal of meat or fish and drinks plenty of nonalcoholic beverages. Her recovery should be almost instantaneous."

The doctor was right. Halfway through her meal, while sitting in Cornelius Vanderbilt's dining room with George later that night, Mary felt her energy return.

"You told me you gave blood to Sean," George said, recounting the events of the day, "but you neglected to tell me you hadn't eaten all day."

"So much was happening that eating didn't enter my mind."

"Well, the important thing is you're all right."

"You've saved my life twice now. Is this going to be a habit with you?"

"I hope not. I'm not sure if my heart can take it."

"If yours fails, you can always have mine." Mary paused for a second then cringed, her face crinkling up, "My lord, did I really say that?"

George nodded. "Most definitely."

"It's tragic. Look what you've turned me into: a sappy, lovesick fool."

"It's catching. I'm similarly afflicted." He took her hand and kissed it as Cornelius entered.

"Well, it looks as if you're feeling much better, Miss Handley," Cornelius said.

"Yes, thank you, and please call me Mary."

"Of course, Mary."

"I'm sorry for anything I might have said this evening. I wasn't myself."

"You know what they say about people who are out of sorts or even drunk?" He stopped and stared at her. "That's when their true selves are revealed."

George turned to Cornelius and gave him a disapproving look. "Since you are not out of sorts or inebriated, dear brother, I will assume this is not your true self, and I forgive you for your behavior." He held out his hand to Mary. "It's time for me to take you home, Mary."

On the way back, Mary and George sat for a while in the carriage without speaking until she broke the silence.

"Well, I certainly made a wonderful impression on your family."

"Don't mind Cornelius. He's a twit, and a pompous one at that."

"I can't completely blame him. I did insult his guests."

"They pushed you into a corner. Did he expect you to lie or to not have an opinion? That's part of what I love about you, Mary. You don't shy away from your beliefs."

"Thank you, George, but telling Andrew Carnegie and John D. Rockefeller that their charitable instincts were motivated by guilt might have been going a bit too far."

He laughed. "I so enjoyed the looks on their faces. Then you had to go and spoil it all by fainting."

"I am quite the spoilsport." She laughed too, then they both got quiet, almost solemn.

"Mary, don't let my brother bother you. He's very old-school and a monumental hypocrite. He talks about the importance of associating with persons of breeding and substance, yet he prefers the company of ruthless businessmen like Carnegie and Rockefeller. They both came from very poor backgrounds, and Rockefeller's father is a bigamist, a cheat, and an all-around flimflam man. In essence, what Cornelius admires is wealth and power. They earned theirs, and he's insecure that he inherited his."

"I just don't want his silly prejudices to affect you in any way."

"They do. They provide me with constant humor."

When they arrived at Mary's tenement building George walked her upstairs and kissed her good night, but not before getting her to promise to rest the next day. After all, it was Sunday. Mary agreed and was eager to get some sleep, which took a while to happen. She had an anxious feeling. It might have been her worry over Sean's predicament, or possibly not. But something was off.

Had she looked out her window and gazed across the street, she would have known what that something was: Shorty, standing in the shadows, watching her. He had decided to follow Mary like he had her brother. Then he could determine the right time to act, and he was sure it wouldn't be long.

31

As usual, Hugh McLaughlin was the first one in the office Monday morning. The first, that is, after Liam Riley. Liam was always there, waiting for him in case he had some pressing work for him to do. McLaughlin didn't on this particular Monday, but under his arm he was carrying the architect's drawing for his North Shore home, given to him by its former owners, and he wanted Liam's opinion. He started talking as he entered the outer office.

"Liam, my lad, I need yer fine eye. The question is, where in blazes do I put my swimmin'—" He stopped as he looked up for the first time and saw Liam's anxious face.

"You have a visitor, Mr. McLaughlin." Liam nodded in the direction of the corner where Collis Huntington was seated.

"I heard you were an early riser, Hugh, though not as early as me apparently," said Huntington. Instead of standing, he sat back more comfortably in his chair.

"Well, well, if it isn't Collis fuckin' Huntington. What the hell do ya want?"

"A word to the wise: you really need to clean up your language if you intend to mix in with the North Shore crowd."

"Oh, ya know about that, huh?"

"I know more about you than your little lackey here."

"This is the second time ya attacked Liam here for no good reason. Are ya put out 'cause no one gives a rat's ass about ya or is it that *I* have a loyal fella who—"

"Please stop," said Huntington as he stood up and straightened his clothes. "Whatever kind of perverse activity the two of you engage in is of no interest to me. What does interest me, and should also interest you, is that you're being investigated for multiple murders and some very shady financial dealings."

McLaughlin looked at Liam, who shrugged his shoulders. "Yer lyin'," he replied.

"Am I? You'll find out." He started to slowly stroll toward the door.

"Who cares? I didn't kill anybody."

Huntington stopped and turned. "So that's your defense: maintaining that you're just shady and not a killer? You may want to reconsider that."

"I don't need a defense. I didn't do anything wrong."

"I'm surprised, Hugh. Surely you're aware it doesn't matter what you did or did not do. It's what they can prove that counts." He started to go once more but soon stopped. "Oh, and another word to the wise: I'd put that swimming pool in the backyard instead of the front, or your neighbors will think you're *très* gauche."

"*Très* fuck ya. Is that French enough for ya, Collis?"

"Language again, Hugh. Language."

∼✑∽

HAVING THOROUGHLY ENJOYED his short stay, Huntington felt chipper enough to bypass the elevator and walk down the three flights of stairs. As he exited the building, he saw a familiar face heading for the entrance.

"Good morning, Miss Handley."

Mary was taken aback. "Mr. Huntington, what are you doing here?"

"Gloating. It's a much-maligned activity, but it's making a big comeback with me. Have a wonderful day." Smiling broadly, he got into his carriage and rode away.

∼

WHEN MARY GOT up to the third floor, she could hear McLaughlin shouting from the hall.

"What the hell does that bastard Huntington have on me?"

"I have no idea, sir. None," said Liam, obviously shaken by McLaughlin's bluster.

"Ya better find out and find out soon. He's settin' me up for a fall, and if I go down, Liam, you know who goes with me, don't ya?"

Liam's mind was rapidly searching for an answer. "Maybe he's bluffing."

"Bluffin'?"

"He could be. That *is* possible."

"Have ya learned nothin' from me? Men like him don't bluff. They destroy."

The voices started to quiet, and, no longer able to hear them, Mary decided to go inside. The second Mary had closed the door Liam popped his head out of McLaughlin's office.

"Who is it? Is that ass Huntington back?" McLaughlin called to Liam from inside.

"It's that lady detective. . . ." Liam paused, trying to remember Mary's name.

"Lady detective?" McLaughlin responded as he quickly emerged from his office.

Mary stepped forward. "How do you do? I'm Mary Handley."

McLaughlin suddenly calmed and started oozing charm. "I know who ya are, girl. I'd be ashamed to say I was from Brooklyn if I didn't know Mary Handley." He walked over and shook her hand, then pointed to Liam. "This is my associate, Liam Riley."

"Mr. McLaughlin, Mr. Riley, pleased to meet you both."

"What brings you here, Mary? I hope ya don't mind if I call ya Mary?"

"No, of course not, go right ahead. I was hoping we could have a word."

"Certainly. Please step inta my office."

Mary did just that, followed by McLaughlin and Liam. McLaughlin nodded to Liam, and he closed the door. As McLaughlin sat at his desk, he gestured to Mary, who sat facing him. Liam plopped down on the windowsill behind the desk. When they were all settled, McLaughlin began. A consummate politician, he made it his business to know something about each one of his constituents, especially the Irish ones.

"So, what can I do for the lady whose father has the best butcher shop in Brooklyn?"

"Thank you, but it's not his. He just works there."

"For goin' on twenty years. Believe me, that place would shut down without him."

"That's very kind of you." Mary cleared her throat. "Mr. McLaughlin, as you probably know, my brother has been arrested for murdering his fiancée."

"Yes, a terrible, terrible tragedy. Isn't it, Liam?"

"Awful. My sympathies, Miss Handley."

"The point is, he didn't do it, and I've been reviewing the evidence. Some odd occurrences have arisen, and I was hoping you could help me explain them."

"I'll do whatever I can," said McLaughlin, then he looked at Liam.

"Anything to help," Liam said.

"On the day my brother was arrested, you made a call to District Attorney Ridgeway's office. Do you remember what that was about?"

"Let me see—"

"I'm sure you remember the day. It made big headlines in all the newspapers."

"I remember, all right. It's the phone call. Ya see, I make a bunch of 'em. But I'm pretty sure I haven't spoken ta Ridgeway in, oh, weeks." He looked at Liam, who nodded.

"What about Judge Moore?"

"The judge? Whew, that's been longer. The last time I saw the good judge was at my New Year's Eve party. I throw a fine party, Mary. Yer family should come this year—"

"Thank you. I look forward to the invitation." Mary knew not to hold her breath for it. "So you haven't spoken with Judge Moore?"

"Not in a month of Sundays."

"Then I don't suppose you spoke with Ridgeway when my brother was arraigned or on the day he was transferred to the Raymond Street Jail."

"I just heard about Sean being stabbed. It's an awful thing and I know yer upset—"

"There's no question I'm upset, Mr. McLaughlin, and I want to find out why, on each day there was a major decision affecting Sean's case, the person responsible for that decision got a phone call from you."

"I see," said McLaughlin, pausing to size Mary up. "I don't like what yer implyin', young lady."

"I'm not implying anything. I'm just asking a question that you refuse to answer."

Liam jumped in. "Better watch your mouth. Do you know who you're talking to?"

Mary held her ground. "I know perfectly well who Mr. McLaughlin is, and I didn't say anything disrespectful."

"Ease up on the girl, will ya, Liam? She's been through hell." He turned to Mary. "Sorry, he's just bein' loyal ta me. The fact is, I don't remember makin' those phone calls—the last one fer sure. I was out on Long Island buyin' my new house."

"Well, there it is then." Mary rose to leave. "Nice meeting you, Mr. McLaughlin and Mr. Riley. Thank you for your time. And congratulations on your new house, Mr. McLaughlin."

There were handshakes, pleasantries exchanged, and another hollow offer by McLaughlin, this time inviting the Handley family out to his house on the North Shore for a summer weekend. McLaughlin and Liam were sure they had evaded what might have been, at the very least, a political nightmare and maybe much more. When Mary got to the door, she turned to them.

"By the way, gentlemen, aren't there telephones on Long Island and don't they have records?"

The truth was, if McLaughlin had called from Long Island, it wouldn't have been from his private phone. He had just bought the house and probably hadn't moved in even if he had intended to get a phone. Most of the phones at that time on Long Island were not in private residences but rather in stores, and on the slim chance Mary could prove McLaughlin had placed a call from one of those stores, she couldn't prove what they'd discussed. Mary just wanted to see their reactions when she made them aware she knew the phone records could be checked. McLaughlin's and Liam's faces had dropped, but it was hard to tell if it was because of the call or the realization that they hadn't bamboozled her, or both. So, knowing full well that they weren't going to divulge any more information, she left.

Walking downstairs, Mary was frustrated. Nothing had changed. Huntington and McLaughlin were still strong suspects, but despite the evidence she'd uncovered against Shorty, she was no closer to finding the person who was truly behind the murders. She needed that person in order to free Sean. Mary started to pore over the facts yet again. Besides Shorty, she had thought that she was the connecting piece between Abigail Corday's murder and Patti's. However, it was conceivable Gabrielle Evans was just another murder Shorty had committed that he'd tried to cover up by framing Sean, and Mary wasn't part of the equation. It was all too coincidental, though, that three unrelated murders involving her and her family would occur separately in a fairly short amount of time. So where did that leave her? It was almost impossible to find a trail leading to the person who hired Shorty to kill Gabrielle Evans and Patti. That left one alternative. She would have to start back at the beginning—or at least the beginning for her in all of this—and find out who hired Abigail Corday to impersonate Emily Worsham.

It was upsetting. She had spent a lot of time chasing down leads, finding Shorty, questioning Huntington, trying to determine McLaughlin's role in all this, yet she was really no further along than when she had returned from Biltmore. She'd had no idea then how to find out who hired Abigail, and now was no different. The clock was ticking away. She didn't have time to waste and neither did Sean.

She walked down the busy Brooklyn street, crowded with people rushing to work, and racked her brain, reviewing all the facts over and over. Then it dawned on her. There was one person who might be able to help.

She chastised herself. *Why haven't I thought of it before?*

32

THE MARQUEE OF the Brooklyn Academy of Music read THE ROBERT DAVIES PLAYERS PRESENT: A ROBERT DAVIES PRODUCTION OF WILLIAM SHAKESPEARE'S *HAMLET* STARRING ROBERT DAVIES. Mary looked at it, thinking that this was a long way to come for an actor who, not long ago, was playing the bit role of the porter in a production of Ibsen's *A Doll's House,* and naturally she wondered how he'd managed such a dramatic turnabout. She had gotten his address from the police, but he had moved, having bought a spacious new brownstone in Clinton Hill. His neighbor, a round woman wearing too much jewelry, had told Mary where she could find him.

"He says he's a Danish prince," the neighbor had said. "If that pompous blowhard is a prince, I'm Pocahontas."

None of this seemed to fit the man she had met who was wailing over Abigail Corday's body the night of the fire, devastated by her death. When questioned further, the neighbor had very little other information about Robert Davies and emphatically stated that she had no desire to find out any more about him.

Inside, the theater company was in the middle of rehearsal. It seemed as if no expense had been spared for this production. The sets were already up and quite magnificent. There was no scrimping on the size of the cast either. If the play called for a crowd, there was going to be one, no matter how many actors with nonspeaking roles had to be paid.

When Mary entered, they were rehearsing act 3, scene 2 of *Hamlet,* where Hamlet instructs the actors how to perform a play, hoping the reaction to the play will help reveal that Claudius killed Hamlet's father. The scene hadn't gotten very far when Robert Davies stopped and turned toward the director.

"This doesn't feel right."

The director, the same one who had directed *A Doll's House,* approached Robert. He seemed weary, as if this was a regular occurrence.

"What's the problem now, Robert?"

"Robert? Who is this Robert? I am Hamlet, prince of Denmark."

"Yes, you are. What can I do for you, Lord Hamlet?" The words "Lord Hamlet" came off his lips with a tinge of disdain, which either Robert didn't pick up or he just ignored.

"It's the early seventeenth century. I'm royalty and there is nothing more common than actors. Why would I be walking amongst them?"

"Because you want to convince them to perform the play the way you want it done."

"I'm a prince. I can convince them from anywhere. Say . . . over there." He nodded toward an isolated part of the stage.

"We need movement in this scene, and the problem we have if you deliver your speech from over there is that it becomes static and less interesting."

"I see what you mean."

"Good." The director thought he was done, but he wasn't.

"I know what we can do. When I'm over there, you can shine a light on me."

"Shine a light on you?" The director obviously thought this idea was insane.

"Yes, that should make it more interesting."

The director started to protest. "I think it's a mistake to—"

"I want a light. If you don't like it, there's the door." Robert pointed to the exit.

After the fiasco of *A Doll's House,* the director, who had a wife and child to support, desperately needed a job. His relation to Louise Carnegie was very distant, his branch of her family tree being far from wealthy. Aware of the director's desperation, Robert knew he could control him. It was an extra bonus that he got to order around the man who thought he was worthy of only a tiny role in *A Doll's House* and wouldn't even let him understudy the lead part of Torvald for no pay.

"All right, you'll get your light," the director said, exasperated at dealing with Robert. "Take a break, everyone."

As they all went their separate ways, Robert picked up a copy of the play and sat in the first row of the theater by himself, studying it. Mary approached him carefully.

"Excuse me, Prince Hamlet, might I have a word with you?"

"Why certainly," responded Robert as he turned to face Mary.

"Do you remember me?"

"You're Mary Handley. How could I forget? What a tragic, awful evening that was. Almost as tragic as when that bastard Claudius killed my father."

Robert had merged his realities: Prince Hamlet in the play and his own experiences as Robert Davies. Abigail evidently had never allowed that to happen. When she "lived a part," she only recognized the world of that role. Robert obviously didn't have the dedication or the talent that Abigail had, and Mary viewed that as a fortunate circumstance. It seemed he wasn't denying the memories of Robert Davies as Abigail Corday would have denied hers, but she would soon find out. Mary decided to play along, acquiescing to his desire to parade around as a prince.

"If it pleases you, my lord, I would like to discuss that tragic evening."

"Of course," he said, beckoning her by patting the seat next to him. "Sit down. No need to be in awe of royalty. We have real emotions like you common folk."

"Thank you. I was hoping you might be able to answer some questions about Abigail."

"Ah yes, Abigail was a very dear friend. Her death was devastating to me."

A good start. Needless to say, Mary wondered how an actor could gain any insight into his character amid the confusion of two opposing realities, but then reminded herself she wasn't there to give acting lessons. She needed information.

"Are you aware that Abigail impersonated Emily Worsham in order to engage my services?"

"Yes, a thoroughly misguided decision."

258 Lawrence H. Levy

"Why was it misguided?"

"Abigail was a true people's performer. She would assume characters and go out onto the streets and entertain the masses for free. People started noticing her brilliance and began hiring her to perform characters at parties and other such whatnot." He waved his hand in what he thought was a royal manner. "The people who hired her to play Emily told her she was doing a good deed, that John Worsham had been murdered and that the killers needed to be caught. It turned out to be an elaborate plot to embarrass an influential family."

"The Huntingtons?" Mary asked.

"Yes . . . nouveau riche," he said with disdain. "That kind doesn't know how to deal with such matters."

Nothing Mary had ever read suggested Hamlet was a snob, but she had no desire to contest Robert's choices as an actor. It would only delay the relevant information she was seeking, so she proceeded. "Did Abigail ever mention that they had threatened her?"

"I don't think those people give warnings. Besides, by the time the plot was exposed, she had gotten the part of Nora, and, deep down, though she'd never have admitted to thinking as Abigail since she was now Nora, she had to have been having second thoughts. She was on her way to becoming a huge success, and it could have all become undone with a scandal, like that actress/producer of *An American Cousin* when President Lincoln was shot."

"Laura Keene? She continued to work after the assassination."

"Yes, but her career was never the same. And what did she do? Simply produce and act in a play. Booth wasn't her ally. He wasn't even in her play. And by agreeing to hire you,

Abigail was in the thick of a huge scandal involving very influential people."

The more Robert talked, the more he dropped out of his Hamlet character. Finally, Mary couldn't resist. "Prince Hamlet, I'm fascinated by your keen mind. Here you are living in the early seventeenth century, and yet you have knowledge of events in the nineteenth century. Are you clairvoyant?"

Robert froze, then finally dropped all pretenses. "You caught me, Mary. But you wouldn't have caught Abigail. I could never get her out of character. That's probably why she's dead today."

"Why do you say that?"

"She always took on the characteristics of the person she was playing, sometimes exaggerating them to truly understand who that person was. In a way, getting the part of Nora was her downfall."

"Since Nora Helmer becomes a liberated woman and freethinker, Abigail became one."

"She wanted to go public, naming the people who had hired her, revealing that they had lied to her and that she wasn't aware the coffin was empty. It was part of Nora's compulsion to be open and honest. If she were playing Lady Macbeth at the time, this never would have happened."

"If she were Lady Macbeth, we'd have infinitely more corpses."

"But not hers. I warned her not to cross these men, but I was just the lowly porter to her."

"Did she ever mention who they were—the men who duped her into playing Emily?"

An announcement came from the director. "Break is over. Everyone back to rehearsal."

Robert instantly became Prince Hamlet again. "Be there presently." He then turned to Mary and shrugged. "She wouldn't divulge any names, but I sensed they were powerful. Of course, since Abigail was playing Nora, she was fearless. It was frustrating. She wouldn't heed anything I said."

"You realize that no one would take the chance of going after Collis Huntington unless there was considerable remuneration?"

"I have to go, but you should really see this production. I have spared no expense. It's going to be brilliant, a *Hamlet* like no one has ever seen before."

"Yes, I'm sure it will be," Mary said, trying to hold back the sarcasm that was fighting its way into her every syllable. His conceit not allowing him to think otherwise, Robert thought Mary had agreed with him. He nodded to her and started back to rehearsal. He had avoided her question, and it set her thinking. She called to him, "Of course, one does wonder how you came into all of this so directly after your friend's demise."

Upon hearing her words, he tripped, falling on the steps leading to the stage. The cast broke out laughing.

"Are you all right, Lord Hamlet?" said the director, stifling his own derisive laughter.

Robert looked up, trying to save face. "Yes, yes, I just wanted to provide all you commoners with a bit of amusement." He then whispered intensely to Mary. "If you must know, a long-lost relative, someone I didn't even know, died and left me a considerable sum. And I'd never have harmed Abigail. Because of her talent, I thought Abigail would get her break first and then help me." Then he returned to being Prince Hamlet. "But as fate would have it, I had no need for her."

"How fortunate for you."

Mary's tone didn't provide Robert with the absolution he was seeking. Miffed, he turned and stomped onto the stage. Mary watched a few more minutes of rehearsal. If the words on the marquee outside weren't enough evidence, what she saw onstage completely confirmed that it was clearly a vanity production. Robert didn't seem to have the commitment or insight Abigail had. It was also entirely possible he had put too much of himself into the role. Instead of playing Hamlet as a tortured soul, he was mistakenly playing him as an insecure peacock. Now that he had money and was in charge, maybe that's exactly what he was.

Of course, the money presented another problem. His proclamation about "a long-lost relative" was at best flimsy. He could've been involved in Abigail Corday's death, especially if someone promised him enough money to advance his stalled acting career. But even if that were true, and Mary highly doubted it, she still had to find out who that person was in order to tie the three murders together.

Fib or not, Robert's "inheritance" started Mary thinking about the old lady who had been killed: Gabrielle Evans. A fire was never set in her house, which upset the pattern in Mary's theory. Maybe whoever hired Shorty had told him not to burn it because that person was going to inherit it. The question was: who would benefit from Gabrielle Evans's death?

33

LESTER HACKEL JR. was a very organized lawyer who believed there was a definite order in the universe and lived
his life that way. He carried fastidiousness to its ultimate level
and then some. Every paper in his office was in its correct
place, as was every pen, chair, table, and picture on the wall.
If at one point a picture had tilted ever so slightly to the
side, Lester would notice it and immediately straighten the
offender. He had two windows behind his desk covered by
two shades. Every morning when he entered the office he
would lower each shade exactly halfway, then study and ad-
just them to make sure both shades were the same distance
from the tops of the windows and completely even with each
other. Anything otherwise was disturbing. It led to chaos,
and Lester couldn't get his work done when there was chaos.

Lester was in his late thirties and had taken over the law
practice from his father, Lester Hackel Sr., who had retired two
years earlier only to tragically die when he was kicked in the
head by a horse whose shoe he was trying to straighten. It was

early afternoon, and Lester had just returned from Schmidt's Bean House, where he had his regular Monday lunch of sausage and baked beans. Sitting at his desk in his Monday outfit—brown suit, brown shoes, and a brown tie—he had an unexpected visitor. Anything unexpected gave Lester a nervous stomach. And his reaction didn't vary one iota even though his visitor was an attractive young woman.

"How do you do, Mr. Hackel? I'm Mary Handley." Mary stuck out her hand to shake his but she was left holding air.

"Junior," he said.

"Excuse me?"

"I'm Mr. Hackel Junior. My father was Mr. Hackel, but he is no longer with us."

"Oh, I'm sorry." Mary finally lowered her hand to her side.

"No need to be. He went as he would have wished: trying to restore order in the world."

"Oh, well then, that must be very . . . comforting."

"It is, but what is not comforting is that I don't seem to remember us having an appointment, Miss . . ."

"Handley. Mary Handley."

"Yes." He glanced at a paper on his desk. "I make a specific notation of all of my appointments for each day—"

"I'm afraid I don't have an appointment."

"Well then, Miss Handley, you must make one, and then we can speak."

"What I have to say won't take long."

"Good, then make a short appointment."

Mary could see Lester would be hard to dissuade. "When is your next appointment?"

He looked at his paper again, then checked his pocket watch. "In fifty-eight minutes."

"Then I'd like to schedule an appointment in two minutes."

"I'm sorry, but I need at least fifteen minutes' lead time. That's my policy."

"All right, fifteen minutes."

"Splendid. I'll put you down."

As Lester wrote Mary's name on his appointment sheet, she walked out into the hall and waited. It was maddening to waste fifteen minutes when time was so precious, but she knew that she would waste even more time trying to convince the officious Mr. Hackel Jr. otherwise. Exactly fifteen minutes later Mary walked back into the office. Lester stood.

"Ah, Miss Handley, good to see you," he said as he rose while checking his pocket watch again. "And right on time." This go-around they shook hands, and he offered her a seat. Lester was a step or two beyond odd, but he had information she needed, and she got right to it.

"Mr. Hackel Jr., I understand you are in the possession of Gabrielle Evans's will."

"I'm afraid you've been misinformed. It's not a will but rather a revocable living trust. My father originally drew it up, but when he retired, the responsibility of her trust was passed on to me. I am also the executor."

"Good, then you can tell me about her heirs."

"I'm afraid I can't. I am not bound to reveal that information. Besides, there has been a delay in the distribution of assets."

Mary knew this was not the type of man who would break protocol. "Can you tell me when the assets will be distributed?"

"Sometime this week. That's all I will say."

"It's been many weeks since her death. That's quite a delay."

"It's called doing my job. As executor, I was also given the duty of making financial decisions for the estate. Mrs. Evans owned a considerable amount of stock in one company that was involved in a buyout. As the executor, I decided it would be in the best interests of the estate to sell the shares, and that transaction was just completed this past Friday."

"What was the name of the company?"

"It's all a matter of public record now. The Long Island Water Supply Company."

"And who bought it?"

"I'm not at liberty to tell you that. I promised to let it come out in the newspapers first."

"Really, and whom did you promise?"

"If I told you that, I'd be telling you who bought the company. But very clever, Miss Handley, very clever indeed."

"Thank you. It was worth a try, but you're too smart for me." She smiled, hoping her compliment and friendly demeanor might convince him to reveal more than he was willing to divulge. "And would you say the estate was worth five thousand dollars, ten thousand, a hundred thousand?"

Lester didn't respond.

"You won't disclose that information either?"

"I will. I'm just waiting for you to reach a number that's high enough for me to confirm."

Mary was speechless. Gabrielle Evans's estate was worth north of one hundred thousand dollars! That was more than enough motive for murder.

❧

ANDREW HASWELL GREEN was not having a good day. As days went, this one exceeded lousy and was bordering on miserable, even worse than the day when he had punched the wall. The extortionists had carried through on their threat. They didn't openly accuse him of anything. Instead, they were torturing him by placing items in the newspaper filled with innuendo.

The latest attempt to unmask him was particularly annoying. It was a line in a newspaper article concerning a benefit he had attended to expand Central Park. An excerpt from the article read, "And Andrew Haswell Green attended, accompanied by his male companion."

Green was livid. His "male companion" was his brother John, a doctor who had just returned from working in Chile and was visiting from Worcester, Massachusetts. Of course, there was no mention of that. *If they did mention John,* Green thought, *those vultures probably would have alluded to some sort of incest.*

He knew Joseph Pulitzer, the owner of the *World,* the newspaper in which this garbage was printed, and contemplated paying him a visit. He soon decided it would be unwise. Even if Pulitzer backed him, he would eventually be faced with the question "Are you or aren't you?" and that would be problematic. If he denied being a homosexual, he was implying that homosexuality was evil and wrong, an implication he surely didn't believe. He was also honest to a fault and absolutely refused to lie. Besides, any denial would just bring more attention to it. Of course, some would claim that making no response was an act of admission. However, he was a lawyer, and he knew there was no concrete proof of anything. Reasonable doubt was ever present.

It was late afternoon, and Green was in his study sipping chamomile tea, hoping it would calm him. It didn't. His butler entered and informed Green that he had a surprise visitor: Collis Huntington. That increased Green's anxiety level. He had no idea why Huntington had come or what he might want, but he told the butler to show him in.

"I understand you've been dealing with some adversity," said Huntington before tossing a newspaper onto the coffee table in front of Green. It was the *World*.

"Collis, don't tell me you're the one who—"

"No, no, it's not my style. When I attack, I start with a little scratch and allow it to build over a long period of time, letting it get larger and larger until the person bleeds out. It's obvious this garbage is purely for motivational purposes."

"So, you've come to revel in my problems because I forced you to withdraw over yours?"

"I prefer commiserate. We have both been attacked by the same man, and I've already set in motion plans to get him off our backs."

"I'm glad you know our adversary, because I certainly don't."

"Hugh McLaughlin. It's really quite obvious when you think about it. That sneaky mick desperately needed to stop the consolidation project in order to retain his little fiefdom of Brooklyn. So he went about attempting to remove the two biggest obstacles to his success: me and you."

"And you're certain of this?"

"As certain as I am about anything, but if I'm wrong, he still goes down and not us."

Green wanted to know more. "Would you like some chamomile tea, Collis?"

"Don't mind if I do, Andy," Huntington said as he sat down on the club chair facing Green. "I usually prefer something a bit stronger, but this will be a nice change."   .

Green called to his butler and asked him to bring another cup and saucer for Huntington. "And see what proper snacks we have. Is that all right with you, Collis?"

Huntington nodded and the butler left. He nestled himself into the club chair, getting comfortable as he looked around the room and then at Green.

"I want you to know, Andy, I count several sodomites as my good friends."

Green winced but decided not to protest. What would be the point?

GEORGE'S BUSINESS DEALINGS were finally complete, and Mary asked him to watch Lester Hackel Jr.'s office. The meeting of Gabrielle Evans's heirs could be at any time, and since the officious Mr. Hackel Jr. would not reveal their identities, they had to keep a vigil. Meanwhile, she paid a visit to the Long Island Water Supply Company.

It was in a town called New Lots that had been annexed by Brooklyn four years earlier. Mary stood across the street and stared at it, the irony fully implanted in her brain that this unassuming building could hold the key to Sean's freedom. All records that contained lists of stockholders were routinely sent to the state capital. Albany was far away, and hoping that she could save precious time, she had decided to go right to the source.

When she entered the building, she was immediately struck by how small the office space was. It was one large room with a desk for the secretary up front and three larger desks in the rear, presumably for the executives. Only the secretary was there, which was part of Mary's plan. She purposely arrived at lunchtime, thinking that the fewer people present, the less chance she would have of someone objecting to her request.

"May I help you?" said the secretary, a thin brunette about Mary's age who sat with her back as straight as a ballet dancer's. Mary couldn't help thinking that she should have been her mother's daughter.

"Yes, as a matter of fact—"

"Wait one minute. I know you."

Mary played along. "Yes, you do look familiar."

"Don't tell me. I know." And she thought for a full ten seconds until you could almost see her revelation. "You went to Girls High, didn't you? That's it! That's where I know you." Girls High School was the first public high school in Brooklyn. It had originally been designed for boys and girls, but there were too many students and, hence, it became a girls' school.

"Yes, of course," Mary replied. "You have a great memory." Mary had never attended Girls High School. After eighth grade, she was sent out into the working world. Instead, she had attained her considerable knowledge from the encyclopedia her parents had bought for Sean, which he never used, and the volumes of secondhand books she routinely absorbed that her father would borrow from a bookstore owner he had befriended. In all likelihood, the secretary had seen her face in the newspapers, but Mary wasn't going to correct her.

"Miss Crabtree's shorthand class. That's where we met. I'm certain."

"Miss Crabtree. That woman was a real hoot."

"Two hoots if you ask me, but I wouldn't be here if it weren't for her. Her class has come in very handy. Very handy indeed."

"I'm glad you have such a good job."

"Don't worry, honey. You'll get one someday."

"Why thank you. That's very heartening. You are a perfect sweetheart."

"My husband tells me I'm too nice."

"Don't you listen to him. You keep being just the way you are."

The secretary chuckled. "That's what I told him. I said you conduct yourself the way you see fit, and I'll behave the way I see fit."

"Good for you. Now, I wonder if you can help me. I've lost touch with my aunt whom I understand was a stockholder here."

"If she was, she isn't anymore. The company was just bought."

"Really? Well then, I hope you had stock. You could've made some good money."

"Just a little, but a little was very nice." She leaned over to whisper as if someone else were in the empty office to hear. "Three hundred dollars a share. I only paid twenty-five for it."

"I'm very happy for you."

"It almost fell through. A big stockholder didn't want to sell."

"Some people are so selfish."

"You're telling me. But it all worked out."

"Good. Who bought your company?"

The secretary looked around, then whispered again. "The

city of Brooklyn. I'm not supposed to tell anyone, but why not? It's going to be in the newspapers soon enough."

That was interesting information, but Mary needed to know more if she was going to find a specific person. "Really? You wouldn't happen to have a list of the old stockholders? Maybe it will have my aunt's address."

The secretary shrugged. "I don't see the harm. After all, they're no longer part owners."

She went to a filing cabinet, removed a folder, and then gave it to Mary. She quickly perused the papers and soon came upon Gabrielle Evans's name. She was by far the largest stockholder. If she had refused to sell at that inflated price, she would have made many enemies among the other stockholders and any relatives who were positioned to inherit her fortune.

As her eyes scanned the rest of the list, she saw several Brooklyn politicians who stood to make a nice amount of profit on the deal. Then the name of the second-largest stockholder in the company popped out at her. It caught her by surprise and she momentarily stopped breathing. She checked it a second and third time. By now, her head was reeling, but there was no mistake. It was right in front of her in black and white: Patrick Campbell.

The second-largest shareholder was Superintendent Campbell!

34

MARY KEPT TELLING herself it wasn't possible. Maybe it was a different Patrick Campbell. Superintendent Campbell had devoted his life to police work. He believed in the law. He wasn't a murderer. Besides, he was her mentor and her good friend. He liked Sean. He would never do this to her and her family no matter how much money was involved. Then the ugly thoughts took over, and unfortunately, they fit together too well. Superintendent Campbell was bound to know Shorty. Billy did, and probably most of the police in Brooklyn. He also hated his new job and hadn't been himself since he started it. He was getting fat and complacent. Maybe he'd made the conscious decision to cash in, and Sean was a complication he hadn't expected. These were all theories and suppositions. Mary hoped that she could find some logic that would absolve him, but she kept returning to the fact that he was a large stockholder in the Long Island Water Supply Company. The second largest, in fact. That was too big to be a coincidence. And the more she reviewed the events, the more damning it was.

She had asked Superintendent Campbell to help her every step of the way, and he had always failed miserably. He couldn't get the police to drop the charges against Sean. He couldn't stop his transfer to the Raymond Street Jail, and he couldn't protect him while he was there. He just plain couldn't. But maybe he never intended to help and . . . it suddenly hit her. Dr. Lansing had said Superintendent Campbell had placed a guard at the infirmary to protect Sean. She had to get there as soon as she could, and it would take longer now. It had started to rain.

&

GEORGE WAS WATCHING Lester Hackel Jr.'s office from across the street. He stood a few buildings down, where he had sought shelter under a tree. It had started raining hard, with lightning and thunder, and he cursed himself for not bringing an umbrella. The danger of standing next to a tree during a lightning storm was obvious, but he ignored it in favor of staying dry. Earlier, when it wasn't raining, he had let his driver wander off with the carriage to the closest saloon, which was a few blocks away. Since George had already been there for several hours, he figured his driver was feeling no pain by now.

George was contemplating going for a cup of tea or anywhere that he could attain proper shelter when he finally saw some activity across the street. A tall, comely Nordic woman, Scandinavian or German in origin, approached the law office carrying a big box. Having no hands free, she kicked the door a couple of times and Lester Hackel Jr. opened it, beckoning her inside. Not long after that he saw a man pull up in a carriage and get out. He was wearing a trench coat, another item George regretted leaving at home, and quickly opened an umbrella before George could see his face. In true cloak-and-dagger fashion, George stayed low as he stealthily made his way across the street, hoping to catch a glimpse of the man. He planted himself behind a milk wagon and carefully moved around it to get a better view.

The man knocked on the door and waited impatiently for Lester Hackel Jr. to answer. He was fidgety. He pulled out his pocket watch and started to turn to the left in order to read the watch in a better light. This was it. The man was about to show his face, and though George was tense, he was excited and ready. It felt odd that even without Mary, he was enjoying himself. *I'm beginning to really like this sleuthing business,* he thought.

That's when he was struck on the side of his head with what felt like a sledgehammer. It wasn't. It was Shorty's fist.

∽

THE RAIN MADE the journey to the Raymond Street Jail seem longer and far more miserable. Once she arrived, it took a while but Mary talked her way in to see Sean after invoking Warden Wilson's name no less than a dozen times. The guards finally checked with him, and she was given clear passage.

When Mary entered the infirmary, out of breath from rushing to get there, she saw a guard bent over Sean's bed. She prayed she was in time.

"Stand away from my brother's bed! Stand away now!"

The guard slowly straightened and raised his hands, then turned around.

"Billy! What in blazes are you doing here?"

As Billy put his hands down he said, "I'm the one who should be askin' that question, lass. The way you were screamin' I thought you had a shotgun in your hands."

"I didn't know it was you, and it was scary the way you were hunched over Sean."

"Well, chess *is* a scary game." He stepped away, revealing Sean lying in the bed, his head propped up with pillows, with a chessboard and pieces next to him on the bed.

"Relax, sis," Sean said. "Billy's just trying to teach me a few moves so that I can give you tougher competition."

After what had seemed like an eternity, Mary exhaled, smiling as she walked toward them. "You should have started years ago. I'm already eons ahead of you."

"That's our plan. Make you feel cocky and then blindside you."

"How's the leg?"

"It hurts. I don't know how useful it'll be, but the doc said it'll take time to find that out." Sean didn't want to talk about his leg. He pointed to Billy. "How do you like my poor excuse for a bodyguard?"

"You're guarding him, Billy?"

"I asked Chief McKellar if I could watch the lad until he got on his feet."

"And Chief McKellar approved it?"

"Ya still don't understand us, do ya, lass?" Billy turned toward Sean. "He may be a filthy, low-down murderer, but he's our murderer and we look after our own."

"Thanks, Billy," Sean responded sarcastically. "You make me feel really special."

"The guard at the station certainly didn't share your sentiments," Mary remarked.

"He's a bit dim-witted," replied Billy, "but most guards

are. That's why I told the one that was here to scram, and I took over."

"You're wonderful, Billy. Thank you."

Mary hugged him, and Billy raised his hands in the air again.

"Careful, girl, or you'll anger the missus, and she's handier with a firearm than I am."

Mary told them she was just there to check on Sean and had to go. She didn't mention the Long Island Water Supply Company and what she had discovered about Superintendent Campbell. She was still formulating what she was going to do. If she let others know, it might get back to him, and he could have time to prepare an excuse or, worse, take action.

When Mary left the Raymond Street Jail, she still hadn't decided where she was going. Should she go directly to Superintendent Campbell's office and confront him, or relieve George and discuss the situation with him? That question was soon answered, because as she stepped out into the pouring rain, Superintendent Campbell's carriage was parked in front.

"Mary, what are you doing here?"

"I could ask you the same question."

"And I can answer it. I was in a meeting when I was interrupted with a telephone call from Warden Wilson informing me you were demanding entry."

"And you allowed it? I'm surprised." Mary regretted those words the second they came out of her mouth. She knew Superintendent Campbell wouldn't let them go unchallenged and she wasn't ready to reveal her suspicions yet. She started walking, hoping she could avoid the inevitable. At best, it was wishful thinking.

"Come back here, Mary."

She kept walking. "I hate to disappoint you, but I have a brother in this jail whose innocence I still have to prove."

Superintendent Campbell told his driver to follow Mary, and the carriage started moving. "Get in the carriage. I'll take you where you need to go."

Mary stiffened. "No, thank you. I can find it on my own."

"Mary Handley, get in this carriage now, and explain to me why you're acting so incredibly bizarre. Now, Mary!"

She stopped. Mary was soaking wet, still mourning Patti's death, devastated over Sean's arrest, and heartbroken over Superintendent Campbell's betrayal. She wouldn't have chosen this time as the moment to confront Campbell, but it was as good as any. She got in the carriage.

Superintendent Campbell offered her a towel. "I keep this in my carriage for emergencies. Dry yourself."

She shook her head. "It's not necessary."

"It's not a choice. You're dripping all over my carriage. Now dry yourself."

Mary took the towel and started wiping her face and hands, then proceeded to her hair. She didn't want to admit it, but it felt good.

"Where are you going?" he asked.

"Why do you want to know?"

"So I can tell my driver. Do you want him to guess?"

Mary told Superintendent Campbell Lester Hackel Jr.'s address. She figured that was the most logical place to go. Maybe George had found something out, and besides, she desperately needed his support at that moment. When Superintendent Campbell gave the address to the driver, she asked, "Do you know who Lester Hackel Jr. is?"

"He's handling Gabrielle Evans's estate." Mary looked surprised, and he continued. "Don't you think I follow the crimes being committed in my city?"

"Then you must know about the Long Island Water Supply Company."

"I've heard of it. Why?"

She had to let him know. She informed him of everything she had found out as Superintendent Campbell listened intently. By the time she finished, her voice and temperament had risen to a very intense level.

"Imagine my disappointment, my anger, my complete outrage to discover the man I admired, *my mentor, my friend*, was not only involved in murder for profit but committed crimes *against my family*. How could you have become so completely depraved?! Have you no shame?!"

Superintendent Campbell didn't so much as flinch at the news. He slowly sat back and scratched under his chin, a habit he had while thinking, and calmly responded.

"I'm proud of you, Mary. You've done some very fine detective work."

"Thank you. I had a good teacher," she said pointedly.

"What's your next step? Are you going to arrest me?"

"You know I can't do that. I have to inform the proper authorities." Suddenly, Mary's emotions took over. Her outrage exploded out of her body. "Damn it, Chief! I don't understand any of this. I thought you cared about us. Why the hell did you do it?"

Superintendent Campbell remained calm. "I said you've done some fine detective work. I didn't say it was correct."

"Prove me wrong, Chief. I'd love you to prove me wrong."

"First of all, I don't and never have owned stock in the Long Island Water Supply Company."

"Then how come your name is on the list?"

"I don't know for sure, but I have some suspicions. I do know this. I have been an honest policeman my whole career, and there is no possible way I could have made enough money to buy that amount of stock, even at twenty-five dollars a share."

"And I should just take your word for it."

"No, but there are other facts to consider. Do you know who just bought the Long Island Water Supply Company?"

"Yes, the city of Brooklyn."

"Mayor Chapin orchestrated the sale."

"So?"

"He doesn't need to steal. He has family money. But he does want to be governor, and he needs Hugh McLaughlin for that."

"That still doesn't explain—"

"Hold your horses, Mary. I'm getting to it. I've been trying to bring down McLaughlin and his damn Brooklyn Ring for years now, and he knows it."

"So he buys stock using your name, he has Chapin buy the company for an outrageous profit, and in case anyone investigates, you're the one who will look crooked."

"By the time I proved I never bought the stock and didn't have the money, I would have been forced to resign and been out of his hair."

"But in all probability no one investigates, and the money is his. I only stumbled upon it because of Sean being framed." She paused, nodding. It all made sense. "I'm sorry, Chief."

"I'd have thought the same thing if it were you. Except, you'd be locked up by now."

Mary smiled as Superintendent Campbell called to his driver and changed their destination to Hugh McLaughlin's office. Her reunion with George would have to wait. She was happy that she might be wrong but would reserve final judgment until they spoke with McLaughlin. The way things were going, anything was possible. She had to watch Superintendent Campbell carefully. She hadn't crossed him off her list yet, and she had no doubt that he knew it.

35

It was late afternoon and Hugh McLaughlin had just decided where to build the swimming pool at his North Shore house when a drop of water splashed onto the architect's plans that were spread out on the desk in his office. He looked up at the origin of the leak, a wet spot on the ceiling. *Damn it! Not again!* He ripped the plans off the desk, then folded them and shoved them into a drawer. He grabbed the wastepaper basket to the right of his chair and placed it on the desk under the drip. He then went to his door, swung it open, and roared to his secretary.

"Helen, tell Liam ta get that moron roofer he hired back in here and—" He stopped when he saw the two people standing next to Helen's desk.

"I'll inform Liam about the roofer, Mr. McLaughlin, and I was just going to inquire about your availability." She gestured toward their visitors. "Superintendent Campbell and Miss Handley would like to speak with you."

Helen answered the ringing phone as McLaughlin instantly turned on his charm, an ability he had no matter how annoyed he might have been. He went over and shook their hands.

"Why, Patrick, it's good to see ya. You should stop by more often. And, Mary, a beautiful Irish lass is always welcome. Please, come in."

He waved for them to follow him into his office. He closed the door and pointed to the wastepaper basket sitting on his desk.

"The *Brooklyn Daily Eagle* calls me a kingmaker, and I can't even get a leak fixed."

Mary responded with pointed words. "The *Brooklyn Daily Eagle* gets many things wrong. They call my brother a murderer, and now I have proof that he's not."

If McLaughlin was concerned, he didn't show it. "Well, that must be a great relief for ya and yer family." He gestured. "Please sit down, both of ya. Make yerselves comfortable."

They both did, Superintendent Campbell on a couch and Mary on a chair facing McLaughlin, who sat at his desk.

"So, what can I do for ya?"

Superintendent Campbell started. "I wonder if you can tell us something about the Long Island Water Supply Company."

"Ah yes, the water supply. I can tell ya buying it was a masterstroke by Mayor Chapin. Those damn New Yorkers—excuse my language, Mary—"

"It's okay. I've heard and spoken much worse."

"All right. Those damn New Yorkers wanted to take over Brooklyn and ruin our fine way of livin'. They could have, too. We needed water, but the good mayor's takin' care of that."

"You left out the part where I become a major stockholder in the company, having never invested a nickel."

"You caught that, Patrick. Good for you. Well, no gall, no glory."

Mary was surprised to see Superintendent Campbell, who usually stayed cool in any number of tense situations, lose his temper and pound his fist on McLaughlin's desk. "No gall, no glory! That's your excuse for framing me for stock manipulation?"

McLaughlin looked at Superintendent Campbell's fist, which was still on his desk, and responded, completely unruffled, "I apologize if I caused ya any consternation. I changed my name on that list 'cause that company was gonna save Brooklyn. People are suspicious, and I didn't want a whole hullabaloo croppin' up over my good investment, holdin' up the progress of our great city. If it makes ya feel any better, Patrick, I've written a letter to the water company explainin' the mistake and askin' 'em to change the name back."

"And I should just believe you?"

"Ya want proof? The letter's sitting on Liam's desk for him to personally take over to 'em when he gets in tomorrow. Helen!"

"Don't bother her, Mr. McLaughlin," said Mary. "The poor woman is swamped with work. I'll get it for you."

"Thank ya, lass. It's right across the hall. Yer such a lovely, considerate girl. Yer parents must be very proud."

Mary wanted to tell him where he could stick his Irish malarkey, but that would cause a row that would defeat their purpose for being there. Instead, she went across the hall to Liam Riley's office. It was tiny with just enough room for a small desk and one thin filing cabinet. McLaughlin wasn't lying. She saw the letter addressed to the Long Island Water Supply Company sitting on Liam's desk. She picked it up and was on her way back when a framed letter on the wall caught her attention. It was from Abraham Lincoln.

When Mary returned to McLaughlin's office, he was laughing.

"I committed murder? Not just one but three? Ya have got to be jokin', Patrick!"

"I couldn't be more serious."

Mary interrupted. "I found the letter. Here it is, Mr. McLaughlin." And she handed it to him.

He held up the letter. "See, Patrick? I wasn't lyin'. I don't have to."

"Well, I guess that settles it," said Mary. "We should be going, Superintendent Campbell." He looked at Mary as if she were from another planet, and she continued. "Mr. McLaughlin has answered our questions satisfactorily, and I just realized it's my mother's birthday today. Her celebration will start any minute now."

Superintendent Campbell didn't move or say anything. He just stared at Mary, trying to figure out what was going on. She looked at him, her eyes telling him to hurry up.

"Please, Superintendent Campbell. I'm already late."

"What a thoughtful daughter," oozed McLaughlin. "Yer a rare breed, Mary Handley. There aren't many of ya left."

"Thank you, sir. Superintendent?"

Superintendent Campbell was still dumbfounded, but he rose, they all said their good-byes, and he and Mary left. When they were outside the office in the elevator, he turned to Mary.

"Okay, what was that all about?"

"McLaughlin didn't do it. Commit the murders, that is."

"That's an interesting conclusion. I suppose there's some reasoning that comes behind it. At least, I pray there is."

"McLaughlin wouldn't kill for profit and take the chance of it getting messy, like this one has. He's too powerful. Why risk it when he can just move on to another scheme?"

"That's it? You pulled me out of there because of your analysis of his personality!" Superintendent Campbell was about to explode when Mary spoke.

"That, and I know who hired Shorty. It was Liam Riley."

36

S HE LEFT IT all to the cats?!" screamed Liam Riley. "Fuck, no, that can't be right!"

Gabrielle Evans's cats, Vicky and Albert, had been carried to Lester Hackel Jr.'s office in a box by the tall, comely Nordic woman, Miss Amundsen, who had been asked to be their new caretaker. They were busy investigating the room, and upon Liam's outburst, they turned toward him. Vicky jumped up onto the desk to get a better look.

Lester Hackel Jr. was mortified by Liam's behavior. "Mr. Riley, there's no need—"

"That was my uncle's money! He promised my mother. She can't do that!"

"I'm afraid she can. He left it all to your aunt, and she had the right to do with it whatever she wished."

"She talked to these damn cats and made up voices for 'em. She was completely daft, mad as a hatter!"

"I'm sorry, but if your uncle had wanted to protect you, he should have had a proviso written." Then Lester Hackel

Jr. wiped his nose with his handkerchief. He was allergic to cats and couldn't wait until this piece of business was over and the cats were gone.

"I'm the only living relative, and I get nothing?"

"You do or you wouldn't be here. Mrs. Evans wanted you to have her King James Bible." At the moment, Vicky was perched on top of the Bible. As he struggled to get her off of it, sniffling all the time, he continued. "It's a nice memento, Mr. Riley, a very fine—"

"What happens to everything after the cats are gone?"

"Ah, yes, interesting." He turned and read from the paper in front of him, " 'When my dear Vicky and Albert pass, and I hope that never happens and they live forever—' "

"Just get to it, please."

"All the assets left in my estate will be liquidated and used to create a home for the care of stray animals. It's to be called Vicky and Albert's Place."

"This can't stand! I'm telling you, that woman was a lunatic!"

"That's one man's opinion, and you can contest it if you wish, Mr. Riley. But my father prepared this trust and when a Hackel prepares a document, it is ironclad. Ironclad, I assure you. Now, if you don't mind, as you can see, I am allergic to cats and there are specific instructions I have to give Miss Amundsen about the care of Vicky and Albert before they can leave and I can stop sneezing." As if on cue, he sneezed.

Still livid, Liam put on his trench coat, grabbed his umbrella, and headed for the door.

"Mr. Riley, aren't you forgetting something?" Lester Hackel Jr. held up the Bible.

"Give it to the cats. Maybe one of them'll become a priest."

With that, Liam marched out into the rain.

∾౿〜

THE NOISE FROM the dripping water was unnerving. The constant plop distracted McLaughlin, preventing him from discerning why Mary Handley's behavior had changed so radically.

"Helen," he screamed, "did ya get that roofer yet?"

"Liam hasn't checked in, sir."

Annoyed and antsy, McLaughlin decided to find the roofer by himself. He charged into Liam's office and started rifling through his desk. After searching through several drawers, he found the roofer's address.

On his way out, he glanced at the letter from Abraham Lincoln that was hanging on the wall. It had been there for a long time and he had never paid much attention to it. But now certain words stood out as if they were magnified. It explained why Mary Handley had been so anxious to leave, and now he also knew exactly what he had to do.

∾౿〜

GEORGE WOKE UP in an alley not far from Lester Hackel Jr.'s office with the rain pouring down on him. It was now dark outside, he was soaking wet through and through, and his head was throbbing. His first instinct was to go to the office to see if he could peek inside and determine who had entered, but after a few steps, he thought better of it. He was woozy and stumbling, and then he touched his head. He was bleeding. He knew he wasn't going anywhere, and so he sat down in the street about ten yards from Lester Hackel Jr.'s door. He thought of his plight: a Vanderbilt found lying in the street bleeding. His brother Cornelius would be mortified. Just thinking of Cornelius coping with the family scandal put a smile on his face.

George had to decide what his next move would be. His driver was in a saloon blocks away, and he was sure he couldn't make it that far. If he were in Manhattan, he'd know where the nearest doctor's office or hospital was. But he was in Brooklyn, and Brooklyn was a strange land to him. He felt completely lost, but he knew he had to get up and keep moving. It was either that or stay put and catch pneumonia. He'd try to get up soon. He just needed a minute to gather his strength.

∽

"WHAT DID THE letter say?" asked Superintendent Campbell as he and Mary sat in his carriage.

"It was addressed to Major Thomas Evans, to whom President Lincoln had just presented the Medal of Honor at the White House. Besides once again thanking him for his bravery and service to the country, the president mentioned what a pleasure it was to meet his wife, Gabrielle, and his son, Paul. He then went on to write that his son Tad hadn't enjoyed himself so much since Tad's brother William had passed away. He asked Major Evans to commend his nephew Liam for playing so well with Tad."

"So Liam Riley is Gabrielle Evans's nephew."

"And probably in line to inherit her estate, which would

be significantly reduced if she refused the Long Island Water Supply Company buyout. It all fits. He's McLaughlin's right-hand man and has probably been making telephone calls in his name all along."

"Good work, Mary. How I wish I could hire you." Superintendent Campbell pulled a folded paper out of his jacket pocket, opened it, then called out the window to his driver and gave him an address.

Mary looked at him strangely. "What is that?"

"Liam Riley's address. McLaughlin said he wouldn't be in the office until tomorrow."

"I figured as much, but—"

"Oh, this," Superintendent Campbell said, holding up the paper. "I always research and write down all pertinent information about people involved in a case, so I can have it at my fingertips at a time like this. You should try it, Mary. It comes in very handy."

"I'm sure it does," said Mary as the carriage took off and started gaining speed.

❧

Liam fumed as he walked to the stable. He had rented a horse and carriage to go to the lawyer's office and back even though it was a short distance from his apartment. Now he wished he hadn't. He could no longer afford the luxury.

The question that he couldn't avoid was: what now? He had planned out in detail what to do once he had the money. It involved moving far away from Brooklyn, going out west to San Francisco. He had already purchased the train ticket. There would be mansions and fine dining and beautiful women at his beck and call. But he didn't have the money.

He could go back to work for McLaughlin, hoping that he'd come through with his promise that Liam would eventually take his place, but he just found out how empty those promises can be. Besides, he was tired of kissing McLaughlin's ass, and he was sure that if the police ever got any real evidence, McLaughlin would sacrifice him in an instant. These thoughts were rumbling around in his head when a hand shot out of a dark storefront and yanked him inside.

"Well, well," said Shorty, "if it isn't little Liam Riley."

"I'm not so little anymore."

"You're not, but I bet I can still kick your arse like I used to."

Liam and his mother had lived in a shanty on the poor side of Brooklyn in Young Dublin, not far from the shanty where Shorty lived, while their rich relatives resided in Clinton Hill. Countless childhood memories of being beaten and terrorized by Shorty immediately came back to him like the nightmare that they were. "What do you want, Shorty?"

"Did you really think you could fool Shorty?"

The obvious answer was yes, but it would anger Shorty, and Liam knew all too well what happened when Shorty got angry.

"Not really, but I had to try."

"All I did was bark a little at that kid and he gave up his contact, who gave you up even faster." Shorty let go of Liam, but there was no chance of running. Shorty had blocked him in.

"What do you want?"

"Sean Handley's sister won't stop. I need to get out of Brooklyn for a while, and three hundred is all I need to do that."

Liam didn't have the money. He had spent almost everything he had paying Shorty for the other three jobs. He also knew he was in for a lot of pain if he answered anything less than yes. "Sure. I have to get it from my boss. You know I work for Hugh McLaughlin, don't you?"

"I shoulda known he was the guy. A little twit like you couldn't pull this off by yourself."

"Me? I'm just an errand boy. Give me a few hours to get it from him."

Shorty thought for a moment, then said, "Okay, but don't try anything. I'm watching."

"I wouldn't dare cross you, Shorty. Certainly you know that."

Shorty stepped aside, and Liam took off back into the street, glad that he had already purchased his ticket to San Francisco and even happier that Shorty was just as stupid as he had remembered.

∼⚬∼

AFTER LIAM HAD left his office, Lester Hackel Jr. droned on to Miss Amundsen about the care of Vicky and Albert. They had been staying with someone else who could no longer care for them, and the instructions in Miss Evans's will were very detailed. By now his nose was red, his eyes were tearing, and Miss Amundsen was yawning. Somehow sensing that he was allergic, Vicky sat on his lap, rubbing against him, making it worse. But Lester Hackel Jr. was not one to give up.

"And at five o'clock every day, not a minute before or after, you feed them their second meal. Now, about the second meal—"

A light, intermittent knock at the door interrupted them,

but he kept going. The next knock was still intermittent but much louder.

"Aren't you going to answer that, Mr. Hackel?" asked Miss Amundsen.

"Jr., Mr. Hackel *Jr.,* and no, I'm not going to answer it. Whoever it is doesn't have an appointment, and I'm in the middle of important business."

As he returned to his paper, there was another knock.

"Well, I'm going to answer it," said Miss Amundsen. "It's miserable outside and somebody might need shelter or help." She got up and opened the door.

Propping himself up in the doorway was George, drenched and bleeding. "Do you know where the nearest hospital is?" he asked, then collapsed into her arms.

"Oh, you poor man," Miss Amundsen exclaimed, then helped George inside and placed him on the couch. He was conscious but weak from everything that had happened.

Lester Hackel Jr. protested, "Not on my couch. He'll ruin it."

"Can I use your phone, please?" George asked.

"Absolutely not. Do you know how much each phone call costs me?"

"I'll pay you back. In fact I'll pay your whole phone bill."

"That's not the point. It's the principle of the thing."

"I'll take you," Miss Amundsen said. "Brooklyn Hospital is only a few blocks away."

As she helped George up, Lester Hackel Jr. objected. "Where do you think you're going, Miss Amundsen? We haven't finished yet."

"We have as far as I am concerned. I could never work for a man like you." And she left with George.

Lester Hackel Jr. wanted to stop her. He wanted to apologize, though he didn't know for what. His pride prevented him from doing so, and he was left alone, helplessly staring at Vicky and Albert. Outside, in spite of the pounding of the pouring rain, George and Miss Amundsen could still hear his loud sneeze.

IT WAS CONVENIENT investigating a crime with the superintendent of police. In a pinch, he could always gain immediate access to almost any place, and Liam Riley's apartment was no exception. The landlady gladly opened the door for Superintendent Campbell and Mary, then left them alone.

Liam wasn't there, and to say his apartment was a mess would be a gross understatement. It looked like a hurricane had just blown through. As Mary and Superintendent Campbell searched, hoping for some clue to his whereabouts, Mary called out to Superintendent Campbell, "You realize, of course, we don't have a search warrant and are breaking the law?"

"Really?" Superintendent Campbell responded slyly. "I could've sworn I heard screams coming from inside the apartment, signaling someone was in danger."

Mary had a better idea, having already come to a quick decision.

"Use pursuit of a felon as an excuse," she said. "He's left town or is leaving."

"How do you know that?"

"Several things. Clothes have been tossed around, hanging out of drawers, left on the floor of the closet, as if he never intends to wear them again."

"Maybe he's just a messy person."

"That is possible, but it's what's not here that convinces me. He may not own a suitcase, but there's none here. There's also no comb, no hairbrush, no razor, and no toothbrush. It's highly unlikely all of those items would be missing unless—"

"Liam Riley is taking a trip."

"Exactly. Let's hope his train hasn't left yet."

And the two of them hurried out the door on their way to Grand Central Depot.

37

In the summer of 1869, Liam Riley's wealthier relatives had taken one of the first trips in history on the transcontinental railroad. He had always wanted to take a trip like that, and here he was, twenty-one years later, finally doing it. Before he found out that he was not about to inherit a fortune, he had bought a first-class ticket to San Francisco with most of the money he had left. It was a simple matter to change the date, and he was excited about putting Brooklyn behind him and finally setting out.

The train hadn't departed yet, and Liam was sitting at a table in the dining car. No food would be served until they were on their way, but Liam wanted to be the first. Because of all the activity that day, he hadn't eaten since breakfast, his pangs of hunger confirming it. He had very little money, but with what he had, he was determined to treat himself to a good meal. Liam had already gotten a menu and was perusing it.

"You should order the steak, Liam. There's nothin' like the steak in first class."

Liam turned to see Hugh McLaughlin standing by his

table. McLaughlin had called Liam's apartment, and when there was no answer, he had called Liam's landlady, with whom he knew Liam was friendly. Liam had told her he was leaving for San Francisco, so she could rent out his apartment. He had also asked her not to tell anyone, but McLaughlin wasn't just anyone.

Standing next to McLaughlin was Sean Callahan. Liam knew Callahan all too well. He was a six-foot-four-inch mountain of a man who was made of solid muscle. Callahan was McLaughlin's enforcer and part-time bodyguard. He sat down next to Liam, and McLaughlin took the chair across from him.

Liam was scared. "Hugh, I know this looks strange, but I can explain."

"I'm sure you can, Liam." McLaughlin took out his pocket watch and looked at it. "The train takes off in thirteen minutes. . . . I'm waitin'." McLaughlin stared at Liam with a hard look. Callahan edged closer to Liam, blocking him in.

Liam knew McLaughlin had already made up his mind. What he had to say at this point was insignificant, but Liam had to try, if for no other reason than to stay alive those extra few minutes.

MARY AND SUPERINTENDENT Campbell were at a meeting of ticket agents at Grand Central Depot. Campbell had convinced their supervisor to temporarily pull them all off duty. If any of the agents had remembered a Liam Riley purchasing a ticket, it would be a lot faster than painstakingly going through the list of passengers departing the depot that evening.

Luck was on their side. One of the agents remembered that a Liam Riley had changed the departure date on his ticket.

"He originally was supposed to leave this Friday but changed it to this evening. I explained to him that Friday's train was more modern than tonight's, but—"

"What train, where, and when?" Mary hastily interrupted.

The agent explained that his eventual destination was San Francisco and that the train was leaving from track eight in a little over ten minutes.

Mary and Superintendent Campbell charged out of there as fast as they could. The agents stared after them, wondering what it was all about, until their supervisor screamed at them and they begrudgingly returned to work to deal with the irate customers who had been kept waiting.

∽

LIAM WAS BEGINNING to sweat as he told McLaughlin and Callahan his woeful tale. He knew he was talking for his life.

"Just as you asked me, Hugh, I paid a woman to impersonate Emily Worsham in order to hire Mary Handley to investigate John Worsham's death. And it worked like you thought it would. Andrew Green got rid of Collis Huntington, and it weakened their consolidation bid."

"The problem is, Liam, even after takin' ya under my wing and all the tutorin' I gave ya, ya still don't understand what I do. Ya ruined a plan that was twenty years in the makin'."

"Twenty years? The water shortage hasn't been that long."

"Twenty years ago, Ryan Gleason, a lovely fella who's long gone now, got soused with me over ales at O'Hara's saloon and told me a doozy of a tale. He worked in the cemetery, and he was loadin' a coffin inta a carriage when it slipped and opened up. There was nothin' but rocks in there. But ol' Ryan didn't give a hoot. The rich people were payin'. As far as he was concerned, they could bury whatever the hell they wanted."

"You've known for twenty years that John Worsham wasn't in that grave?"

"The rest of the information was just the usual highfalutin society rumors about Arabella Huntington, but the coffin was different. I keep information like that, waitin' for the time it'll benefit me the most. Twenty years, Liam. This was the time."

If it was possible, Liam was getting more scared than he had been earlier. "I didn't know, Hugh. I—"

"Of course ya didn't know. I was the only one who knew. But ya need to do what I tell ya, and I didn't tell ya to have that woman killed. Ya screwed up, Liam."

"Abigail Corday was a starving actress who lived in my neighborhood. I didn't know she was crazy. She got a part in a play and all of a sudden she thought she was that person and . . . she was going to tell everything, Hugh. Ruin your plan, and everything we worked for."

"We?"

"I mean you, but I do help. I do."

"No, Liam, I'm pretty sure yer meanin' *we* with a decided emphasis on *you*. Yer the one who suggested the Long Island Water Supply Company after what ya called *exhaustive research*. Yer the one who had Gabrielle Evans killed, didn't ya?"

"She was stopping the sale of the company. We wouldn't have gotten the water Brooklyn needed, and you wouldn't have made your money."

"I would have just sold my shares and invested in another water company without it bein' tied to a murder. But that wouldn't do for you since Gabrielle Evans was yer aunt."

"She was what? I have no idea what—"

"I finally read that stupid Lincoln letter ya hung on yer wall." McLaughlin leaned over the table toward Liam and whispered intensely. "Her death led to Patricia Cassidy's and got Mary Handley and Superintendent Campbell on my arse. Did ya hear that, Liam? My arse, not yers!"

By now, it was obvious that Liam had no chance of talking his way out of this. He had a pistol in the right pocket of his coat, which was draped over the back of his chair. He'd never intended to use the pistol but rather planned to sell it for cash when his money totally ran out. He was glad that time hadn't arrived yet. He slowly slipped his hand into the right pocket. He was ready.

"It's time for us to go, Liam," said McLaughlin. "All of us."

Liam knew what that meant. "What happens if I refuse?"

"Well then, I would get up and leave the train. Callahan here would give me a few minutes to strike up a conversation with somebody, then he'd lean over and snap yer neck."

"I see. Okay, Hugh, you win." Liam started to slowly rise, as if he were going with them, then he quickly pulled the gun out of his pocket. Callahan saw it coming and grabbed Liam's hand. In the struggle the gun went off, and Callahan was shot in the stomach. He screamed in pain as the other passengers gasped in fear, and in his last act before crumpling to the floor, Callahan knocked Liam's gun out of his hand, sending it sliding down the aisle of the dining car. Liam had never shot anyone before. He paused for a brief second as everyone stared at him, then he charged out of the car as fast as he could. McLaughlin didn't make a move. Besides being too old for physical confrontation, he needed to be able to deny involvement in any violence.

"Is there a doctor here?" he called out. "This poor man is bleedin' to death!"

∼⦿∼

MARY AND SUPERINTENDENT Campbell were on track eight and had just begun going from car to car looking for Liam. They decided it would take less time if they split up, so Mary started at the back and Superintendent Campbell at the front. Just after the gun had gone off, Superintendent Campbell had made it to the dining car in time to see Liam flying out, taking off in Mary's direction. He stepped out on the platform and screamed as loud as he could.

"Mary! On the platform! Coming your way!"

Mary stepped out of her car, and sure enough Liam was running wildly toward her. Mary was very proficient at jujitsu, but there was no time for that. She quickly stuck out her foot and sent Liam sprawling to the ground, landing on his back. When he started to get up, she grabbed him by the shirt with one hand, and then, using the space between her thumb and pointer finger, she drove her other hand into his windpipe. He was immediately helpless, gasping for air.

"Don't worry, Mr. Riley. You'll breathe again. I'm not letting you off that easily. You framed my brother and you had three innocent women killed, including my good friend Patti. And you're going to pay for all of it."

Superintendent Campbell arrived, out of breath. Mary

looked at him. He nodded, took out his handcuffs, and gave them to her. She turned Liam around and started putting them on him.

"I once saw Thomas Edison demonstrate the barbaric power of the electric chair, using a calf as his test subject. It burst into flames, emitting a shriek so horrifying that it made me sick and I couldn't eat for days. But I'm still going to be there when they strap you in, and then I'm going out and having a steak dinner."

Once the cuffs were on, she helped him up to his feet and turned him to face her.

"Liam Riley, it gives me great pleasure to say . . . you're under arrest, you bastard!"

38

I<small>T WASN'T LONG</small> before Liam confessed to everything and named Shorty as the man he'd hired to commit the murders: Gabrielle Evans for the inheritance he didn't get, Abigail Corday to keep the John Worsham plan silent, and Patti to stop Sean from discovering Gabrielle Evans's murderer. Chief McKellar sent a dozen policemen out to scour the streets for Shorty. Mary stayed for a while to tell what she knew, and then she was done. The rest was police work, and she still wasn't part of the force. When she and Superintendent Campbell delivered Liam to Second Street Station, Mary asked to use their phone. Her parents couldn't afford a phone, so she called the people down the block, who went to get them. Needless to say, when her parents heard the news that Sean would soon be free, they were beyond thrilled.

Mary then called George to also let him know and to apologize for leaving him alone so long at Lester Hackel Jr.'s office. George's butler told her that he was at Brooklyn Hospital.

"What? Is he okay? What happened?" Mary asked, both surprised and concerned. The butler had no details, and she quickly prevailed upon Superintendent Campbell, who lent her his carriage.

"Keep it for the evening, Mary. I'll get a ride home. Don't worry."

"Thanks, Chief."

"Thank *you,* Mary Handley. Very nice work."

When Mary arrived at Brooklyn Hospital in downtown Brooklyn, George's brother Cornelius was helping him check out. Miss Amundsen had also stayed to make sure he was okay. And thankfully, George *was* going to be okay. The doctors had stitched up the cut on his head, and any scar would be covered by his hair. The weakness and temporary dizziness he had been experiencing were the result of a concussion. The symptoms were presently gone, but they would probably return, and he had been told to limit his activity for a while. George seemed himself at the moment, and the doctors said the odds were good that he would eventually experience a full recovery. Of course, he needed to see a doctor for periodic check-ups.

Mary felt awful about what had happened. "If I hadn't asked you to watch—"

"Stop it, Mary," said George. "The only way I'll allow you to take responsibility is if you personally bonked me on the head yourself."

"I didn't, but I reserve the right for some time in the future when you're being difficult." She kissed him on the cheek, and they hugged, which prompted Cornelius to interrupt.

"I hate to shorten this touching reunion, but I need to get home. Shall we, George?"

"I have a carriage, too," said Mary. "Cornelius has done plenty. Let me take you home."

George turned to Cornelius. "Go ahead. Mary and I will be fine."

"I can't thank you enough for taking care of George when I couldn't be there."

"Just performing my sibling responsibility. Aren't I, George?"

"Yes, Cornelius, and you do it so well."

Mary noted the coldness of this exchange, but this wasn't the time to address it.

Cornelius turned to Miss Amundsen. "Can I drop you someplace, young lady?"

"As a matter of fact, you can. I don't live far from here."

"Good, you can direct my driver."

The four of them said their good-byes, with George and Mary thanking Miss Amundsen profusely for bringing him to the hospital. In no time, George and Mary were alone, and she asked him about the specifics of what had happened.

Unfortunately, there were very few specifics. George had no idea who or what had hit him. It wasn't robbery, because nothing had been taken. His wallet was completely intact, his money all still there. Mary suspected that it was Shorty, and when she informed him about the events of her evening, he agreed. Who else would have a vested interest in seeing that Liam Riley was not caught? They were both thankful that George wasn't one of Shorty's assignments and that he didn't view George as a serious threat or he wouldn't still be alive. When they finished speculating, George congratulated Mary for solving the crimes, showing genuine excitement that Sean would be set free.

The rain was as strong as ever, and so was the thunder and lightning as they made their way in Superintendent Campbell's carriage to George's house. As they were crossing the Brooklyn Bridge, Mary asked George about the odd exchange between Cornelius and him.

"What odd exchange?" asked George as if he knew nothing about it.

"You know," said Mary, "the one that was colder than Arctic winds in January."

"Please be more specific. There are so many." Mary looked at George, and he knew he needed to explain further. "My brother and I don't see eye to eye on the minor things: politics, art, social associations, how we spend our money, and generally what we do with our lives. On the other hand, we do agree on our lineage."

"I'm sorry, but thankfully he's your brother and not your father."

"No doubt. Unfortunately, though, there is a hitch to that."

"If you're about to reveal a deep, dark secret of perverse family behavior, please don't," Mary joked. "Just know that I love you even if you have six toes on each foot. And by the way, I have seen your feet, and even though they don't possess six toes, they are suspect."

"Ah, you noticed. My feet are always the last thing I reveal to anyone with whom I wish to become intimate. People have been known to shriek in fear and run off."

"I must've passed the test, because I'm not running off any time soon."

He put his arm around her and hugged her tightly. They remained that way in silence until they passed over the bridge into Manhattan. Then Mary broke it.

"What's wrong? And don't tell me it's the conk on the head. I know that isn't true."

"It's useless trying to hide anything from that brilliant mind of yours."

"Then don't hide it. I promise I won't bite. I gave that up when I was four and bit Sean. He didn't taste very good."

George smiled wryly, then let it out. "I told you that until today I had business for a few days concerning Biltmore and couldn't sleuth with you. That's true, but it isn't what you might have thought. I wasn't buying more land, hiring more workers, or anything of that sort. I was fighting to keep it."

"I don't understand."

"My father passed away five years ago. Since I was always more concerned with the arts instead of business and since Cornelius was older than me—nineteen years older, to be exact—he thought Cornelius would be a good person to oversee my inheritance, protecting me from careless expenditures and from getting swindled. Cornelius has taken that a step further. He has decided to become my moral compass."

"What is he trying to do?

"Take away Biltmore and most of my inheritance, leaving me with only my house in Manhattan and whatever is already in my bank account from my monthly trust allotment. He says he could take it all, but since I'm his brother he's decided to be generous."

"Obviously, you're going to fight him."

"That's precisely what I've been doing the last few days. Regrettably, his lawyers must be better than mine, because it appears that he has won."

"He can't do that!"

"You haven't been listening, darling. Apparently, he can."

Mary sat there for a while, absorbing everything George had told her, then turned toward him and very seriously asked, "Is it me, George? Am I the one who has offended his moral compass? Have I made you wander off course?"

"Why discuss his skewed logic? Cornelius is—"

"I knew it. It was my dreadful performance at our engagement dinner, wasn't it?"

"He had made up his mind before that. The dinner was a setup, to bring me to my senses, as he put it. He doesn't want me to marry you."

"I'm sure tonight only reinforced his belief that you are in league with the devil."

"Mary, there is absolutely no way I'm going to let him and his twisted values control us."

"But he is. He's destroying your dream. He's taking away Biltmore."

"Sometimes there are sacrifices a man has—"

"Damn it, George! I won't allow it!"

"As brilliant and as resourceful as you are, my darling, I'm afraid you have no control over this."

"What if we don't get married? What if we just live together in sin? It might be fun. We could be that notorious couple who causes everyone's eyebrows to rise when we enter a room."

"As delicious as that sounds, it would just cause his moral compass to spin out of control and explode."

"At least we'd be doing something. We can't just take it."

"I'm afraid there are some things in life you just have to accept and move on. Cornelius's idiotic and prejudiced behavior happens to be one of them. He's threatened to disinherit his son Neily from money Cornelius didn't even earn but was given by right of his birth. And Neily is dating a banker's daughter."

"I see, and I'm a mere butcher's daughter."

"That's him, Mary, not me."

"I know. I'm trying to see it from his side. Here I am: a poor butcher's daughter who is, of all things, a female private detective. My brother's been arrested for murder—"

"And he's just been proven innocent."

"That doesn't matter. It's the publicity, the headlines, the constant scrutiny, and possible scandal with which I will always be associated. I'm surprised Cornelius hasn't suffered a heart attack already."

"To hell with Cornelius!"

"Easier said than done."

"A phrase originated by William Horman, a former headmaster at Eton College in England. See how good you are for me, Mary? You're getting me to read and broaden my mind."

Mary wasn't listening. She was trying to figure a way out of their situation, but she could only come to one upsetting conclusion.

"We can't get married, George."

"No, Mary! You can't allow him—"

"But he has. I know what it's like to have a dream, and I refuse to let you give up yours."

"That's my choice, Mary, not yours! I'd much rather have you than any piece of land!"

"Listen to your words. You're already lying to yourself. Biltmore is much more than a piece of land to you and you know it."

The two of them were silent, letting the difficulty of their situation consume them as the carriage pulled up and stopped in front of George's house. Mary spoke first. Her heart was breaking, but Mary was never one to shy away from any problem, no matter how painful.

"I don't see a way out of this. Even if I'm willing to give up my dream of being a detective, and I'm not sure I am, I'm still a butcher's daughter. There's no changing that."

George grabbed her and held on tight. "I love you, Mary, and I'm not giving you up."

"And I love you, more than anyone I have ever known or will ever know." Mary's voice started to crack, causing her to stop, but every ounce of her body told her she had to push on or she never would. She gazed into his eyes. "What happens three, five, seven years from now when you realize you will never get to accomplish what you know in your heart you were put on this earth to do? How will you feel then?"

"As long as I have you—"

"Damn it, George! We can't lie to ourselves! This is too important!"

George decided not to debate her any further, at least not that night. His voice softened. "You're right, Mary. This is too important, and it is much too important to decide right here and now, especially after such a long and active day. Promise me that you will not come to any conclusions now, and you will think about this for a while."

"I will, George, but—"

"Promise me you'll give it time, Mary. You already know what my decision is."

"I promise."

"Good. I love you, Mary Handley."

He kissed her. The passion was still there, but lack of passion had never been their problem. They finally broke, and

George alighted from the carriage. He went to his front door, Mary watching him all the way, and then he turned to blow a kiss before he went inside.

A sense of paralysis came over Mary. She couldn't move. She couldn't even speak the words to the driver to take her home. She just sat there, stunned, as the tears started to come. There would be no stopping them. The pain was too great. Then the rage came and she lost control. She started wildly kicking the floor, banging her hands on any hard surface she could find. She was smoldering inside. Mary flung the door open, jumped to the ground, and marched up to George's house.

He instinctively knew the loud knock on his door was her. George waved off his butler and answered it himself. The rain was pouring harder than ever, and Mary was getting wetter by the second.

"Tell your brother he's an ass."

"Gladly. Now come inside. You're getting drenched."

She surprised George by throwing her arms around him and kissing him. It was a different embrace. There was a ferocity to it that was unlike her. When she let go, she placed something in his hand. It was the ring case containing the engagement ring he had given her.

"Mary—"

"It's completely reusable. We never did have time to get it sized." She started back to the carriage, and he stepped outside.

"I refuse to accept this."

"And I refuse to let you ruin your life." She got into the carriage.

"Mary—"

"Good-bye, George," she said, then signaled the driver to take off.

George took a few more steps out into the rain. As the thunder exploded in the sky, the lightning crackled, and the water dripped down his face, he screamed, "Mary! Mary, come back here!"

But she wasn't coming back, and he knew he had lost her.

39

MARY LET THE driver go after he dropped her off at her tenement building on Elizabeth Street. She went upstairs, got out of her wet clothes, and dried her hair as well as she could. She put on her robe and sat down on her bed to read an Edgar Allan Poe story, hoping it would divert her attention. It didn't. She tried to focus on the joy of Sean's imminent release, but even that couldn't change her mood. She knew what she needed: an old-fashioned venting to a friend. Maybe that would put George out of her mind long enough so that she could sleep. Unfortunately, her options were limited.

Patti was dead, her good friend Sarah was pregnant again and no doubt in bed at that hour after chasing her three children all day, and . . . that was it. Her mother was certainly the last person Mary wanted to see. She was in no mood to be showered with "I told you so's."

Then she thought of Lazlo. He was terribly verbose, and he would probably bombard her with platitudes from Benjamin Franklin, but maybe that would lull her to sleep. Besides, she knew he cared about her as she did about him. Add to that the fact that he always stayed up late and his shoulder seemed to fill the bill as the perfect one on which she should cry.

Mary put on dry clothes. Considering the rainstorm outside, they were the clothes she cared the least about. She slipped on her coat, grabbed her umbrella, and ventured out into the elements.

Lazlo's Books was a short five blocks from Mary's apartment, but the inclement weather and empty streets made it seem like a longer journey than usual. Thankfully, it didn't take much to raise Lazlo from his reading chair. A few quick knocks and a minute later he was peering through the glass portion of the door to see who was disturbing his intellectual tranquility. He was always happy to see Mary, and he promptly opened the door to welcome her. She was delighted that he was wearing his kimono and carrying a small kerosene lantern. It gave her an immediate chuckle and also solidified that she had come to the right place for the diversion she sought.

"Thank you, Lazlo. I've always wondered what the Japanese version of Diogenes would look like, and now I know."

"Sorry to disappoint, but you'd never catch me searching for an honest man. I'd have more luck finding Ebenezer Scrooge's Christmas ghosts." He indicated his lantern. "This is purely for purposes of illumination. But come inside. I doubt whether you came visiting at this hour to discuss Greek philosophers, ghosts, or literature."

Lazlo's welcoming and warm voice was just what Mary needed. She stepped inside the store to close her umbrella, and she was just about done when she saw a glimmer of fear flash in Lazlo's eyes. Before she could turn around, she was hit from behind and hit hard. As she fell to the floor, she instinctively knew it was Shorty, cursing herself for being so careless just before passing out.

Mary had been out for less than a minute when she woke up. Lazlo was lying next to her, unconscious. Noticing that he was breathing, she was relieved that he was still alive, but she doubted whether Shorty intended either of them to remain in that state much longer. As she slowly rose, she saw Shorty in the main part of the bookstore. He had knocked over one of the large bookcases, dumping a pile of books onto the floor. She had started to pull Lazlo out the door to safety when Shorty spotted her.

"Well, well, awake so soon?" he said as he walked toward her, Lazlo's kerosene lantern in his hand. "Your friend Lazlo's a real generous sort." He pointed to the pile of books. "He left plenty of kindling and a beautiful flame." He held up the lantern before he threw it into the pile, where it shattered and the books started to burn. Then he went for Mary.

She had to drop Lazlo and figure out some way to combat this monster of a man. She was still a little groggy from the blow she had suffered, but fortunately Shorty was talkative. Apparently, he needed to vent for a much different reason than she did.

"The flatfoots are out in force lookin' for me, and I got you to thank for it."

"You're forgetting your buddy Liam Riley. He couldn't stop talking about you."

Shorty's harrumph was full of disdain. "That poof."

"Right, he mentioned that, too. I forgot. Was it your ass or his that did the receiving?"

Her experience had told her it was easy to anger Shorty, and she had accomplished that. He roared as he charged at her, but Mary was ready. Besides being proficient in jujitsu, she was also well practiced in the French art of kickboxing called savate. When Shorty got close, she let loose with a *fouetté,* a roundhouse kick, aimed at his one good knee. It landed, and Shorty went down.

Mary went to finish him with a kick to his head, but at the last second he threw up his right arm, blocked the kick, and grabbed her foot with his left hand, yanking her to the floor. Once Shorty got hold of anyone with those massive arms of his, it was almost impossible to get free.

He started pulling her toward him. She thrashed wildly and screamed, but it was in vain. He had her. Then, almost out of nowhere, Shorty got kicked in the back of the head. It was Lazlo, who had just regained consciousness. The kick wasn't devastating, but it was enough to shock Shorty into loosening his grip, and Mary slid free. Shorty punished Lazlo with a powerful punch to his face that broke his cheekbone and knocked him out again.

By the time Shorty turned his attention back to Mary, she had gotten Lazlo's old musket, his Brown Bess, out of the hall closet and was pointing it at him.

Shorty slowly got to his feet and scoffed at her. "You're going to shoot me?" He laughed.

"I've done it before, and it will be my pleasure to do it again."

She aimed it at his chest and pulled the trigger. Nothing happened. She pulled it again and again. Still nothing. Lazlo probably hadn't kept it up over the years and odds were it was rusted. *What a hell of a time to find this out,* she thought.

Shorty slowly made his way to her. The cocky look on his face said it all. He could smell victory. Using the musket like a baseball bat, she swung it at him. It landed the first time on his arm, but with all that muscle he hardly felt it. The second time around he was ready and caught it, then pulled her to him. When she was close, she started kicking again, but when it came to fighting and nothing else, Shorty was a fast learner.

With both of them holding on to the musket, he swung her around, then released his right hand and punched her in the stomach. The pain was instantaneous, causing her to let go of the musket. In control, Shorty threw the musket aside, then disdainfully shoved her, and she tumbled outside into the rain. He methodically followed her like an animal stalking his wounded prey as the fire inside grew. There was plenty of paper to burn.

By the time Mary started to get up, Shorty was there and had her in his clutches.

"This is the part I've been waitin' for," he said. He put his right arm around her neck and dragged her to the alley on the side of the bookstore, so he could do his special work in private. It occurred to him that he liked the rain pouring down on them. It added a certain excitement. *I'll have to remember that,* he thought.

Mary flailed her arms and legs, but to no avail. When he got to the alley, he turned her to face him and put both hands around her neck. Mary was scared.

"You're not such a snotty bitch now, are ya?" Then he started squeezing.

Swinging away at him was doing no good, and trying to pry off his powerful hands was useless. Mary knew it would only be a matter of seconds until she lost consciousness, and panic set in. Then she remembered what her jujitsu teacher, Wei Chung, had taught her in one of her first lessons when she was a young girl.

When fighting a larger and more powerful adversary, you can't wrestle with him or you will lose. You must always use the element of surprise.

Wei's words resonated with her. She took her two thumbs and thrust them into his eyes, digging deeply. Grunting from the shock, he reflexively released his grip on her in order to assess the damage.

Now free, Mary tried to run away, but she was gasping for air and too weak to go anywhere. She stumbled to the ground and wound up sitting with her back against the side wall of the bookstore. She was trying to catch her breath and mount some plan, but there was little she could do. She didn't even have the strength to outrun Shorty, and he had a leg brace. Mary watched as he quickly recovered, turned around, and stood in the puddle next to her, fuming. She looked skyward as if asking for divine intervention . . . and it came!

Lightning struck Lazlo's lightning rod. The grounding wire was in reach. Mary yanked it out and threw the now exposed wire into Shorty's puddle as she rolled out of the way. Shorty had no idea what she was doing until the water and his metal leg brace proved to be excellent conductors, and then it was too late.

Mary watched as the electricity passed through Shorty's body and he started shaking violently. The absolute horror of not knowing what was happening to him was firmly planted on his face as he emitted a terrifying scream that lasted a full thirty seconds before he fell into the alley face-first. His head bounced back up, and his face landed on its side, his eyes blankly staring at Mary. Whatever light had once been in them was out, and she was sure he was dead.

Mary smelled the fire and realized she had to get to Lazlo. She forced herself to rise and carefully walked around Shorty, making sure to avoid any electricity from the lightning that might still be there.

By now the fire was raging inside the bookstore. Luckily, Lazlo was near the entrance, and though there was plenty of smoke, the fire hadn't gotten to him yet. Mary summoned whatever strength she had left and dragged him by his feet out into the storm. As she sat on the ground, cradling his head in her lap, the rain splashing on his face, he eventually started to come to.

"Lazlo, thank God you're okay! I'd never be able to forgive myself if something happened to you because of me!"

He was weak and had to speak carefully because of his broken cheekbone, but Lazlo was never one to stay silent for long.

"I see. And this isn't something?" He indicated his beaten-up face and burning store. Mary chortled at his ability to toss out a quip in even the direst circumstances.

"You'll be pleased to know that your old friend Ben Franklin saved us."

"Really? Did he ride up on his trusty steed with a lance in his hand like Don Quixote?"

"I'm serious, Lazlo. It was your lightning rod. I obliterated the bastard with it."

He smiled. "Well, what do you know?"

The fire was growing and Mary pulled Lazlo farther away from the building.

"I feel awful about your home and store. It's all my fault."

"Don't fret, Mary. Ben will save it for me."

"Look at it. I'm sorry, Lazlo, but there's no saving this building."

"Ben will get me another one." About this time, Mary was thinking he might have some brain damage and maybe she needed to get him to the hospital sooner rather than later. She was looking around for some sort of transportation when he explained further.

"You see, Mary, Ben was one of the first people to suggest fire insurance, and I always follow Ben's suggestions." The wily look in his eyes surfaced through his broken face.

As the firemen arrived, they were surprised to see two very battered and very wet people lying on the sidewalk laughing hysterically.

40

MARY AWOKE THE next morning feeling the residual effects of her struggle with Shorty. Her ribs were sore, and she could still see the imprint of some of his fingers on her neck. The events of the previous day raced through her mind as if they were a bad dream, but they were real. She thought of George and tried to push him out of her head to concentrate on something positive. Sean was being released that afternoon, and she had a couple of loose ends to tie up before that. She was thankful that she was busy. Maybe that would keep her from thinking of George. If that failed, it was still raining. Maybe being annoyed about the weather would work.

On her way out of her apartment, she stopped to check her mail, which she hadn't had time to do the day before, and she found a letter from Emily Worsham. She thanked Mary profusely once again for flushing her uncle John out of hiding so the family could spend some time with him before he passed away. And he had just passed away. They had buried him in

Richmond in the same grave that had contained an empty coffin for the past twelve years. Emily wrote, "Uncle John went as he had always wished: in the arms of a lady of the evening after an all-night poker game." Mary could just picture it, too, and the vision of that old rascal made her chuckle.

Her first stop of the day was William Gaynor's office. He welcomed her with open arms.

"Mary, my dear. My God, you've been a busy one, haven't you? I must get George to recommend more clients. I so enjoy winning cases without having to do anything."

His mention of George hurt, but Mary decided to ignore it and move on or she might turn into the type of person she detested: the kind who pours her guts out to everyone she sees.

"The important thing is that Sean is free. I'm glad I could help. The way it all started out I was more of a detriment than anything else."

"About that, by the way. You deliberately ignored my instructions."

"What instructions?"

"I specifically warned you about staying out of the newspapers." The impish grin on his face gave away his delight as he held up a copy of the *Brooklyn Daily Eagle*. The headline read, HANDLEY CAPTURES ONE MURDERER, KILLS THE OTHER. "You must tell me all the details," he said. "Newspapers never get it right."

"I promise I will someday when I have more time. Presently, I believe that I have some information to impart to you that you will find far more interesting."

Mary informed him about the Long Island Water Supply Company and, as the second-largest shareholder, the un-

godly profit Hugh McLaughlin was going to make on Mayor
Chapin's purchase of the company for Brooklyn. As she had
expected, Gaynor was outraged and went off into one of
his rants about dishonest politicians and how they make life
harder for common, decent people.

By the time Mary had left, she was convinced that she had
made the right decision in leaving this matter in Gaynor's
hands. Pretty soon all of Brooklyn and New York would
know of it, and at the very least, it would be a boon to the
consolidation project and mean much trouble for Hugh
McLaughlin.

Mary's next stop was in Manhattan. She owed Collis
Huntington a visit and also an apology. She had inadvertently
exposed his family to scandal, and she was truly sorry for it.

Once again, Huntington's nephew Henry was visiting,
and he, Arabella, Huntington, and Archer were chatting in
the drawing room. The butler showed Mary to Huntington's
office, where she sat on a comfortable and cushy leather club
chair. He joined her shortly thereafter, and she rose only to
be signaled by him to sit back down. He went to a small bar
and started to pour himself a drink as the butler left, closing
the door and leaving them all alone.

"Would you like a drink, Miss Handley?"

"No, thank you, but please go right ahead."

"Oh, I fully intend to."

As he finished pouring his drink and took a sip, Mary
made a mental note that it was early in the day to be drinking, but she was not there to monitor his habits.

"So, Miss Handley, I see you've solved your brother's
problem," he said as he sat on the couch opposite her.

"Indeed I have, Mr. Huntington, but not without costs. I

want to apologize for what this mess has done to your family and the slights they have suffered. Certainly if I had any inkling I was being used as a pawn, I never would have taken the Worsham case in the first place."

"That's very kind of you. Of course, that doesn't change our circumstances any."

Lively laughter could be heard from the other room. He took another sip of his drink. She somehow got the feeling that Huntington was referring to more than just the Worsham case. Whatever it was, it was indeed private and not something she felt comfortable pursuing. There were other matters to discuss. She told him about her experiences down in Virginia with John Worsham and how she had gotten a letter saying that he had just passed away.

Huntington laughed. "That John was such a rogue, but hiding out in the woods for twelve years? That really tops everything."

"He also told me who Archer's real father is. It must be very difficult to live with your son and not be able to tell him you're his true father. I'm sorry you have to suffer that pain."

Huntington paused for a moment as if he was not certain he wanted to discuss this matter. Then he shrugged as if saying, *Why not?*

"We all have our burdens to bear, Miss Handley. Even though Archer is my son, he'd still be labeled a bastard and that would destroy Arabella."

"And what about Archer? Doesn't he have a right to know?"

"Well, as far as Archer's concerned, the apple doesn't fall far from the tree—Arabella's tree, that is. I highly doubt he would be able to deal with it and could very possibly be scarred for life."

"Where does that leave you, Mr. Huntington?"

He sighed, trying to hide his emotion. "It leaves me where I am and have always been: as the man willing to do the dirty work to get the job done. Surely you've heard that about me."

Mary saw a vulnerability in Huntington she had never seen before and had never thought she would ever see. She actually felt sorry for him. "Well, you can rest assured I will never divulge that information to anyone."

"I'm not a person who takes people at their word, but I'm going to trust you. Please don't disappoint me."

"I wouldn't dare now that I've seen you in action. But I do have questions, the answers to which might tie up some loose ends that are puzzling me."

"Go right ahead."

"Have you heard of the Long Island Water Supply Company?"

He stared at her, then without a trace of acknowledgment asked, "What have you heard?"

Mary explained what she knew about the mayor's buyout and McLaughlin's ownership of shares. Huntington nodded and didn't say a word even when she was done. She decided to ask him a question that was nagging at her.

"I would appreciate your insight, Mr. Huntington. No matter how deplorable their actions, I understand Liam Riley's and Shorty's behavior. I can even comprehend Mayor Chapin's ambitions. What I don't understand is Hugh McLaughlin's role in all of this."

"Isn't greed simple enough?"

"I understand greed, but McLaughlin is not a stupid man. Surely he had to know that this amount of greed would raise eyebrows."

"Do you mind if I speak hypothetically?"

"No, of course not."

"Let's say some individual had been wronged by Hugh McLaughlin, and he wanted retribution. And let's say this person had many contacts in the financial community, found out what company Mayor Chapin was trying to purchase, and determined that the profit the stockholders would make, though large, wasn't enough to appear egregious. So let's say this individual—"

"The person who'd been wronged?"

"Yes. Let's say he was a man of means who had the resources to bid up the price of the company until Mayor Chapin had to buy it at an absurd profit for the shareholders."

"McLaughlin could have said no and stuck the man with an overpriced company."

"No doubt. But let's also say this very same man of means was an excellent judge of character, and he knew that once a financial windfall of this size was placed in Mr. McLaughlin's lap, he wouldn't be able to resist it."

"So in spite of the saying, you can lead a horse to water, and you *can* make him drink."

"All you need is the right incentive."

"Hopefully, one day I'll meet this hypothetical man of means, so I can tell him bravo."

Laughter once again floated in from the other room. As he got up to pour himself another drink, he commented, "Well, they seem to be having a lot of fun, don't they?"

"Yes, sounds like a jolly time."

"That Henry can be very funny." There was an odd mixture of admiration and contempt in his voice. He downed the second drink in one gulp, then poured himself another. "So, you had quite a day yesterday, Miss Handley."

"Yes, indeed."

"You caught a murderer, killed another, saved a man from a burning building, got incriminating information on a crooked politician—"

"Not your ordinary day."

"No, and to top it off, you and George Vanderbilt ended your engagement."

This prompted Mary to stand. "Do you pry into everyone's personal lives?"

"Only those who spark my interest."

"Well then, put this in your bank of knowledge. George and I love each other very much. I broke up with him because I didn't want to see stupid upper-crust prejudices ruin his life. You people are insane."

"Be careful who you lump into the same category."

"I'm sorry. Are you not upper-crust or is all this wealth around me a façade?"

"There is wealth, and then there is *wealth*."

"And there is clarity, and then there is clarity," Mary quickly quipped back.

Huntington laughed. "I like your fire, Mary Handley. And just think. Not too long ago I wanted to bury you. I apologize for that."

"I was aware of it, and it was why I suspected you at first. But you cleverly used my suspicions to point me in the right direction in order to get everything you needed."

"But I didn't get everything. In fact, I didn't get the one thing I wanted most. You see, you and I have a lot more in common than you think."

"I know it's not our bank accounts. What is it?"

Huntington poured himself another drink. He was becoming decidedly tipsy, and therefore less guarded. "I want acceptance for the woman I love, as you wanted acceptance for the man you love. You and I don't give a hoot about the Vanderbilts or Carnegies or any other of those stuck-up snobs with their silly parties and rules. But for various reasons, their approval means something to our loves. You lost George because of it, and I often feel as if Arabella is slipping away. Arabella may seem tough, but she is a sensitive soul who constantly seeks recognition. The social snubs we've suffered, people staring at us in the street, gossiping about us, are devastating to her. I've accomplished many impossible things in my life, but I'm at a loss as to how to reverse that, make it all better, so to speak." Real emotion began pouring out. "I do want to please her so."

Laughter drifted in from the other room again, and Huntington flinched as if it pained him. Mary started to see him in a different light: not as the ruthless businessman who regularly stepped on those in his way, but rather as a man desperate to please the woman he loved and felt he was failing. It wasn't enough to forgive his faults, but it did humanize him, and Mary was able to feel sympathy.

There was a quick couple of knocks at the door, and Archer entered without waiting for a response. He was laughing.

"You must come and hear Henry's story about—" He stopped when he saw Mary and he became anxious. "Hello, Miss Handley. Have you come with news of my father's body?"

"As a matter of fact, I have, Archer."

Mary saw Huntington stiffen, his eyes filling with anxiety. Mary looked at Archer and did what she thought was best.

She lied. She told him that shortly after John Worsham was buried twenty years before, his body was stolen. She didn't know where the body was now, and the only reason she had found out this much was by interviewing an old former cemetery worker who knew someone who sold bodies back then.

"I'm sorry, Archer, but that's all I could uncover."

"I don't know why," Archer said, "but somehow that makes me feel much better."

"I'm glad to hear that. I'm sure he would be extremely proud of the fine young man you've turned out to be."

"Thank you, Miss Handley."

"But remember, a major part of who you are is a direct result of this man right here." She pointed to Huntington. "I don't think you could have wished for a better father."

"You're right, Miss Handley," Archer said, then turned to Huntington and smiled. "Are you ready to eat?"

Huntington smiled back. It was warm, a rarity for him. "Certainly, son. Would you please join us for lunch, Miss Handley?"

"Is it lunchtime already? Regretfully, I have to be going. Thank you all again for your time." Satisfied that she had somewhat corrected a wrong of her doing, Mary quickly said good-bye and ran out.

41

THE RAIN HAD finally stopped, and the sun was shining brightly as Sean stepped out of the Raymond Street Jail and onto the sidewalk a free man. He was walking with a cane, but he was *walking*. And Mary was waiting. She had splurged and rented a carriage for the occasion.

"Welcome to the outside world, Sean."

He took a deep breath. "It's good to smell the air instead of decades-old prison dust."

"What do you want to do now? Your choice."

"You know, Mary."

She did know. The two of them got in the carriage, and they were off. During the ride, Mary filled Sean in on the final details of the case. Sean listened and nodded his head once or twice but stayed silent. After she was through, he spoke.

"Funny thing is, I originally became a policeman because it was a job—a job I could get. God knows I wasn't going to be a doctor."

"Or a lawyer or anything that required a lot of schooling," Mary teased.

"I hated school all right, but what I hated more was the thought of working in a butcher shop. The idea of spending the rest of my life immersed in animal blood and flesh was scary."

Mary shuddered. "I don't know how Dad does it."

"Neither do I," Sean said, shaking his head in wonder. "And the longer I was on the job as a police officer, the more I began to like and respect it. I loved the idea of protecting decent people from the animals that prey on them."

"You'll be back on the force. The doctor says you'll make a full recovery."

"That's not the point, Mary," Sean said, trying to be logical, fighting his emotion. "I couldn't protect the person I loved most. I couldn't protect Patti."

"You can't beat yourself up for something over which you had no control. Like you said, there are animals out there, and sometimes they commit acts that no reasonable person would ever consider doing. You couldn't have predicted it."

"Maybe someday I'll get to believing that, but right now . . ."

Not wanting Sean to fall back into a funk, Mary changed the subject. "On the contrary, I should have been able to predict what happened with George."

Sean looked puzzled. "Something happened with George?"

Mary slumped in her seat. She had forgotten that Sean didn't know, and now she had to relate all the unpleasant details. It was painful rehashing them, but when she finished, she tried to be philosophical about it.

"Maybe Mother's theory of Handley symmetry is correct.

When something good happens to one of us, something bad happens to another. I get George, you get arrested. I lose George, you get out of jail."

"I'm not sure Mother's going to be in a philosophical mood when she finds out you gave back that very expensive engagement ring."

The two of them instantly burst into laughter, and they didn't stop for a while. It was a great release.

Green-Wood Cemetery was just a few blocks from Prospect Park. It was built in 1838 and was known for its natural parklike surroundings. As Mary and Sean walked through the grounds, it occurred to them that this was the kind of place Patti would have loved. They stayed silent for a while. It seemed appropriate, as if the tranquility demanded it. Finally, Sean spoke.

"I'm not sure if I said it yet or not, sis, but I'm really sorry about George. It's not right."

"Many things aren't, but thanks, Sean. I really appreciate it." Her look told him she meant it.

They stopped at Patti's grave and stared at the headstone. It read, PATRICIA CASSIDY, 1868–1890. Underneath that was the inscription WE DIDN'T NEED POETRY. WE HAD EACH OTHER.

Mary took a deep breath and then said, "Good choice, Sean. Nothing by Walt Whitman could have been more appropriate or heartfelt."

Standing over Patti's grave, they felt a closeness they had never felt before. Then they did something that they hadn't done since Mary was born and Sean asked to hold his baby sister.

They hugged.

EPILOGUE

A MONTH AFTER SEAN was released from prison he was back at work. During that period, Mary had taken the time to heal. It was a month full of news. In exchange for Huntington not exposing more of McLaughlin's misdeeds, the items in the newspaper about Green's homosexuality stopped. Instead, gossip linked him to several actresses of the day, much to Green's amusement. It gave Huntington pleasure to pull McLaughlin's strings, but it didn't get him back into the consolidation project, and his family still didn't attain the social acceptance Arabella desired. The Robert Davies Players' production of *Hamlet* had opened and closed on the same night after disastrous reviews. One critic ventured to say that the curtain should have come down the moment Robert Davies first entered as Hamlet. However, Robert Davies was not deterred. He still had plenty of his inheritance left and was planning a production of *Macbeth*. Mary assumed that Shakespeare was rolling over in his grave.

George was persistent and he and Mary met three more

times, trying to find a way out of their dilemma. They couldn't. At each meeting, George tried to convince Mary once again that he could easily live without Biltmore but not without her, and each time she became more resolute that he was deceiving himself. It was painful for both of them, and though it had become too much to bear, they agreed to see each other one final time. They met at Café Roberto, a coffeehouse in downtown Brooklyn. By then, George had come to accept the inevitable. He even spoke of Biltmore. When he did, his eyes lit up, and Mary knew she had made the right decision. They tried very hard not to make this last parting difficult on each other, but that was not possible.

"I'm sure you're right, Mary. I guess I'm just not used to losing."

"We clearly differ there. I've had a lot of practice."

She watched him ride off in his carriage and somehow instinctively knew he was going to be okay. What she hadn't gotten a grasp of yet was whether she would be.

The newspaper headlines concerning the Brooklyn Bridegrooms' efforts to become the first team to win a pennant in both the American and National leagues had been pushed aside by the Long Island Water Supply Company scandal. William Gaynor had turned out to be the tenacious bulldog that Mary thought he was. He sunk his teeth into that piece of political corruption and wouldn't budge. It was now pretty clear that Alfred Chapin's political ambitions had been seriously derailed. He would finish his term as mayor but he would never be governor or senator. He eventually went back to practicing law.

Hugh McLaughlin would not go quietly. He fought back, trying to emphasize the good that the water company would do for Brooklyn and portraying New Yorkers as evil city dwellers who were trying to ruin the tranquil community of Brooklyn. But no matter how vehemently he argued, McLaughlin couldn't explain away the huge profit he had made on the water company purchase, and William Gaynor would not let anyone forget that. He even filed a lawsuit against the city of Brooklyn for misuse of funds.

The consolidation of New York and Brooklyn was now inevitable. Green led the charge for New York, while the Brooklyn Ring tried to fight by planting controversial articles in the *Brooklyn Daily Eagle* that stirred up the fear of conservative Protestants who were concerned about immigrants corrupting their wholesome values. Still, the scandal of the Long Island Water Supply Company was the haymaker that ended this fight. They would argue back and forth over the details for a while. Complicated annexations took time, often many years. Votes had to be taken and bureaucratic traditions had to be observed, but Brooklyn's most powerful political cabal was tarnished and would not be able to recover in time. More importantly, Hugh McLaughlin's clout had quickly begun to wane, and Mary would enjoy watching him disappear from the political scene.

On this particular day though, Mary was not concerned with Hugh McLaughlin, the water company scandal, the consolidation project, or even Brooklyn. This day was special because it was the grand opening of Lazlo's new bookstore. With the insurance money from the fire, Lazlo had secured a building three blocks from the old bookstore, furnished it, and filled it with books. It was larger than his previous one, and even his upstairs quarters were more expansive.

Mary beamed when she saw the huge front window with

giant gold letters spelling out LAZLO'S BOOKS. However, what took her by complete surprise were the words in smaller print on the bottom right section of the window. They read, OFFICE OF MARY HANDLEY, CONSULTING DETECTIVE. Thrilled, Mary rushed inside.

The store was already crowded. Lazlo was at the far end regaling a group with the tale of his encounter with the infamous, and now departed, Shorty. He spotted Mary, excused himself, and made his way to her.

"Lazlo, your new store looks fabulous!"

"Thank you, but did you really expect anything less?"

"Of course not, especially not from a renowned genius such as yourself."

"I suspect your flattery is derived from seeing your name out front."

"It's quite an incentive. Hopefully, a compliment a day will keep my name there."

Lazlo got serious. "It's not necessary, Mary. You saved my life, and I'm very grateful."

"I also was the one who put your life in danger."

"True, but think of the excitement with which you provided me, and the fascinating story I can relate ad infinitum well into my declining years." Lazlo and Mary shared a smile, then she looked around the store.

"It appears you've attracted a goodly bunch. I suppose I should get to work."

Lazlo stopped her. "Your services are not required here." Mary was stunned, but before she could question him, he pointed. "They're required over there." Sitting in a corner on a bench were two women and a man. "Prospective clients, I presume?"

Mary walked over to them, introduced herself, apologized for keeping them waiting, and asked if they were all together. They weren't. They were three separate cases! Mary was delighted inside but hid it in order to appear professional. She asked them who had arrived first and when a woman stood, Mary instructed her to follow her into her office.

After a few steps, she stopped, begged the woman's indulgence, and went to Lazlo.

"By the way, Lazlo, where is my new office?"

"I thought you'd never ask." He pointed to a room in the back. This room was larger than her previous office, and as an extra perk, it had a window. There was a brand-new desk, a couch, two chairs, three filing cabinets, and, to top it off, an electric lamp!

Mary found it hard to contain her excitement, but she managed. There was a client present. Mary's business cards had been destroyed in the fire, but Sarah had already had new ones made for her. She took one out of her purse and gave it to the woman as she offered her a seat.

Mary walked behind her desk and sat. She gave herself a moment to take everything in. Her dream of being a working detective was finally starting to come true. She sat erect, folding her hands on the desk, and leaned forward as she looked the woman in the eye. She then spoke the words that she hoped to say many more times over the years as her business continued to thrive.

"Now, how may I be of service to you, madam?"

AUTHOR'S NOTE

Though my story is fictional, there are many historical facts intertwined with the fiction. The Arabella Huntington/Collis Huntington/John Worsham triangle is based on truth down to its Richmond, Virginia, roots, as is their son, Archer. Andrew Haswell Green was a real man who was the catalyst and proponent of much of what people admire about New York today. He was the architect of New York's consolidation and the one responsible for getting it done. The Long Island Water Supply Company scandal did indeed happen, and Hugh McLaughlin and Mayor Alfred Chapin were involved. William Gaynor was the lawyer who exposed the scandal and campaigned against them. George Vanderbilt did build Biltmore down in Asheville, North Carolina, and it still stands today as a monument to his ingenuity and foresight. John D. Rockefeller and Andrew Carnegie are American icons, and I tried to portray them truthfully.

There are two interesting footnotes to this story. Ten years after Collis Huntington died in 1900, Henry Huntington divorced his wife, and three years afterward he married Arabella Huntington. Also, Cornelius Vanderbilt II eventually disinherited his son Neily, who married the banker's daughter in spite of his father's protests. They stayed married for the rest of their lives.

Mary Handley and Superintendent Campbell were also real people who worked on the Goodrich case together. She was the one who caught the Goodrich killer, proving that "even females" can be competent detectives, an undeniable fact that prompted me to send her off on more adventures.

ACKNOWLEDGMENTS

My editor, Sarah Bedingfield, has done an amazing job with her notes and positive guidance. Thank you, Sarah. I hope I always have someone as smart and as centered as you for my editorial champion.

My team at Random House: publicists Rachel Rokicki, Hanna Frail, and Dyana Messina, and marketing specialist Danielle Crabtree have been incredibly enthusiastic and have worked tirelessly. I greatly appreciate their efforts.

I'd also like to thank publicists Howie Simon and Amy Sisoyev for their wonderful enthusiasm and their efforts on my behalf.

My agent, Paul Fedorko, has been a great champion of my writing, and I can't thank him enough for his belief in me and his counsel.

Paul's assistant, Sammy Bina, has also been extremely helpful, and I thank her for it.

My wife, Fran, my son, Josh, and my daughter, Erin, have all been fantastic. Their support as I have ventured into novel writing has been unyielding and overwhelmingly positive. My love for them is boundless, and I am way beyond fortunate to have them.

Michael, Helen, and Adam Levy have also been tremendously supportive, and their actions have gone above and beyond anything that could possibly be suspected.

As a young boy, Roz and Elliott Joseph did everything they could to encourage my love of books, and I hope it shows here. Marilyn Lichterman was also a champion of my ventures into the arts, and I want to thank her.

My close friend David Campagna has always been extremely supportive and positive about any endeavor I've decided to tackle. This one was no different, and I want him to know how much I appreciate him.

My fellow writer David Garber and I have a habit of bouncing ideas off each other. I believe every writer needs a buddy like David, and I'm lucky to have him as a friend.

I'd also like to thank Nikki and Charley Garrett, Stan Finkelberg, and Lois Feller for reading early versions of this novel and encouraging me with their enthusiastic responses.

A READER'S GUIDE FOR *BROOKLYN ON FIRE*

IN ORDER TO provide reading groups with the most informed and thought-provoking questions possible, it is necessary to reveal certain aspects of the story in this novel. If you have not finished reading *Brooklyn on Fire,* we respectfully suggest that you wait before reviewing this guide.

1) The book opens with Alice B. Sanger becoming the first woman to work on the president's staff at the White House. How does this give context to Mary's achievements and struggles as a consulting detective in an all-male profession?

2) Arabella Huntington and Mary Handley appear to be direct opposites as characters. However, they're both able to exert power over others in order to accomplish their goals. Considering the era, discuss the ways in which they both have carved a desirable space for themselves in New York City.

3) "Could it be that weeks with George, regularly experiencing the life of the privileged, had somehow seeped into her bones and made her dissatisfied with her situation? . . . Maybe the comforts of riches really were addictive, and she was getting hooked." This is a pivotal moment for Mary. How would you describe her philosophies toward money—of having it and of not having it—up until this point? What do you think is at the root of her inner conflict in this moment? How do you think this struggle manifests in her relationship with George, before their breakup?

4) In learning of Shorty's background at the beginning of the book, it's clear that he's had a difficult life. Does his background evoke sympathy in you as a reader? If so, does your sympathy toward him change throughout the course of the book? Do you feel sympathetic toward any of the other criminals in *Brooklyn on Fire*? Why or why not?

5) False accusations (whether made intentionally or not) happen throughout the book. Which seems the most unfair in this novel? This was an era where evidence available was limited; how do you think these accusations would have unfolded in the present day? How would Mary's methodology and research be different today?

6) Compare Elizabeth Handley with Cornelius Vanderbilt and their respective relationships with Mary and George. They are both very protective and critical, and

they do not seem to trust the decisions that Mary and George make. How are their aims similar and different? Despite their actions, do you think they both want the best for their loved ones?

7)   How do Mary and Sean compete, professionally and at home? What characteristics do they share? What do you think is next for Sean at the police department?

8)   *Brooklyn on Fire* takes us out of New York and into rural areas of the South. In what ways does this change the way Mary pursues her investigation?

9)   What makes Lazlo a good sidekick for Mary?

10)   How does danger play a role in *Brooklyn on Fire*? How does Mary handle danger? Do you think she's brave? She puts her loved ones in danger, too; what are your thoughts on this?

11)   Hugh McLaughlin and Collis Huntington are master manipulators in their own right. Who do you think was more powerful? Ultimately, who was more dangerous? Do you believe either of them had good intentions, in any capacity? If so, what were they, and could these motives have led them to handle things differently and possibly more fairly?

12)   How has Mary changed since solving the Goodrich murder in *Second Street Station*? In what ways has she developed as a young woman and as a detective?